FALL
FROM
GRACE

AVENGING ANGEL **BOOK ONE**

TONY C. FRANKLIN

FALL FROM GRACE

Avenging Angel Book One

Tony C. Franklin

Published by TCF Books

Special thanks to all who read and critiqued this wild meandering story and helped me focus on the meaningful parts. Thank you, Karen, for editing and helping me see the bigger picture. Judy, Jesse, Mike, Sharon, Patti, Ryan, and Tiffany of the Kindly Critics, for your encouragement and advice early on. Your comments and encouragement helped this story become a reality. Thanks to Kiri, Kanika, and Sasha for helping me cut to the chase and eliminate the unneeded backstory. Last, thank you Betty Jean for being my Beta Reader.

If you can just make it through the pain and keep breathing, you can survive anything.

JONATHAN COT

PROLOGUE

Arkansas Game and Fish Commission

Daily Log Book

Officer Jonathan Cotton

November 26

I arrested hunting guide Danny Ray and five of his clients for violating federal and Arkansas migratory bird hunting laws this afternoon. Broken laws included hunting on a baited field, exceeding the daily bag limits, and the daily possession limits of geese and Mallard ducks. They will be charged in federal court, and not in state court. There will be a better chance of the charges being upheld in Federal Court. One client was the son of U.S. senator Thomas, and another was the son of a state District Judge Boone. They laughed and threatened me until the local deputies hand cuffed them and I had their trucks, boats and guns towed and impounded. If convicted, the guide will lose his right to hunt, fish, or work as a guide anywhere in the United States. All offenders will lose their material possessions impounded at the time of arrest, including trucks, boats, boat trailers, and guns. I didn't pay any attention to threats against me, but threats against my family, I take seriously. It amazes me they think the law doesn't pertain to them.

February 17

I found a note under the windshield wiper of my truck. It was a picture of me with my wife and daughter out for dinner on Valentine's Day. Written in block letters under the picture was "Who dies first?"

It's time to request a transfer. I cannot put my family in danger.

CHAPTER 1

Angel

I'm a runner. I'm addicted to the euphoric feeling that occurs just after you break through the pain of the stitch in your side and the inability to catch your breath. Somehow, the mind and body compensate and allow you to continue running and ignore the pain. It allows you to push yourself through walls and limitations you didn't know existed.

Life is like that. If you can just make it through the pain and keep breathing, you can survive anything. That's what my dad always says. He was a Marine and now he is a Wildlife Officer for the Arkansas Game and Fish Commission. He taught me to push myself and never quit, no matter how much exhaustion or fear I felt.

It was the first Monday of August. The first mandatory cross-country practice was today, and we didn't want to overdo it, so we only ran a mile around the farm that morning. Our coach would time us to see what kind of condition we were in. School begins in a week, and our first cross country meet would be at Lyon College in Batesville by the end of August.

Dan and Ben Brock were brothers who lived next door to us on the farm where my parents rented a house. Dan wanted to be a farmer, and Ben wanted to be a preacher.

Ben will start college in a few weeks at Harding University in Searcy, where he will major in theology. He confessed to me and Dan that he would miss the routine of running and morning chores. I told him I would try to cover for him and help Dan. They amazed me. Most siblings had a love-hate relationship. Not Ben and Dan. It was obvious they loved and respected each other. They both enjoyed hunting and fishing as much as I did, but Dan enjoyed the farm work, and Ben enjoyed the Bible. They both enjoyed the cross-country running, but they didn't try hard either. Even though Ben had finished high school, he wanted to run with Dan one more time.

My parents had rented the old house on the Brock's farm about two months ago. Since then, Dan and I spent most of our waking hours together, which started at five each morning with a four or five-mile run around the farm.

We moved away from the town where I grew up in the summer of my senior year in high school. And this is where we ended up, living in a rentcd house on the Brock family farm. I don't mind, because it's beautiful here, and I made a friend in Dan. We have a view of the river and the mountains from the back porch. There is the forest to the east, and the farm everywhere else.

I'm an only child and grew up as a daddy's girl. He taught me to hunt, fish, and enjoy the outdoors. He is six foot five inches tall and muscular. Everything about Dad is big, including his smile and personality. He takes his job seriously though, and that has gotten him into trouble. We moved because he began receiving threats and he felt he was being stalked.

Coach Taylor would be in for a pleasant surprise. He knew Dan and Ben would be at practice, and he knew I was coming. But he didn't know I was an eight-hundred-meter district champion. The team averaged eight to ten guys, but rarely had a good female runner. There were enough girls to form a team, but they rarely placed in the top five. I might change that. I had been keeping up with Dan and Ben easily the last week. We hadn't pushed ourselves yet, but we decided we would start this week.

Sometimes, the team held practices in the U.S. Army Corps of Engineers Dam Site Park. The trail wove through the shaded pine and post oak woods. We just had to watch out for the poison ivy and the occasional snake. But we were accustomed to that.

Coach Taylor was excited to meet me, especially after he learned my track history. Last year I won the eight hundred meters at district and placed fifth at state. Mom and I planned to go to school the next afternoon to sign up for classes. Coach reminded me I needed to sign up for cross-country and track and to schedule a physical.

There were fifteen runners to show up, nine guys and six girls. Dan and Ben started at a slow pace, but I took off ahead of them. Ben yelled something at me and I shook my head. It was a beautiful morning, and I felt that urge to run. We were halfway through the one-mile lap when they caught up to me.

"Slow down there, Cotton Top. We have three laps to make," Ben said as he passed me.

I laughed and almost lost my breath. It's hard enough to run and talk, it's harder to run and laugh. Cotton Top, he made that up from my last name Cotton and my blonde hair. My name is Angelina Cotton, but I go by Angel.

Dan ran up beside me. "Come on Cotton Top, you started this." That brought a smile to my face. No one had ever given me a nickname before.

I finished under nineteen minutes, which would win most races. I finished fourth out of our group that day. The person between me, Ben and Dan was another high school senior, John Parker. He placed tenth at the state meet last year, Dan said. John wasn't even breathing hard when he finished. He was giving Ben and Dan high fives when Ben started yelling.

"Come on Cotton Top! Kick it, you got this!"

Dan joined him, "Come on Angel. Finish strong!"

Dan caught me as I crossed the makeshift finish line. He put his arm around me and kept me walking. Walking keeps your muscles from cramping. Coach Taylor whooped and yelled out my time. I was gasping for air and my legs were wobbly, and had that rubbery feeling of pure exhaustion. Dan handed me a towel and a bottle of water. I didn't really need his help to stand up, but I kind of liked his arm around me and leaned in a little closer to smell the faint scent of aftershave and sweat.

Even John Parker looked impressed and laughed when I huffed, "I can't believe you guys ran off and left me."

Dan and Ben started a little tradition two years ago. They brought their party barge and invited the boys' and girls' teams to go to the lake with us after the first practice. We launched at Dam Site Marina and motored a little way to some bluffs and spent the afternoon swimming and relaxing. The bluffs weren't tall, and people climbed up and jumped off. They were still inside the park, so if anyone needed to, they could walk to the park's restrooms or to where they parked their car and leave. The barge was fun, and we kept the ice chest and snacks on it.

CHAPTER 2

Dan

The sunlight sparkled off the water as the pontoon boat gently rocked on the waves. Our cross-country team members were lounging on the boat or cooling off in the lake by lazing in the water on pool floats or various life jackets. We anchored about twenty feet from the base of the bluffs with about five other boats.

The other boats included a mixture of ski boats, bass boats not being used for fishing, and another pontoon. Their occupants were climbing the bluffs and jumping into the lake. Our cross-country team must have been tired, because no one had gone over ten feet from the boat yet.

Angel and I were sharing a blowup pool float. Instead of laying on it, we were using it as a floating bar. Our elbows and sports drinks were on the float side by side. We accidentally played footsies a few times; we grinned at each other, but never apologized.

"Where is that squirrel?" Angel asked, frustrated.

Somewhere on shore, there was a very loud and agitated squirrel barking his little lungs out. We had searched the oak and pine trees above the bluff and couldn't find the squirrel.

"I've got an idea," I said. "I think the bark is bouncing off the bluff. Let's look for him on the opposite shore."

"How do you know it's a male?"

"You're right," I said. "Only a female would chatter that much."

That's when she punched me in the arm. Then she dunked me. We forgot all about the squirrel as the others joined us in a big splash water fight.

After our water battle ended, we were all hungry, and someone suggested a pizza run. We pulled up the anchors and motored closer to the roped-off swimming area and tied up to shore. None of us had changed into swimsuits. The guys were still wearing our cross-country practice shorts, while the girls wore their sports bra tops and shorts.

I had rarely seen a girl as lean as Angel, and she was the first I'd ever known to have better-looking six-pack abs than me. I had more of a four-pack, and most of the time it was just a flat stomach. Mom was an excellent cook, and I loved to eat.

I jumped off the barge into the shallow water and waded to shore with the anchor. I tied the rope around a small boulder and looked up to see Sarah, my ex-girlfriend, walking straight toward me. Angel and I were having fun, and I really didn't want to deal with my ex-girlfriend.

Sarah was a pretty brunette with waist-length hair and big brown eyes. Her smile could make anyone return the smile. The sunlight sparkled off her shoes, and I noticed she was wearing black sequined slip-on sneakers.

"Hi, Dan."

"Hi," was my simple response as I frowned at her. I would not make it easy for her. She was not someone I wanted to see today, but I dropped my hands to my sides and stood there. I broke up with her near the end of our junior year because I felt our relationship wasn't going anywhere. We had different goals and plans after high school.

"Can we talk?"

I felt an arm slip around mine. Angel asked, "Who's your friend?"

A chill ran down my spine. This was not how I wanted one girl to meet the other.

"Angel, this is Sarah. Sarah, this is Angel."

"I'm his girlfriend," Sarah said.

"Ex-girlfriend! We broke up, remember?" I said with all the aggravation I could muster. My face felt hot from the anger. I turned to leave, but she spoke again.

"You're going to hook up with someone else and forget about me? I thought we might make up."

Angel stepped up to Sarah and leaned in closely. She said something to Sarah, but I couldn't hear it.

Angel grabbed my arm, and sweetly drawled, "Come on, Dan." And we walked back to the pontoon boat. I realized then, I had stronger feelings for Angel than I'd ever had for Sarah.

Ben met us and asked, "Was that Sarah?"

"Yes," I said. "She said she wanted to talk, but Angel showed up and she accused us of hooking up."

"Dan, she's been sick. She had to go back to St Jude's for treatment for leukemia," Ben said.

"What?" The joy drained from me and I experienced a verbal punch in the gut.

"Oh God, I was rude to her," Angel said. "I have to apologize."

Angel took off running. I turned to go after her, but Ben grabbed my arm.

"Stay with the boat. I'll make sure she's okay." I had learned to trust Ben's instincts with people. Apparently, I had screwed this one up royally.

My head spun, and the bile rose in my throat, but I kept it down. If I had known she was sick, I would have acted differently. I felt the darkness that envelopes you when you've hurt someone without meaning to. I didn't love Sarah, but I still cared about her. If she had told me she was going for chemo, I would have been there to support her. Yes, I knew I would. And I wouldn't have given Angel a chance.

I crawled back on the pontoon and waited. It wasn't long before Angel showed up. She sat on the seat beside me, a little away from me, letting me know she was keeping her distance. Earlier, she had sat next to me and our legs had touched.

"You're an asshole, Dan Brock," she muttered.

"I didn't know she was sick."

"It doesn't matter. She thought you knew. She thought you took the easy way out," was Angel's angry reply.

I said nothing. What could I say? It didn't matter if I didn't know, I should have noticed. But we were going different ways after high school. Why continue a relationship we both knew was going to end?

Angel looked at me. "I started having feelings for you, but I need to wait and see what kind of person you really are. Do you stand by your friends or do you walk away when they need you?"

She stood and walked to the back of the pontoon where the other team members were. I was sure they had seen our confrontation, and they were leaving me alone.

Of course, I stood by my family and friends. Truthfully, I hadn't paid enough attention to Sarah's needs and therefore; I hadn't been there when she needed me. I guess, in Angel's eyes, that made me an asshole.

A whirlpool of thoughts dragged me down, causing my head to spin as it sucked me under. The wind caught the pontoon boat, shifting it under my feet and caused my stomach to lurch. In two steps I was off the boat, wading to shore. I was barely ashore and into the trees before I went to my knees and vomited.

I'd never been this emotional. Could emotions make you sick? Ben was watching me when I looked up.

"Are you okay, little brother?"

"I don't know. Angel and I were getting close to each other, then Sarah showed up, and you dropped this bombshell on me and now Angel doesn't trust me to stand by my friends when they need me." I sat back on my heels, took a deep breath, and exhaled.

"You're not exactly at the top of Sarah's list right now, either. But she admits she didn't handle the breakup well. She should have told you the truth and she would have, but she didn't expect you to break up with her."

"I guess I need to talk to her," I replied.

"Yes, you do," Ben said. "But it can wait. Get your head clear first. You're dealing with too many emotions right now." My brother gave me a pat on the back. "Angel likes you. She's not going anywhere." Ben squeezed my shoulder. "Your one fault is not paying enough attention to the people around you. You focus on your plans and goals. You're there if we ask for something, but you never ask if we need anything."

Ben paused and removed his hand from my shoulder. "I understand that tomorrow is not guaranteed to us. Slow down and love the people around you. Come on, John is back with the pizza."

He placed his hand on my forehead. "Let's get you cooled off and get some fluids in you. You're running a fever."

If I had a fever, maybe it wasn't emotions making me sick.

CHAPTER 3

Angel

Today I'd been happy, upset, sad, and confused. Over the last two months, Dan and I had gone from neighbors to friends to what? I thought after cross country practice and swimming, we would become a little more than friends. Then his ex-girlfriend showed up. Dan had broken up with her over three months earlier. I didn't care what she said about me, but it upset me that she was toying with Dan. I leaned in close to her face and whispered, "Dan is too nice to be played like a yo-yo."

It was Ben, Dan's older brother, who told us that Sarah was being treated for leukemia. How horrible was I for being rude to a cancer patient? I ran to find her. She wasn't far from where Dan met her. Fortunately, there wasn't much brush between the trees and you could see people easily.

I called her name. "Sarah, wait!"

She stopped and stared at me. "I'm sorry. Ben just told us about your treatment. If I had known, I wouldn't have been so rude. Are you okay?"

She was still upset. There was a tear rolling down her cheek. "I'm okay. What you said to me hurt more. Dan didn't know my leukemia had returned?"

"No. And Ben acted like he hadn't known very long."

"Are you and Dan dating?"

"No. We've only known each other for the summer break. My dad is a game warden, and we moved into his grandparents' house. We've spent a lot of time together. We have a lot in common."

"He's one of the good guys. I should have told him about the leukemia before we broke up. I saw you and assumed he had moved on. For a moment, I guess I got jealous."

I didn't tell her about my feelings for Dan. There would be time for that later.

Ben's voice came from behind me. "Sarah, are you okay?"

Before I walked back to the pontoon boat, I apologized again, and gave her a quick hug.

I was very familiar with dehydration and heat exhaustion from running track. I was convinced Dan was experiencing heat exhaustion. He had worked in the hot dusty hayfield all day on Saturday. The temperature was in the high nineties. Sunday afternoon we were outside at shooting sports practice. And today, we ran our fastest times in our cross-country practice and headed to the lake in the blistering sun. In hindsight, I knew he had not consumed enough fluids. I rode the four-wheeler and took him water in the hayfield several times and encouraged him to drink more, but he was focused on completing the job. It caught up with him and he was paying a double price now.

First, he was an asshole, not for breaking up with Sarah, but for being blind to her health. And second, he was dehydrated, something that rest and fluids would fix. But I was seeing a different side of Dan. This side was a workaholic, like my dad. I wasn't sure how I felt about that. Dad could get so focused on his cases, he would ignore me and Mom. I know he didn't do it intentionally, but it still hurt. Was work more important than your wife and daughter? Was Dan going to be the same way?

He was in the lake, cooling off near the boat.

"Dan? How are you doing?" I called from the pontoon.

"I'm better," he replied, moving the float toward the boat. The sun was setting and would quickly disappear behind the mountains in the west.

"It's time to head home," Ben yelled for everyone's benefit. "Dan, do you want to drive the pontoon, or get the truck?"

One look at Dan told me he wasn't ready for a rocking boat.

"I'll go get the truck and meet you at the launch ramp."

He and I walked to the truck. I really liked Dan, but I needed some time to sort things out. Twice he stopped to lean on a tree until he could steady himself. I finally grabbed his arm and slowed his pace down. We walked to the truck with me holding his arm.

The sun was setting and it would be dark when we got home. We still had chores to do. It would serve him

17

right to let him do the chores by himself, or let Ben help him.

The launch ramp was wide enough for three trucks and trailers. I'd watched Ben and Dan driving trucks and pulling hay trailers around the farm and knew they were skilled at backing trucks and trailers. Our timing was good. No one was on the ramp, and Dan whipped the Green Machine, his truck, around and backed down the ramp, leaving plenty of room for others to back in.

He backed the trailer into the water, and we got out to winch the boat onto the trailer. Ben was fighting waves to get to the pontoon to the trailer. Someone in a thirty-six-foot Baja Outlaw was gunning his boat and making waves in the no-wake zone. No doubt showing off for the two girls in skimpy bikinis in his boat. People on the nearby docks were yelling at him to stop. He kept driving in circles and waving at people with his middle finger. His waves were rocking the boats tied to the docks and knocking people off their feet. I went fishing with Dad often. I knew the boating laws and regulations because he drilled them into my head. This guy was breaking the law, and he didn't care.

There was always someone who couldn't back up a trailer if they had an automatic pilot. It was the buddies of the show-off driver of the Baja. They drove a Hummer H3, with an empty forty-foot trailer behind for the Baja. The driver was either drunk or couldn't back a trailer. Probably both. I looked around the truck when I heard yelling. The driver had almost jack-knifed his trailer right into Dan's truck.

I ran up the ramp, waving my hands above my head, and yelled, "Whoa, whoa, stop, stop!"

18

I'll call the first guy in the Hummer idiot number one. He jumped out of the passenger side, yelling at me, and stumbled to one knee and stood back up, continuing to yell and cuss. He was a small skinny guy wearing cut-off jeans and an unbuttoned shirt open to show his lack of chest hair.

"Hey, bitch. Get that piece of shit out of the way. We got a real boat to load up."

The driver pulled up a few feet to try again. He hadn't pulled up far enough. That was idiot number two in my book. He couldn't back up a trailer. Dad had taught me to pull up as straight as I could before trying to back straight up.

"Stop. Stop." I yelled again as the trailer headed in the same direction toward Dan's truck.

I looked back at the pontoon, and I honestly thought Ben was swearing. Maybe he was praying, but only the good Lord knows which. The waves pushed the boat over two feet from where he needed to line up with the trailer, just missing the pontoon guide which doubled as a tail light holder.

I turned to find idiot number one just a few feet away. He grabbed his crotch and said to me, "You look pretty good sweetheart, why don't you come home with me and big John and we'll show you a fucking good time."

I assumed he was calling his pecker big John. I slapped him. That's when he really earned the name idiot number one. He laughed and reached out and touched my face. Dad had taught me how to fight and we still sparred often. This idiot would pay for touching me. I threw a straight right punch that bloodied his nose. Then I kicked him in the groin with a kick that would have made a football player proud.

I didn't notice Dan running up the ramp to us. But he was there, holding the electric cattle prod from the back of his truck.

The guy was rolling on the launch ramp with one hand on his nose and the other on his crotch. He was wailing and cussing, "Am gone kit thu bish." Which I interpreted as, "I'm going to kill you, bitch."

Dan was standing two feet down-ramp from him. I was to his side, about three feet from him, in the martial arts fighting stance Dad had taught me. Dan had locked eyes with idiot number two. He was sixty feet away, leaning on the hood of the Hummer, with his arms crossed, holding a pistol loosely in his left hand.

"Stand back, my friend. It's been a fair fight so far. Except Little John has had a half-case of beer to drink today, and your girlfriend here seems to be some kind of karate expert."

Five things happened almost simultaneously, except one started it all. Little John, that's what idiot number two called him, pulled a pistol from his waistband, and screamed, "Die, bitch."

I hoped Little John didn't live up to the title of idiot number one, and have a live round in the chamber of his pistol. Most southerners kept the chamber empty to avoid an accidental discharge. I kicked out with my right foot, hitting Little John's hand and knocking the pistol free. Thank goodness it did not go off.

Dan stuck Little John with the cattle prod, lighting him up with about five thousand volts of electricity. It was enough to shake up a person, but not enough to hurt them. The typical taser produces ten times the voltage of a cattle prod, so the cattle prod just startles a person or a cow. Little John went back to rolling on the launch ramp and screaming, "Sh, sh, sh, shit!"

At least I think that's what he was saying.

A siren and red and blue lights came rolling down the ramp in the form of a sheriff's patrol. And the pistol that Little John's buddy was holding magically disappeared.

We all stopped and watched as Sheriff Bull Tatum got out of his SUV. Dan introduced me once when he dropped by the farm to visit Mr. Brock, Dan's dad. The sheriff was a large man. He was well over six feet tall, and two hundred pounds. He had a flattened nose that looked like it had been broken several times. Dad said the nickname Bull came from his high school days of playing football.

"Put the cattle prod down, Dan," he said in a tired voice.

Dan put the cattle prod on the ground at his feet. Little John was coming around, but he did not get up.

"She attacked me, deputy. Beat the shit out of me. And her boyfriend electrocuted me with that cattle prod."

Sheriff Tatum sighed. "It's Sheriff, not deputy. And I watched the whole thing, Little John. She was trying to keep your cousin from backing into Dan's truck. You're under arrest for carrying a concealed weapon. And he shocked you with a cattle prod. Electrocution would have killed you."

That confirmed it. Little John was an idiot.

CHAPTER 4

Dan

The sheriff and his family went to Dad's church, our church. He had known me and Ben since we were adopted. I had been to his farm many times to help work cattle. I had never seen the Sheriff performing his job. In this position, he scared and intimidated me.

"I've got a permit to carry that," Little John said when the sheriff asked about the pistol.

"Then I'll add public intoxication and drunk and disorderly conduct. Get up and turn around." The sheriff pulled the cuffs from his belt and headed toward Little John. Little John didn't resist. He cuffed his hands behind his back, then walked over and picked up the pistol. He released the clip and put it into his pocket. Slowly, the sheriff turned away and slid the slide back and caught the cartridge that had been in the barrel. He was hiding the fact that the pistol had a round in the chamber from me and Angel.

"Are you Danny or Donny?" he asked, looking toward the Hummer.

"I'm Donny. Danny's on the boat," he said, pointing toward the lake.

"Why don't you walk over here and join us? You're not under arrest," Sheriff Tatum said.

The sheriff looked at Angel. "Young lady, grab that cattle prod and go get in Dan's truck."

Angel did as she was told. Sheriff Tatum looked at me and grinned as Angel told Little John, "Hope you and Big John have fun in jail."

"Bitch," Little John spat at her.

When Donny got to the County SUV, the sheriff looked at me. "Dan, back their rig down the ramp so they can load their boat and get out of here."

"Now wait a minute," Donny argued.

Sheriff Tatum held his hand up. "He'll have it backed up and we can all be out of here in ten minutes. I've seen this young man back a forty-foot gooseneck trailer a quarter mile down a muddy road. He won't hurt your Hummer."

I walked up the launch ramp to get to the driver's side of the Hummer. For the first time, I saw a deputy sitting in his patrol vehicle with the barrel of a shotgun sticking out of his window.

Then I noticed the olive-green truck of Angel's dad parked at an odd angle in the nearest parking lot. The barrel of a rifle just barely showed above the window opening of his door.

When I reached the front of the Hummer, there were no trucks with trailers waiting for us. My eyes followed the approach road around until I saw another deputy patrol car stopping traffic from approaching the ramp.

The hair stood up on my neck, and a cold sweat covered my body. Who were these guys?

CHAPTER 5

Dan

The Hummer was trashed. The back seat had women's clothing strewn across it and a black sequined shoe caught my attention, making me think of Sarah. I would have to call her tomorrow. No. I needed to go see her. This conversation needed to be in person.

Backing the trailer up would have been easy, but the Hummer's transmission was slipping. It was still simple work. In two minutes, the trailer was in water.

I got out of the Hummer and stood in knee deep water. The Baja was already on the trailer. I looked at the boat driver and understood why the sheriff asked Donny which one he was. These guys were identical twins, except the personalities were totally different.

Danny said, "Get the fuck away from my rig. I'll get it from here."

I turned and waded out of the water and walked back to my truck. Maybe it was the lake water, but another icy chill ran up my neck. Ben had finally gotten the pontoon boat onto our trailer. Angel was helping to winch it onto the trailer so we could pull up and tie it down.

Ben motioned for me to pull up and he and Angel would ride on the pontoon until I pulled over to tie it down.

I stopped twenty yards down the exit road and pulled over so other vehicles could pass, and we could tie the pontoon down to the trailer.

I had just gotten out of my truck when a deputy pulled up and rolled his window down. The air conditioning escaping his cruiser felt good on my face.

"Sheriff said y'all are to go straight home. The game warden will wait for y'all."

"Yes sir," I said as the window rolled up and he drove away.

Ben walked up to me. "What's going on Dan?"

I shook my head as I heard a whippoorwill call from somewhere nearby. It was dark by now, but the temperature was still hot and I realized I wasn't sweating.

"We have orders to go straight home. Officer Cotton is waiting for us." Then I asked him, "Can you drive? I'm not up to it."

We piled into the truck. Ben drove, Angel sat in the middle, and I was by the passenger window. I looked at Angel and her face was pale; her eyes were moist, and her mouth drooped in horror movie style.

"Are you okay?" I asked.

She shook her head no. "He had a live round in the chamber. He could have killed me."

"Probably not," I said. "He probably shoots as well as his buddy backs up boat trailers. He could have hit my truck, though."

She looked at me with mouth and eyes wide open in horror. Then the joke hit her and she grinned and started giggling. I started laughing with her.

"What?" Ben asked. "What's the joke?"

I explained what had happened on the ramp. Then I asked a series of questions that stumped him and Angel.

"Have you ever seen Sheriff Tatum wear a bulletproof vest?"

"No."

"Did you notice the deputy at the top of the ramp with his shotgun hanging out the window?"

"No," he said, a little slower.

"Did you see Angel's dad in the parking lot with his rifle pointing out of his truck window? Or the deputy that had traffic stopped a hundred yards from the launch ramp."

Ben was getting pale as well. "No."

"We were in the wrong place at the wrong time. Sheriff Tatum may have saved our lives. Let's find out what's going on."

We were at the four-way stop just outside of Heber Springs when Dad called and asked where we were.

"Just turned onto Wilburn Road and we are about to cross the river. We're coming straight home," I said.

"Park the truck and come to the house. You can unhook later. Okay?"

"Yes sir," I answered.

27

"Something is up, Ben. Dad didn't tell me he loved me."

Ben looked at me, raised his eyebrows, and hit the gas. Ben rarely sped or broke any rules. If something was wrong with Dad, though, the rules didn't matter.

It took us fifteen minutes to get home, but it seemed like an hour. Ben parked the truck and boat by the equipment shed where one of us would back it in later. Ben tried to hurry us to the house, but I wasn't going fast and Angel stayed close to me. My head was still pounding, and I was feeling weak. I didn't eat any pizza this afternoon.

Officer Cotton's truck was in the drive, along with another deputy's patrol car. We hurried through the garage and into the mudroom. Dad met us there with a sharp look on his face.

We walked into the living room to find Mom, Officer Cotton, Angel's mom, and an older deputy I didn't know already seated on the couches and chairs scattered around the room and facing the fireplace.

Angel started to give her dad a hug, but he held his hand up. "Y'all have a seat on the couch there."

We sat on the couch with Angel between us.

It was Angel that broke the silence. "Dad, what's going on? We didn't start that stuff on the boat ramp."

"We'll talk about that in a minute. Dan, did you talk to Sarah Young this afternoon?"

I just nodded. I was getting a bad feeling because I had been rude to her and didn't know what Angel said.

Did she decide to file charges against Angel? But Angel apologized and didn't touch her. Would she still do that? What did Ben say to her?

Ben spoke up then. "We all saw her." Then he told them everything that had happened.

"When I found Angel and Sarah, they were apologizing and hugging each other."

Ben hesitated for a few seconds. I'd had my head down, listening. My head was still pounding, but I glanced over at him. He took a deep breath. I glanced at Angel and saw a tear in the corner of her eye.

Ben continued, "I told Sarah I was sorry about everything that happened. She accepted the blame and said she had handled the breakup with Dan badly. She expected Dan to be resistant to breaking up, but he wasn't. Sarah didn't want him to feel obligated to support her through her trips back and forth to Memphis, so she didn't argue about breaking up."

"She got angry when she saw Angel. She didn't blame Angel for being rude, and said what hurt was Angel telling her Dan wasn't a yo-yo to be played with."

I looked at Angel. The tear rolled down her cheek.

Ben said, "I held her hand and prayed with her. Then I gave her a hug before she headed back to her car."

"So, you were the last one to see her?" Officer Cotton asked.

Ben nodded. "The last of us three."

I realized what was happening then. "Is she okay?"

"Her mother hasn't seen her since she left home to go talk to you," Officer Cotton answered. "Her car was still at Dam Site Park. But there is no sign of her."

My head was really pounding now. I reached for my back pocket to get my iPhone. "I can track her phone with mine." She lost her phone once before and we found it using mine.

"We've already found her phone," the deputy said, speaking for the first time.

I tried to recall the conversation we had when we broke up. I wanted to remember her exact words and mine. Too much was running through my head. Was she okay? Then I remembered the Hummer.

"There was a black sequined shoe, just like hers, in the back seat of the Hummer." I was shaking and my voice was cracking. Angel reached over and grabbed my hand.

She asked, "Who were those idiots on the ramp tonight, Dad?"

He sighed. "That was Danny and Donny Ray, and their cousin Little John Johnson."

"Can't you stop them and search their Hummer?" Angel asked.

"We need a search warrant to check their vehicle," he replied.

Angel let go of my hand. "No, you don't. They were on the lake. They had guns. All you need is probable cause, and Dan just gave it to you." Game Wardens don't need search warrants to search for suspected hunting violations.

Her dad looked sick. "I can't get close to them. I have a case pending against Danny that will put him away for twenty years. But he has also got a restraining order against me. I'm not supposed to get within a hundred yards of the twins." He shook his head and added. "They have also threatened to kill me, you and your mom."

"They're your stalkers?" Angel asked.

"I'm afraid they are." I noticed he was holding Mrs. Cotton's hand for the first time.

"What can we do to help?" Ben asked.

"Nothing, I'm afraid," the deputy said. "You need to stay at home for the next few days. These guys are dangerous. They're suspected of drug smuggling, human trafficking, and even murder, but no one has made anything stick." He stood up. "I'll call the sheriff. He was adamant that y'all had nothing to do with her disappearance. But we had to follow procedure and question everyone who saw her."

Officer Cotton added. "I broke the restraining order tonight because you kids were there. But I stayed back, hoping they wouldn't see me. The sheriff didn't use your name, because we were afraid they might figure out who you were, Angel."

I was stunned. They had suspected us, or me, more than likely, of having something to do with Sarah's disappearance. But it had to be those guys. I excused myself and headed to the half bathroom in the mudroom. I was feeling sick again.

CHAPTER 6

Dan

My head was spinning, and the pounding felt like someone was beating a metal building with a sledgehammer. I was shivering and it fit my mood. Sarah was missing. I wasn't in love with her, but I didn't wish for anything bad to happen to her, either. That's where Mom found me sitting on the floor of the half bath, feeling like everything was pushing down on me. I wished I would either throw up, or the feeling would go away.

Mom had a way of reading me and Ben. It was like she knew what we were thinking. Maybe it was intuition, or maybe it was dealing with hundreds of kids during her career as a teacher. Either way, she surprised me when she finally said, "It's not your fault that Sarah is missing. It's not your fault that you broke up. Dan, you knew the relationship would not last, and you did the right thing. It was the best for both of you. This wasn't your fault, okay?"

"Thanks, Mom. I think I needed to hear that, but it still bothers me."

"I know it does. You go take a shower, and I'll bring you some acetaminophen, crackers, and Gatorade to your room," she said.

"Thank you, Mom."

Our mudroom was between our garage and the kitchen. It had a half bathroom. A toilet and a vanity for washing our hands. The other side was our laundry room. Our rule was no filthy clothes past the mudroom. We all had a couple of changes of clothes in the mudroom. Many days, I wished it had a shower, when I came in filthy from head to toe. Today was another day, because I didn't feel well enough to go to my room. One day, I would add a shower.

Ben and I shared a bathroom between our rooms. Mom and Dad's bedroom was across the hall and had its own master bathroom. I dreaded walking through the living room past everyone to go to the shower. I pushed myself up off the floor and started walking. Mom was still in the kitchen getting Ritz crackers out of the cabinet when I walked through. I was prepared to apologize to everyone when I walked into the living room, but there was no one there.

"Where is everyone, Mom?"

"Deputy Williams left. The Cotton's went home. And your dad went to help Ben unhook the pontoon boat and feed the livestock," she said.

"I need to go help."

"No. You are going to take these." She held her hand out. "Drink this Gatorade. Take a shower and go to bed," she instructed.

I took the two Tylenol from her open palm and left the blue pill, which I suspected was Benadryl.

"I don't think I'll need that to sleep."

She stood on her tiptoes and kissed my cheek, "Go get some rest. Your dad and Ben will take care of the chores."

It was almost ten when I laid down on my bed. I don't remember falling asleep, but it must not have taken long. It was after one a.m. when I sat straight up and screamed. I was frightened, trying to figure out where I was, when Ben turned my light on.

"Are you okay, Dan? I'm here, what do you need?" he asked, after sitting on my bed.

I looked around my room. The pictures of our state championship shooting sports teams were on the wall. There were ribbons from fairs and livestock shows. The picture of me and Ben with our grand and reserve champion steers from last year's county fair. I was still breathing hard, but I focused on Ben.

"Have they found Sarah?"

"No, I don't think so."

I held back a big sob and slammed my fist into the bed. I rarely lost my temper. My brother crawled further onto the bed and put his arm around my shoulder.

"What's bothering you? Get it off your chest."

"I dreamed I was back on the launch ramp. That guy." I took a deep breath before I continued. "Little John. He pulled his pistol and shot Sarah."

"You mean Angel?" Ben asked.

"No. In the dream, it was Sarah he shot. She was standing where Angel was standing. I think he really killed Sarah." I was shaking. "The dream was so vivid. It was in slow motion. He pulled his pistol. I screamed no. He pulled the trigger. I watched the bullet leave the barrel and hit her between the eyes, and blood and gore flew from the back of her head. She made eye contact with me as she fell and mouthed 'I'm sorry.'"

I had gotten my breath back.

"Why would she tell me she was sorry, Ben?"

"I don't know. Dreams can be strange. Maybe you wanted to tell her you were sorry."

"She wouldn't run away," I said.

"I know. I don't think she would either. Try to go back to sleep, Dan. You need to rest," Ben encouraged me.

"I don't want to have another dream. Besides, I'm hungry. I think I'll find something to eat."

Ben crawled off my bed and left. My mom stuck her head in my room. "Did I hear you say you were hungry? I'll go fix you something."

I'm sure she heard and watched everything. She had a way of letting me and Ben work out things between us. She also had a way of being there in case we needed her.

I looked around my room for clean clothes. Ben kept his room immaculate. I slept in my room and changed clothes there. That was about it. The dirty clothes were on the closet floor. My clean clothes were folded and stacked on my dresser or hanging in my closet.

The farm I kept clean and organized. I sprayed soil sterilant under the fences to keep brush from growing up through them. The pastures were brush hogged to keep weeds down and encourage grass growth. Hay fields were cut and baled regularly. The livestock barn, equipment shed, and shop were clean and organized.

My room was my crash zone. There were no television or video game systems. I had a laptop, but I seldom used it in my room. That was for tracking business expenses, livestock pedigrees, and doing the occasional school work. When I pointed out to mom and dad, that I kept the farm clean and organized because I lived on the farm, not in my room, they had stopped harassing me about cleaning my room. Don't get me wrong, I pulled the covers up on my bed in the morning, and picked my clothes up several times a week, but it was on my schedule and when I felt it needed it.

I found some torn jeans on the closet floor, a clean 4-H T-shirt, and socks on the dresser, not in it, and got dressed. I grabbed the empty Gatorade bottle and the remaining crackers to take back to the kitchen. Mom had scrambled some eggs and made two pieces of toast with butter and homemade muscadine jelly. There was another orange Gatorade on the table with breakfast.

"Thanks Mom, you're too kind to me. I'm going to go work on the Mustang when I'm finished. Sleep is the last thing I want to do right now."

"I'm sorry Daniel, I heard what you told Ben. Dreams can be harsh sometimes," she said, patting my shoulder.

Mom hugged me, and I leaned down and gave her a kiss on the cheek.

"Take your phone and a radio with you. Your dad and Ben have radios by their beds."

"Okay, Mom."

Mom headed back to bed. I sat down and ate my eggs and toast. It was more like I vacuumed them up. I was hungry. I still had a headache, but not like before.

The dishes went into the dishwasher, and I searched the cabinets for the Tylenol. I popped two pills into my mouth and chased them with the rest of the Gatorade. I wasn't a pill person, but I didn't want a repeat of last night's headache. The second empty Gatorade bottle went into the trash beneath the sink, and I grabbed another cold Gatorade from the fridge.

Ben and I were adopted. The farm belonged to my biological parents, who died in a car accident when Ben and I were two and three years old. My biological parents had owned an insurance agency and took financial planning seriously. Because of that, they left us trust funds funded by life insurance. Ben and I would be well off when we reached twenty-one.

My biological father had laid out our home and the farm buildings in the shape of a capital C. The house was on the south side toward the river. The front of the house faced the livestock barn on the north side.

The house had a deck that ran the full length and faced the river. Our shop was part of the equipment shed closest to the house. The enclosed shop had a wood heater for winter work. During the summer, the doors slid open and the shop fan up near the ceiling tried to suck the hot air out.

The next building was the hay barn. There were a hundred feet of livestock pens on either side. Just in case the hay caught on fire, it was away from the other structures. The last building was the livestock barn. It ran east and west and housed horse stalls, a show pen, and a covered working pen. We had ten calves tied in the show pen right now. Six of them I would show this fall. The other four I was hoping to sell as show calves to other 4-H and FFA members for next year. I wasn't trying to make big money; I was trying to build a reputation, and I was slowly breeding show calves that were winning the big shows.

My pet project, though, was a sixty-five Ford Mustang convertible, cherry red with double white racing stripes on the hood and trunk. It had been sitting in the shop for my entire life. I think it was my biological dad's project as well. It was my way of trying to connect with my biological dad. The green seventy-two Ford truck I drove every day had belonged to my biological grandfather. I named it the Green Machine. It had four-wheel drive and had yet to get stuck in a mud hole.

The Mustang was professionally painted four years ago. The seats were reupholstered three years ago. I had a new convertible top and flooring installed as well. Last year I had the V-8 engine, and the transmission rebuilt. This year I was replacing the wiring. Everything was working, except the brake lights and back blinkers.

The light was barely on in the shop when my phone chimed. It was a text from Angel. *Are you up? I can't sleep.*

I was about to work on my Mustang.

Angel asked, *Do you want to talk?*

Walk to the end of your driveway. I'll pick you up.

Angel must have been sitting on her front porch and saw the shop light come on. I was the only person in my house that would be in the shop or barn area after one in the morning.

I opened the shop doors wide, put the top down on the Mustang, and started the engine. It wasn't loud, but it could be. Most of the car was original, and I did not trick it out, except for the dual exhaust. You could feel the power, though. I eased it out of the shop and onto the farm road. I wanted to floor it and feel the wind swirl around me. But I kept my desires in check and idled down the road until I got to Angel's drive.

She was waiting at the end of the drive. She was wearing jeans and a baggy sweatshirt with a large collar that slipped over one shoulder. Even in August, the nights could get chilly by the river. The air would roll across the sixty-degree water and cool down the areas close to the river. Angel had her hair in a ponytail and stuck out the back of a Realtree camo ball cap.

"Your tail lights aren't working," she said.

"That's what I'm working on. You want to help me?"

"Sure. I didn't know you had a Mustang."

"I've been working on it for the last four to five years. There is a short in the taillights that I can't find. A bad dream woke me earlier, and I didn't want to go back to sleep."

I pulled into her drive, shifted the manual transmission into reverse. I backed out onto our farm road and headed back to the shop. The temptation to floor it came again, but I resisted it. I didn't want to wake up both of our families and I wasn't sure my head could handle it either.

"A bad dream? They seem to go around," she said.

"I'll tell you mine if you tell me yours," I prodded.

I pulled into the shop, instead of backing in. We sat in the bucket seats after I turned the car off. I looked at Angel and she was looking straight ahead and was taking deep breaths.

"I'll go first. We were on the launch ramp again in my dream. Little John pulled his pistol and shot you."

Angel turned her head and was staring at me. Her mouth and eyes were wide open.

"Only it wasn't you. It was Sarah. All I could do was scream, no. I watched the bullet leave the gun in slow motion and hit her between the eyes." I had to stop and take a few deep breaths before I continued.

"She made eye contact with me and said, 'I'm sorry.'"

Angel's eyes were moist. I'm sure mine were too.

"I don't understand why it was her, and I don't understand why she said she was sorry."

Angel got her breath under control finally. She looked at me and took a deep breath.

"My dream was almost the same. Except it was you that got shot."

She took a sobbing breath. "The pistol went off when I kicked his hand and it shot you. He shot you."

I reached over and took her hand and intertwined our fingers so we were holding hands.

"I'm here, and I wasn't shot. Neither were you," I said.

"But we don't know that Sarah wasn't shot. Little John seems the type of creep to do that. I could see it in his eyes. He hated me for beating him," Angel replied.

"Speaking of beating him. Where did you learn how to fight?"

She squeezed my hand. "My dad. He has taught me everything he learned in the Marines and on his job. Mostly it's self-defense techniques, to protect myself if I'm attacked."

We were silent for a few minutes, just sitting there holding hands.

Angel broke the silence. "Do you love her? Sarah?"

I shook my head. "I wouldn't have broken up with her if I did. We were totally different and going in different directions after high school. I enjoyed spending time with her, but I want to stay on the farm, and she wants to get away from the boondocks. That doesn't mean I didn't care about her, though."

Angel asked, "You think something bad has happened?"

"I think the Ray brothers and Little John know exactly what happened," I answered.

I changed subjects. Nothing we said was going to help find Sarah, and I didn't want to think about after the dream.

"So, what are you planning to do after high school?"

"I wanted to get a degree in biology or wildlife management and become a game warden. Last night has made me think twice about facing someone with a gun." She let go of my hand. "You're a strange guy, Dan Brock. You're smart, funny, a hard worker, competitive and compassionate."

I laughed and opened my car door to get out. "According to my brother, I'm focused only on my plans and responsibilities. He says I accomplish more than anyone he knows. I'm there for friends and family, if they ask. But I never ask if they need anything? What do you think?"

"I've only known you for a few weeks, but I think Ben is right only because you don't have weak or needy people around you. I think you would offer to help if they needed your help, like you offered to help me when we first met. Your mom, dad, and Ben are all strong people. You are surrounded by strong people."

"Wow. I never have thought to look at it that way. So, have you decided if I'm the type of person who will stand by his friends?"

She grinned at me and got out of the Mustang. She spoke in her best southern accent, "I think you're the type of friend who brings a cattle prod to a gunfight to protect a lady's honor."

I laughed. "In my defense, I didn't know he had a gun. I was nearly as shocked as he was," moving my hand like I was using the cattle prod.

She smiled and laughed at my joke. "At least you didn't electrocute him."

My smile disappeared, and I said. "I wish I had electrocuted him."

I turned the emergency flashers on and exited the Mustang.

"Help me find this short," I said.

We talked about Sarah and what might have happened to her as I worked on the car. "I'd like to go looking for her," I said.

"Me too, but we were told not to leave the farm, remember?"

Thirty minutes later, we had tracked it down to the rusted connections of the ground wires. After cleaning the wire connectors and grinding the rust off the frame and reconnecting the grounds, the lights worked.

"Whew, now I can get it registered and licensed. Thanks, Angel."

"You did all the work."

"But you saved me from making fifty trips back and forth from the light switch to the taillights."

She walked over to the worktable and stared at the collection of old cell phones laying on it.

"What's this?" She asked.

"I've been making game trail cameras out of old cell phones," I said.

"Do they work?" Angel asked.

I pulled my iPhone out of my back pocket. "My cousin Mike has helped me find an app that lets me check remote cameras. I may have to switch to an Android phone to do what I want. I have two cameras working on Bluetooth connections right now. One is in the barn watching the show calves. The other camera is on top of the hill overlooking the pastures."

I pulled up the live connections, and we watched one of the show calves stand up and stretch in the barn. The camera on the hill was dark. It was working, but it needed light to see anything.

"I still have some battery issues to figure out. It may be easier to go buy some real trail cameras."

She changed the conversation and asked, "So what do you plan on doing when you graduate?"

"I've already gotten a head start by taking AP classes and concurrent classes at ASU Heber Springs. This fall I'm taking an EMT class so I can ride in the ambulance with the local fire department. Next fall, I will start taking nursing classes at Harding," I replied.

"I can't see you as a nurse," Angel said, and frowned.

"I want to work in the emergency room. To assess and treat injuries before the doctors take over."

"Okay," she said, nodding her head. "I can see that. You are the type of person who needs to be doing something."

I added, "And nurses make good money. I can live on the farm and work close to home."

"Why not medical school?" she asked.

"Eight plus years of school after high school? No thank you," I said. "I can become a paramedic quickly. Become an LPN in two years. And continue school to become an RN in four. I can start working almost immediately and still go to school."

She yawned while listening to me.

I noticed and asked, "Are you ready to try sleeping again? I'll walk you home this time."

CHAPTER 7

Angel

The events of last night kept bothering me. I did not know what happened to Sarah.

I could have kicked Dan's butt for not being there for that poor girl. How could you date someone for a year and not know they were sick? But he broke up with her. Why was she yelling at us? She doesn't know me. And Dan and I aren't dating. At least, not yet.

It's all so confusing. Where did she go? I thought we cleared things up when we talked. I expected Dan to show up and say he was sorry. But Ben showed up instead. If I'm not mistaken, she was dating the wrong brother because Ben acted like he had a crush on Sarah.

But what do I do now? I think about Dan all the time. I love to hear him laugh and see his smile. He is so positive and energetic. We've spent every waking hour together for the last few weeks. I can't wait to wake up and see him in the mornings. I get excited to see him jogging down the road for our morning runs. And who else besides Dan would come to my aid with a cattle prod? My knight in shining armor carrying a broadsword is a cowboy with a cattle prod. No matter how badly I wanted to pee my pants when Little John pulled out that pistol, I will always smile when I remember Dan shocking him. How can I be angry at someone who did that? Especially after I dreamed he was shot.

I had dreaded starting a new school for my senior year. Then I met Dan. He was a true country boy, but he was a gentleman as well. I'd never caught him looking at me in a sexual way. If I hadn't known he had dated Sarah, I might have thought he was gay. Maybe he was, but I didn't think so. I think he is very self-disciplined or playing hard to get. Or maybe he still had feelings for Sarah.

I slipped into the house through the kitchen door and quietly closed it. This was the first house we had lived in that really felt like a home. The house had some furniture in it when we moved in. The Brocks had let people live here occasionally when someone lost their house because of a storm or fire. That's why it was partially furnished. We moved most of our stuff in and didn't have to move much of the existing furniture. That's how little we owned.

My room had a full-size bed, not the little twin bed I'd slept in since I was three. I had put away all my clothes in the closet and the dresser. My track trophies and ribbons were on a small shelf that was already on the wall. The house had a washer and dryer, which meant we no longer had to make regular trips to the laundromat.

We never thought of ourselves as poor. But money was always tight and buying extra things for the house was always over our budget. This was the home I'd always dreamed about. Even Mom and Dad said it was the nicest home they ever lived in. Mr. Brock had rented to Dad cheap because they had lost two cows to hunters a few years back and he thought Dad would be a good deterrent.

I slipped into bed thinking about the Rays and their cousin. How could they get away with making threats against Dad?

CHAPTER 8

Dan

Angel and I decided against running that morning. It was only two and a half hours away from our normal wake up time of five thirty when I walked her home. We would start on the morning chores at eight, which gave us more time to rest. If we could rest. Talking about it seemed to help me. But I was getting really worried about Sarah. Where was she? Did she walk away or did something bad happen to her?

That was her shoe in the Hummer. I knew in my heart those guys had something to do with Sarah's disappearance.

I was a preacher's son and brother of a soon-to-be preacher, and I wasn't supposed to feel this way about these guys. But they belonged to the devil, and while the Bible taught us to be wary of the devil's tricks, it did not say we must love him or his associates.

I basically just fell on my bed, clothes still on, when I returned from walking Angel home. That's the way Ben found me when he woke me at seven thirty.

"There's been no word on Sarah," he said before I asked.

Then he added, "When Sheriff Tatum pulled up. The guy in the Baja quit making circles, and I could get the pontoon straightened out. I looked at his boat and he had a death stare on the sheriff. One girl made eye contact with me and I would swear she mouthed, 'Help us.'"

"Do you think the girl really said 'Help us' last night?"

"Yeah." He hesitated before going on. "Yes, I do. The more I think about it, the more positive I am."

"Did you tell the deputy last night? Or call the sheriff this morning?"

"I didn't have to. The sheriff is here now. I told him a few minutes ago. He wanted to talk to you, so come on."

"Alright, let me use the bathroom and I'll be right there."

*****

"Good morning, Sheriff, Mom, Dad," I said, as I walked into the dining room. They were drinking coffee around the table. The sheriff stood and shook my hand.

"Good morning, Dan. I came to visit your dad, but I wanted to ask you a few questions too, if you don't mind," he drawled.

"Yes sir," I replied. "Ask away."

"Now, I know you had nothing to do with her disappearance. You have a lot of witnesses to verify where you were all day yesterday. But I need to review all possibilities. Okay?"

Mom set a cup of black coffee in front of me. I hadn't noticed that she moved. She refilled the sheriff's and Dad's cups before sitting back down.

"I understand," I answered. "But she didn't run away. She wouldn't do that, if that's what you were thinking. Not because we broke up, or because of yesterday. She is too strong to do that."

I took a sip of coffee. It was good, not as strong as Ben and I brewed before our morning runs, but it was much needed. I hoped it would help with my lingering headache.

"Why did y'all break up, Dan?"

"It was my idea. For us to have some space this summer. To see if we still had feelings for each other. I liked her a lot, but I didn't see us having a future together. She dreamed of college in Fayetteville, the University of Arkansas. I dreamed of staying here on the farm. It wouldn't have worked long term."

"Ben said you didn't know that she was getting treatment for leukemia," the sheriff said.

I took another sip of coffee. "No. I might have still broken up with her, but I would have checked on her frequently. We were still friendly."

"Okay, Dan. Her mom said the two of you were good friends, but she never saw the relationship going anywhere either. She thinks like you do, Sarah wouldn't run away."

I looked Sheriff Tatum straight in the eyes. "The more I think about it. The more I believe the Ray brothers and Little John had something to do with it. I believe that was her shoe in the back seat of the Hummer."

"My God, I hope you are wrong, son. Those are some bad guys," the Sheriff replied.

"We are doing an extensive search of the park this morning. Ben and your dad have agreed to help. I wish you could help us, Dan, but I need you to stay here with Angel. Her mom and dad are going to the school to get her registered for classes. No one in the Cotton family is to go anywhere by themselves for the next few days. Understand me, Dan?"

I nodded.

"I know you and Angel are good friends already. You have plenty to do around here."

"Yes sir. Would it be okay if we went trout fishing on the river? I told Angel we could go sometime."

"I don't see why you couldn't."

"Sheriff? Can we carry our pistols? My cattle prod wasn't much of a match against Little John's pistol last night."

"What?" my parents chorused together.

The sheriff held his hand up to my parents. "They were never in any danger. Angel handled it just like her dad said she would. I had a deputy with a shotgun trained on Little John, and the game warden had his rifle aimed at the Hummer driver. And I was right there too."

I noticed the Sheriff didn't mention Little John's pistol. Mom and Dad stared at me. I knew I was going to have to tell them the entire story, eventually.

"Lloyd, I'll see you and Ben in half an hour?" Sheriff Tatum asked.

"We will be there, Bull," my father answered.

"Thank you for the coffee, Sharon. Have a good day," the sheriff said as he headed for the mudroom.

This wasn't the first time the sheriff visited our house. The other times were social calls. Rarely was it business related unless the sheriff was asking dad about someone he knew.

My mom reached and grabbed my wrist. "Daniel Brock. You were going to use a cattle prod against a guy with a pistol? What were you thinking?"

"That I was going to help Angel. She was trying to stop those guys from backing their boat trailer into my truck. When he grabbed his crotch and reached for her, I grabbed the first thing I could find in the bed of my truck and ran to help her. We didn't know he had a gun on him until after she punched him in the nose and kicked him in the groin. He went down crying like a baby."

Ben stepped into the kitchen, dressed in jeans and hiking boots. We kept backpacks loaded with search and rescue gear, first aid supplies, rappelling ropes, and extra clothes. It was just in case he needed anything during the search. We had done this before. As members of the rural volunteer fire department, we knew how to be prepared.

"At least the cattle prod worked. Dan gave him a good buzz."

Dad shook his head. "Son, you're a good man. Naive, but good."

I knew that would be the last I would hear about last night from Dad. Mom would remind me, though, even if I already felt like an idiot for bringing a cattle prod to a gunfight. That's when I realized the sheriff never answered my question. He never said whether we could carry our pistols. On the farm, it wouldn't be necessary. But on the river, I figured the local game warden, Angel's Dad, would overlook that minor issue.

CHAPTER 9

Dan

Angel knocked on the mudroom door about fifteen minutes later. Her eyes were red and her face was puffy. She looked tired and depressed and I'm sure I looked the same way.

"Are you okay?"

"I guess," she replied.

"Any more bad dreams?" I asked as we walked into the kitchen to put away my coffee cup.

She shook her head no. "I still didn't sleep well. What did the sheriff want?"

"He had a few more questions about mine and Sarah's relationship, but he already knew my whereabouts all day yesterday. I think he was here to ask Dad and Ben to be part of the search party that's searching the park this morning."

"Come on, help me feed and water the calves. Why are you so down this morning?" I asked as we left the house. We both squinted at the bright sun, reminding us how little sleep we had.

She said, "I'm not sure how to say this, so don't take it the wrong way. I mean, I love being on the farm, but."

"But you don't like being told you can't leave it either," I finished for her.

"Yeah, I was afraid you wouldn't understand. Guess you do, though."

"I love this farm," I said. "But being told you can't leave is like being held hostage. We can go trout fishing this afternoon. It's technically not leaving the farm."

She finally smiled back. "I've got my trout stamp, but I haven't been since we moved here."

"Alright, it's watering, feeding and bathing some calves this morning, and fishing this afternoon."

She said, "Let's do this." Then she flashed that smile that made my heart skip a beat. The one that starts with the lips and ends in the depths of her eyes. Lots of girls have beautiful bodies and faces, but Angel also has a beautiful soul and that's what attracted me the most.

We were washing down the second pair of calves when my phone buzzed in my back pocket. Caller ID said it was Ben. My hand was soapy and wet, but I answered the call and put it on speaker.

"What's up, big brother?"

"I found Sarah," he cried. "I need you to come to the hospital. Meet me in the chapel."

"We're on our way." Oh God. He hung up before I could ask questions.

"Ben found Sarah. He wants us to meet him at the hospital. Angel, rinse the soap off, please, and untie them. They can roam loose in the lot until we get back.

I'm going to get my truck and tell Mom what's happening."

She nodded and said, "Go!"

Twenty minutes later, we turned into the hospital driveway. Five minutes after that, we were in the chapel. My brother Ben was usually a rock. His faith in God was so strong that you could almost feel God's presence and power when you were around him. But today, Ben was on his knees in front of a cross bearing the likeness of Jesus. He was rocking back and forth with his head bowed and his hands clasped together. If finding Sarah did this to him, it was not good.

I knelt beside him. Angel knelt on the other side. "Ben, I'm here."

Ben turned to me, his face twisted in agony. I reached over and pulled him to me and hugged him as hard as I could. I had never seen Ben cry, much less fall apart like he did now.

"Let it out, brother. Let it go." I said and felt the urge to sob with him.

He cried for several minutes. Angel looked at me and raised her eyebrows. Her look asked, *What's going on?*

I shrugged my shoulders as much as I could while holding Ben.

"Ben? You said you found Sarah?"

He got control of himself finally, although tears were still streaming from his eyes.

"She's alive, but barely. She was naked, tied up, and stuffed in a burlap bag. I've never seen a person beaten so badly. I don't know how she survived," he sobbed.

My stomach dropped. I looked at Angel and I could tell we were both thinking about Little John.

"Oh no. Does the sheriff know?"

"Yeah, he and Dad are searching the cliff face for evidence." Ben answered.

"If dad is helping," I said for Angel's benefit, "it means they may need the rappelling equipment."

"Did you have to carry her up?" I asked Ben.

He nodded yes.

"Dan, they stuffed her into a crevice. Then they stepped on her or kicked her further in and threw rocks on top of her. They buried her alive. I was searching along the cliff and looking over the edge. She was right at the top. I only found her because I heard a rattling, coughing sound."

"Oh my God," Angel said.

Ben had moved until he was sitting on the floor. I was getting uncomfortable squatting on the floor beside him.

"Come on, let's get you into a chair." What was I supposed to say? I understood why Ben was crying. I couldn't visualize Sarah that way. All I could only see was her smiling face.

Ben stood up. His clothes were filthy, but I wasn't concerned about that.

I sat down beside him. "Ben, talk to me. You're never this shaken. What's bothering you?"

"I was the last person to see her," he said.

"No Ben, whoever did this was the last to see her. You may have been the last one to see her healthy," Angel said. "This was not your fault."

"I could have walked her to her car. I thought she was leaving." Ben looked up at Angel.

"Maybe she took a walk around the park to clear her head. It's something I would do," Angel said.

Ben turned to me. "Dan, I have a confession to make. I've had a crush on Sarah since before you started dating. She was the cutest girl in school. I don't understand how someone could do this."

I was stunned. Ben had a crush on Sarah. The door to the chapel opened and Sarah's mother came in.

"Ben? Oh, thank God. Dan, you're here too." We stood up, and Ben moved towards Mrs. Young with hands out. She pushed his hands aside and enveloped him in a big bear hug. Her make-up was smeared from tears and tissues.

"Thank you, thank you, thank you, for saving my girl," she croaked. Tears were still rolling down her cheeks.

She released Ben and looked at me. I wasn't sure what she was thinking until she reached for me and I gave her a hug, too.

"The sheriff told me everything that happened yesterday and last night with you guys." She saw Angel standing out of the way. "You must be the game warden's daughter. When Sarah gets well, I want you to teach her how to fight, okay?"

Angel let out an obvious sigh of relief. "I would be happy too."

She looked back at me and Ben. "They have stabilized her, and are planning to med-flight her to Baptist Medical Center in Little Rock. I need to be there, but I'm not up to driving. Do you think your mom or dad could drive me? Tom's already in Little Rock and he will meet me there."

Ben immediately volunteered, "I'll drive you, but I need to change clothes."

"We can take my van," Mrs. Young said. She was trying to think logically, but holding back the feelings was very difficult. She hugged Ben again as she tried to hold back the tears.

I was still shocked, but I was thinking logically. "Ben, use my truck and take Mrs. Young home to pack some things. She may be there a while. Angel and I will take her van, fill it up with gas, and meet you at their house. I'll stop by the bank and get you some cash. I keep a spare set of clothes behind the truck seat. They should fit you."

They both just stared at me. I handed my truck keys to Ben.

"Mrs. Young, I need your van keys, please."

Ben was used to me taking charge and giving directions with farm chores, or at livestock shows. Mrs.

Young, as far as I could remember, had never heard me take charge, but she started digging for her van keys.

I reached over and pulled Ben into a hug, and whispered in his ear, "Go pray for her health, and love her the way I couldn't."

I touched Mrs. Young's shoulder, and she turned to me, and I gave her a quick hug. "Whatever you need, let me or Ben know. Okay?"

"Thank you," she said as the tears flowed again.

Mrs. Young and Ben left the Chapel. I turned to the cross in front of the chapel and closed my eyes briefly. *God, please make her well.* I was not one to waste time on long prayers. God knew what I needed. He knew what I wanted. My prayer was to let him know what I desired right then. People who call themselves prayer warriors will disagree. They will say that the longer and more fervent the prayer, the better. I would argue that God already knows our thoughts and desires intimately. Therefore, a short direct prayer was better.

Angel and I found the Young's van in the parking lot. She was trying to ask a question, but I was going over the list in my mind to make sure I didn't miss anything. It was difficult to stay focused because I kept thinking of Sarah, Ben, and Mrs. Young.

Angel tried to speak, but I held up my finger and said, "Hold on."

When I had my list memorized, I looked at Angel. "I'm sorry. I was trying to make sure I thought of everything. But it's difficult with what's happened."

I pulled into a station on the bypass around Heber Springs to fill up the Young's van. It was about a third full. The pump seemed extremely slow.

"Dan, what's going on?"

"What do you mean?"

"Did Ben say he had a crush on Sarah?"

"Yes, he did," I said. "But, more importantly, he asked for my forgiveness and my permission to do something about it. And I gave it to him."

"Okay, I think I missed that conversation," she said. "But it explains a lot."

"It's a brother thing. We often know what the other one is thinking."

Angel reached across the void between the van seats and put her hand on my arm. "I heard you tell him to pray for her health, but I didn't catch what you told him after that. What did you say? It looked like you gave him an emotional boost."

I was almost ashamed to admit it, but I made eye contact and held her gaze for several seconds. "I told him to love her like I couldn't."

"Oh," she said, and squeezed my arm. She looked beautiful then. I wanted to lean across that void between the seats and kiss her. But it was the wrong time to be thinking of something like that.

After filling up the Young's van, I stopped by the bank and got five hundred dollars in cash for Ben and a one-thousand-dollar preloaded Visa card. I didn't consider myself rich, but I managed the farm and the farm accounts.

I didn't know Ben's plans, and I figured he didn't know either. The cash was in case he stayed a day or two. He would have his debit card, but cash came in handy. The Visa card was for him to give to the Youngs for their expenses. He would tell them it was from the church. He and I had done that before. Dad didn't let us tithe to the church. He said it was like giving money to ourselves to pay him, so this was our way of giving and dad went along with it. If they told him thank you for the money, he would pass it off as no big deal, and he would know that Ben and I had helped.

The Youngs lived on Eden Isle, which was a peninsula that stuck out into Greers Ferry Lake. It was a golf course community and was considered the wealthy neighborhood. We pulled into the driveway just as Ben was walking out of the house with Mrs. Young's suitcase. Mrs. Young was locking the front door behind him.

I gave him the cash and card with a brief explanation, and he nodded.

"Keep me updated. Let me know what you need. One of us will come get you, bring you your car, clothes, whatever you need. I love you, Ben."

"I will, I will. Thanks, Dan."

"Drive carefully," I said as Angel and I headed to my truck.

CHAPTER 10

Dan

I drove down a few streets to clear my head and to let Angel see the houses. The rumors said that several country music stars from Nashville owned homes on Eden Isle.

"I like your house and our house better. They have that cozy, home feeling."

"I agree. I love the farm and both houses."

"Can we go fishing tomorrow? I feel more like target practice this afternoon," Angel said.

"Absolutely. I'll show you our private target range."

As we drove back through town, I detoured by the high school and I gave Angel the tour up panther hill where painted panther paw prints on the street led up the hill to the school. The paw tracks led to the football stadium, where my cousin Mike was challenging to become the starting quarterback as a sophomore. It was difficult to drive by the school without thinking about Sarah. Which was exactly what I was trying to do.

The entire school system, from kindergarten through twelfth grade, was on one campus. I drove around the block and showed her the elementary schools and then turned in the drive that went between the football stadium, the gymnasium, and the west end of the high school. We exited the high school campus down North Eleventh Street, past the Methodist Church, and back onto Main Street.

As we were passing city hall, Angel looked out her window and said, "Dan, it's the Hummer."

It was in the grocery store parking lot, next to city hall. There was a white Ford F-150, King Ranch pickup parked beside it. One of the Ray brothers was standing beside the truck, looking at the ground. He was talking to someone under the Hummer.

"Let's get out of here," I said.

"Are these guys rich?" Angel asked. "They have a Hummer, and a King Ranch F-150." My mind had switched directions. "I wonder if Little John is still in jail?"

"What?" Angel asked. Then realizing what I was asking. "Surely, he is."

Then she backtracked, "No, he was arrested for public intoxication. They usually let them sleep it off in jail and let them loose the next day. He may be the one under the Hummer."

We passed through the three-way stop and the red light at the courthouse, and we were at the four-way stop when I looked in the side-view mirror. The sheriff was three cars back, and was staring right at me through the mirror.

I sighed. "Oh, man."

"What?" Angel asked as she twisted in her seat to look behind us.

"The sheriff spotted us."

The sheriff pointed to the right. I knew he wanted me to pull over. He was about to chew us out for leaving the farm. I stuck my arm out the window and gave him a thumbs up.

I drove two blocks and turned left at Spring Park, and parked in one of the diagonal spaces close to the playground. The sheriff pulled into the spot beside me and got out of the SUV, and started yelling as he walked to my window.

"Damn it, Dan. Y'all were told to stay home."

"Ben needed me at the hospital," I replied. The sheriff raised his hands and looked around in exacerbation.

"I don't see the hospital, Dan." I had to laugh and grin at him. "I'm sorry Sheriff. Ben is driving Mrs. Young to Little Rock. We helped with a few errands so they could leave as soon as possible. We are heading home now. After we make a quick stop for some ammo. We are target practicing this afternoon," I told him. He calmed down, as I knew he would, and leaned his forearms into the window of my truck. He knew about our shooting sports team and had always been supportive. "What are you shooting today?"

"Probably my Glock, but I need to get some nine-millimeter ammo for it." He grinned, "You need to let Angel shoot the Glock 19 that I traded you for my grandson's show calf.

"Before you head home, I need to tell y'all something, and I don't want to say it in front of your parents." He breathed deeply before he continued. "Since you've talked to Ben, you know how he found

66

her. We're guessing Sarah was raped. It may or may not have been Little John or one of his cousins. They got Little John out of jail this morning after we started the search, and I'm pretty sure they are no longer in the county."

"Maybe Little John is not. But one of the Ray brothers was standing beside the Hummer in the grocery store parking lot five minutes ago," I said.

"You saw one of them?"

"We both did. They also have a white King Ranch F-150," I added.

"Go home," he said flatly, and turned to his SUV. He stopped and came back. "Little John bragged in the jail last night that he'd had sex with over one hundred women." The sheriff hesitated and then continued. "He said he could count on one finger," he held his right index finger up for emphasis, "one finger, how many of those were consensual." He looked at Angel when he spoke. "Don't mess with them. If you see them, run and call me."

"Yes, sir," we said in unison.

The sheriff honked his horn and made a get-moving gesture. I gave a thumbs up and put the Green Machine in reverse. I explained to Angel the trade I made with the Sheriff.

"Let's go get some shells so you can try it out," I said.

"Me?" She grinned.

"He knows what I have. He doesn't know what you own. But the Glock nineteen is smaller and will fit your hand better." I was avoiding talking and thinking about Sarah. The Sheriff's warning quieted both of us. Fishing is a relaxing sport. Target practice is a way to relieve tension. I suspected Angel would visualize Little John's face every time she shot a target. I know I would.

Thirty minutes later, after a stop at the gun shop, we were back on the farm. We picked up four boxes of nine mil ammo, with each box holding fifty cartridges. It was all they had in stock.

I parked in the gravel drive that went to the shop. Dad was waiting for us because he met me as I got out of the truck.

"Where's Ben?" he asked, putting his left hand on my right shoulder.

"He's driving Mrs. Young to Little Rock. Finding her has really shaken him. He was the last person to see Sarah before this happened and the first to see her after. He blames himself for not walking her all the way to her car. I've never seen him lose it that bad, Dad."

"I know he's devastated. We all are."

"I let him borrow my spare clothes I keep in the truck and he's driving her van to Baptist. He didn't call you or Mom and tell you?"

"No," Dad murmured. "Your mom has some lunch fixed in there if you are hungry. Let's go inside. I'm going to call Ben."

I started toward the house. Dad pulled his phone out of his pocket and speed dialed Ben. We immediately heard a phone ringing in my truck. I stopped and walked back to my truck. The ring was coming from behind the seat. I tilted the seat forward and found Ben's dirty clothes and his phone still in his pants pocket.

I held it up to show Dad, "Looks like one of us is going to Little Rock tonight."

"Your brother couldn't have had anything to do with this, could he?" Dad asked quietly.

Angel answered first, "No, sir. He's a good person. He feels terrible that he wasn't there to protect her."

"Lord, forgive me for questioning my son," Dad prayed with his eyes and head bowed.

"Dad, why would you even think that? You know us both better than that. He liked Sarah, and he feels terrible. He blames himself for not walking her back to her car."

Angel walked over to my dad and gave him a big hug. "Mr. Brock, Ben, and Dan are good guys. I trust them both, and Dan is the best friend I've ever had."

He patted her on the back. "Thank you, Angel. That means a lot to me. I'm sorry, Dan, I was wrong to question Ben."

CHAPTER 11

Dan

Mom had fried some burgers for lunch. She never knew what our schedules were going to be like, and often cooked something she could store in the fridge and we could warm up later.

Our house sat about one hundred fifty feet from the river. The trees along the bank blocked most of the view, but we could see the water when the river was up. The deck ran the length of our house and faced the river, and that's where Angel and I ate lunch. I guess we were both distracted, because we talked very little while we ate.

I was thinking about Sarah and Ben and needed to think about something else. Finally, I asked Angel, "Am I really the best friend you've ever had?"

She had the last bite of her burger almost to her mouth when she stopped and set it down on the paper plate.

"I don't fit in with most girls. I enjoy hunting and fishing and being outdoors. Most of the guys I knew thought that meant I wanted to sleep with them outdoors. You and Ben have treated me as a friend. An equal. You've included me in everything. Y'all aren't like the boys I've always known. You two are men. Real men, like my dad, that I enjoy being around."

She looked down and picked up the last bite of her burger. She blushed a little. After she chewed a few times, I reached over and grabbed her hand.

"Hey, mom, and dad are the reason we are this way. And we choose to treat people with respect. I dated Sarah for nearly a year. We were close, but never sexually close. We had our chances, and we talked about it, but we didn't feel that was what held couples together."

"I don't have many close friends either," I continued. "This farm takes most of my time, and with mom and dad's advice, I manage it well. I don't take time to go partying or run around with my classmates. I love every minute that I spend with you on this farm. You have become the best friend I've ever had, other than my brother."

I laughed a little and said, "And he is my brother. It's not like I got to choose him."

She pulled her hand away from mine and placed both hands in her lap. She looked toward the river as if she were listening for advice.

"Dan, the first time a girl has sex, she wants it to be special. She wants it to be with someone she has feelings for. They certainly don't want to get raped, beaten and buried alive, like Sarah." She turned to look at me then.

I started to speak, but Angel held up her hand.

"I don't want that to happen to me, Dan. That shouldn't happen to any girl. Especially with scum like Little John. Now that I know these guys have made threats against Dad, Mom and me, I'm going to be looking over my shoulder constantly."

She stood up quickly. "Let's go do some target practice. I want to be ready if they come after me."

"Alright," I said. I thought about her comments. I felt horrible about Sarah. And I felt horrible for Ben. When I thought about how he felt when he found her, my gut lurched and I thought I was going to lose the burger I just ate. If these guys raped and beat Sarah, what would they do to Angel? No one should be treated like Sarah had been.

When I walked into the kitchen behind Angel, I was walking with a purpose. Dad always told me to improve my attitude, walk faster, work faster, and think about what I needed to get done. I went into the mudroom. Our fireproof gun cabinet was behind a wall panel next to the half bath. I grabbed the Glocks and their holsters, locked up, and closed the panel. From a shelf near the hidden panel, I grabbed two pairs of safety glasses, earplugs, and a cleaning kit and stuffed it all into a backpack, hanging near our jackets and rain gear.

Angel was thanking Mom for lunch when I stepped back into the kitchen.

"Thank you for lunch, Mom. We are going to target practice for a little while."

She gave me that look. The one that spoke volumes without a word being spoken. Then she said, "Be careful."

"Yes ma'am," Angel and I chorused.

CHAPTER 12

Angel

Even with the new pistol Dan loaned me, I needed little practice. I was perfect from fifteen and twenty yards, and slightly missed the bullseye twice from twenty-five yards. We went through one box of ammo each and we were sitting on a log cleaning our pistols. If they wanted me, they would have to get through my dad first. That wouldn't be easy. If they somehow managed that, though, I wanted to be ready.

"I love this pistol, Dan."

He smiled at me. "Yeah, I know. I think you like it more than you like me."

I turned on the southern drawl then and leaned toward him, "Now you know us southern girls like our guns like we like our men. We like straight shooters, and we like them hot."

"Are you calling me a straight shooter?"

"Yes sir," I drawled.

"Are you calling me hot?"

I moved a strand of hair from my face and watched as the sun flickered on his black hair. It bathed him in a kind of halo.

"You're getting there," I said.

We both laughed.

That's when we heard a truck coming down the wooded road. Dan and I walked, hoping to see a deer or two. We had seen several squirrels and a rabbit, but no deer. Anything was a needed distraction today.

"Something is up. Dad is bringing my truck back here. Let's pack up," Dan said, standing up. "You keep the pistol. I want you to have it for protection."

"Dan, that's a six-hundred-dollar pistol," I exclaimed.

"I've got one, and I can change the magazine faster than I can draw another pistol." He hesitated for just a few seconds, "If you will continue to help me with farm chores and during the fairs, we will work out a payment system for you to buy it."

I frowned for a moment, realizing it was a gift, but he was giving me an easy out to accept it. I walked to him, stood on my tiptoes, put my hand behind his neck and pulled his head down, and kissed him hard on the lips. He needed to know how I felt about him. I'd never felt this way about a guy before. It was a strange but wonderful feeling, which had me thinking about him most of the time.

He kissed me back as hard as he could. That was when his dad started honking the truck horn just before he came into view. He didn't know that we had stopped shooting and had taken our ear plugs out. Dan told me it was a family rule to make a noise before approaching the shooting area. We broke apart and started picking up our stuff and putting it into the backpack he had brought.

His dad pulled up with the window rolled down. He informed us, "Sheriff Tatum has been shot. We need you to come home."

Without a word, I opened the door for Angel and she jumped into the middle and I slid in beside her.

"What's happened?" Dan asked.

"We don't know many details, but apparently there was a shooting in the parking lot between the grocery store and the old city hall. The sheriff sustained injuries and two people lost their lives. That's all we know. They have med-flighted Bull to Baptist Hospital in Little Rock. We are going to drive Mrs. Tatum down there. We need you to finish your chores and drive Ben's car down. Bring his phone and some clothes for him."

"No problem," Dan said. "I'll feed the livestock before I leave. Angel, will you help me with the chores?"

"Sure," I said, giving him a questioning look. We were sure the shooting involved the Ray brothers and possibly Little John.

"Dad, I'm going to pay Angel some to help me with chores. She's been helping already, and since Ben is starting college soon, I'm going to need some help."

"You better talk to him about back pay, Angel."

"Oh, I will, Mr. Brock. I will." I gave him a bittersweet smile he didn't see as he focused on driving. He was worried about his friend, the Sheriff, but still joking with us. It was an unusual person who maintained a sense of humor in a stressful situation.

CHAPTER 13

Dan

We said our goodbyes to mom and dad, and headed to the barn to feed and water the show calves. We had done this without Ben before, and we each knew what needed to be done. I found it strange that Angel and I were suddenly not talking. Our thoughts consumed us. We would pass each other, give a slight smile, and glance away. I felt like I should have been thinking about the shooting. But I was thinking about kissing Angel instead.

It finally hit me. Angel had as much as told me at lunch that she had never had a boyfriend or even a best friend. She had never developed that trust. I had, at least, dated Sarah. And Ben was my best friend, as well as my brother. This was all new to Angel. How do you go from being friends, to becoming boyfriend and girlfriend, to becoming lovers? You either jump right in or you go slow. She trusted me because I had treated her with kindness and respect. I didn't want to lose that trust.

Angel and I were finishing up and cleaning the feed room when I stepped in front of her. She stopped and looked up at me questionably. I took her face in my hands and gently kissed her lips. She grabbed my shirt with both her hands and pulled me to her. I wasn't expecting that, and it threw me off balance. We ended up falling on top of a partial pallet of feed.

I put my hands out and caught myself before I fell on top of her. I bent down and kissed her again. Her hands were under my T-shirt, moving up my back. She lifted her head up and responded to my kiss. *She wants me too.* As soon as I thought that, it stopped me cold.

I broke off our kiss and put my lips to her ear and kissed it gently. "I want you so badly," I whispered. She shivered and drew in a deep breath in response to my whisper. "But not like this. I want our first time to be special, not on a pallet of feed in a barn."

I pushed myself to one side of her and lay there, caressing her face. She was breathing hard and her hand was playing with the hair on my stomach.

"Dan, I want you. I don't care when or where," she said.

We looked into each other's eyes. "I don't want you to just be the first girl I have sex with Angel. I want you to be my best friend, my girlfriend. I want you to be the first woman I fall head over heels in love with and make mad, passionate love to." For just a moment, I hesitated. "If it is meant for us to be together, then I want you to be the woman that I marry and raise children with, but there are so many things we don't know about each other yet."

She closed her eyes and leaned her forehead against mine. "When you put it that way, I think I can wait. I don't want to, but I will."

"I don't even know what your favorite color is," I said.

"Blue." Her breath came quickly, as if rushing me to change my mind.

"Baby blue, sky blue, or dark blue?" I asked.

"The blue of your eyes," she said, tilting her head back and staring at me. "Yours?"

"Forest green," I answered.

I kissed her hard and pulled her into a tight embrace. Her hand slipped from my belly button down into my pants and grabbed the erection that had been growing there. I pulled away from the kiss and reached for her wrist. She let go and pulled her hand out. She smiled playfully at me and said, "It will be worth the wait."

I rolled her on her back, put my hand on her flat belly and inched my hand toward her jeans.

"Do it. Do it, please," she whispered.

My phone rang in my back pocket.

I fell back and reached for the phone. "It's probably Dad. Yep."

I answered, "Hi, Dad!" My heart was pounding, and I struggled to control my breathing.

Angel lay back on the feed bags, her wrist over her eyes, looking like the most beautiful young woman I had ever seen.

I turned away to focus on my conversation with Dad. When he finished and said goodbye, I turned to talk to Angel, but she wasn't there.

Was I in love with Angel? I thought so. I had feelings for Angel that I never felt for Sarah. Not just the physical attraction. I wanted to be around her. She made me happy when she was around and I missed her when she went home.

I know tomorrow is not guaranteed. Ben's words came to mind. They were prophetic, given the circumstances of yesterday and today. Little John could have shot us last night. Sarah was raped and beaten, and now Sheriff Tatum had been shot.

Earlier, I had talked myself into taking it slow, but I knew what I wanted and I wanted to jump right into a relationship with Angel. I had this nagging feeling that our time together was going to be short. I wanted to enjoy every minute we could spend together. These guys had threatened Angel's family. Look at what they had done to Sarah and Sheriff Tatum.

I locked the feed room and stepped out of the barn to find Angel staring at the mountain that rose south of the river. I walked up behind her and put my arms around her thin waist and rested my hands on her stomach. She leaned back against me.

"Dan, I'm sorry, I got carried away. I shouldn't have pressured you," Angel sighed.

I shushed her, bent my head to kiss her ear, and slid my hand down the front of her pants.

She gasped, "Mom might see us." You could see the barnyard where we stood from both of our houses.

"She's gone to Walmart and is with your dad in town. We have the farm to ourselves, but your parents will be on their way home soon. Dad said to wait for them to get home before we leave for Little Rock. Your dad needs to talk to us."

She relaxed and turned her head to kiss me.

CHAPTER 14

Dan

We had just broken from our second kiss when Angel's mom called to let her know we needed to be at their house in fifteen minutes.

"Take my four-wheeler, I'm going to go shower and change."

"Okay," echoed behind her as she ran to my four-wheeler.

I took a quick shower and then gathered some clothes to take to Ben. I grabbed his shaving kit from the bathroom. From his closet, I took a gym bag and filled it with three days' worth of clothing. Then I spotted his Bible on the dresser.

I held his Bible in my hands and said a quick prayer and asked for complete healing for Sarah and Sheriff Tatum, and guidance for me and Angel.

I packed his Bible, grabbed his spare car keys from the key rack in the mudroom, and headed to my truck. Grabbing the backpack that still held the Glocks and boxes of ammo, I threw it over my shoulder. I put the bags in the back seat of Ben's Honda Accord and headed to the Cottons.

It was late afternoon, and the sun was setting. The car was extra hot, and I rolled the windows down to air it out. I enjoyed the breeze from the window and the beauty of the sun reflecting off the house and the tree-line just ahead of me. Even with all the tragedies happening yesterday and today, I was happier than I had ever been. I was in love. Then I thought about Sarah and Sheriff Tatum and all the joy came crashing down. How do you feel happy and sad at the same time? This roller coaster of emotion was turning into a storm.

I got to the rental house, now the Cottons' home, just in time to help Mrs. Cotton unload groceries.

She asked me, "Where is my daughter? I thought she was with you."

"She came home to take a shower right after you called."

Officer Cotton pulled into the drive as we carried the last of the groceries into the house.

"Hi Dan," he called from his truck. "I hope you don't mind. I put up a game camera just down the driveway from the main road."

"Don't mind at all. I should have thought of that myself," I replied. The camera would record anyone who turned into our drive.

His size always amazed me. He was six-foot-five and at least two hundred and sixty pounds of muscle.

"I'm taking as many precautions as I can. This situation has gotten out of hand. Come on, I need to talk to you and Angel."

He relieved Mrs. Cotton of her bags and we headed to the house. Mrs. Cotton opened and held the door for us to enter. We put the grocery bags on the dining table. I noticed they had not swapped out my grandparent's old oak dining table and chairs for theirs. It was antique, but still beautiful and very sturdy.

Mrs. Cotton yelled, "Angel, you're needed in the kitchen."

"Coming Mom," she replied.

Mr. Cotton had stepped out of the room to remove his holster and pistol. Angel entered the kitchen and my jaw dropped. She was wearing a white spaghetti strap sundress. Her hair was pulled to the left side of her face and over her shoulder, and she was wearing lipstick. I had never seen her wear lipstick or make-up. She was gorgeous.

"Wow," her mom said. "Who are you and what have you done with my daughter?"

"Mom, I thought you wanted me to act more ladylike," Angel replied as she gave her mom a hug.

Her dad came in and whistled. He looked at Mrs. Cotton. "Did you ask her what she did with our daughter?"

"Would y'all stop," Angel begged, giving her dad a smile and a hug.

I stared at Angel and she finally asked, "What are you staring at, Mr. Brock?"

"You Cotton top, I never imagined you were so beautiful."

Changing the subject quickly, her dad said, "Okay, listen, you two. I have an evidence box in the truck I need you to take to Little Rock. A state trooper will meet you at the hospital. You will give her the box. She will interview the two of you. And Dan, she will interview your brother Ben and your dad."

He hesitated and looked at both of us to make sure he had our attention. "Anytime a city or county officer is involved in a shooting, the state police are called in to investigate. The Sheriff is being investigated for shooting one of the Ray brothers. And accusations are already being made against the sheriff, the chief deputy, and myself. The sheriff's department seems to be in some turmoil right now. Half of the department supports the sheriff and the other half believes the Ray's attorneys."

"How is the sheriff doing?" I asked.

"We have heard nothing. Hopefully, you can give us an update after you get there," Mr. Cotton answered.

My next question was, "Who was killed today?"

Officer Cotton sighed, "Danny Ray, and a city patrolman. I didn't catch his name. He came out of city hall during the shooting and caught a stray bullet."

Angel looked at her dad. "Isn't this against protocol? Having us transport an evidence box to Little Rock?"

"Yes, but it has been approved. I'll put the box into a duffle bag to make it look like luggage," he said.

"Daddy, you're scaring me. Are there police officers taking the Ray's side?" Angel asked.

Her dad sighed heavily. "Yes, and maybe people higher up. But I didn't tell you that, because I can't prove anything. Y'all need to get on the road. Dan, do you know your way through Searcy?"

I smiled. "Absolutely."

"Put your brother's luggage in the trunk on top of the duffle bag. There is a good chance you will get stopped at a sobriety checkpoint between here and Searcy. They can look in your car, but they can't search your trunk without a search warrant. We are hoping they won't bother two seventeen-year-olds and you can get the evidence to the State Police."

I nodded. "Someone wants the evidence lost. So, if it's lost, but not lost, the State Police have time to build a case."

Angel was grinning at me. Officer Cotton said, "You got it. I'm sorry to use you this way. But you have friends who were hurt in this case, and we figured you would help."

"No problem," I answered. A lump formed in my throat. "May I change the subject and ask a personal question?"

Mr. Cotton seemed hesitant. "I guess I owe you that much. What's your question?"

"Mr. Cotton? Mrs. Cotton? May I have permission to date, Angel?"

Mr. Cotton grinned in relief. Mrs. Cotton laughed out loud. "I've been wondering how long it would take. She's talked about nothing but you since we moved here."

"Mom!" Angel pleaded.

"We've raised Angel to be independent," Mr. Cotton replied. "You'll have to ask her." As he nodded at his daughter.

I turned to Angel, "Well?"

"You're not getting off that easy. You asked them properly, ask me properly too."

"Angel, would you go out with me?" I asked.

"Well, of course, you dummy. Do you think I would wear a dress for just anybody, even though tonight is not a date?" She looked hesitant. "Is it?"

"I don't think we can count tonight as a date. It's more like a secret mission, a hospital visit, and an interrogation."

Officer Cotton laughed. "Come on, Dan, let's get that duffle bag."

I looked at Angel's feet. They weren't cute feet. They were runner's feet, long, wide, and callused.

"Where are your shoes?" I asked, following Officer Cotton out the door.

Angel looked at her mom. "Mom, can I borrow your flats?"

We left them to figure out the shoe situation. I followed Mr. Cotton to his truck. He unlocked the toolbox behind the passenger side cab of his truck and pulled out a file box taped closed with duct tape. The tape had evidence written on it in black marker. He pulled out a duffle bag that had USMC stamped on it and put the box inside and clipped it closed.

I opened the back door of the Accord and pulled out Ben's bag. I grabbed the backpack as well.

I unlocked the trunk and Officer Cotton put the duffle in and I put Ben's bag on top.

"Remember, do not open the trunk for anyone except the State Trooper who interviews you. Let them take the bag out of the trunk. Don't touch it, okay?"

"Yes, sir."

Angel and her mom were coming out of the house. As I closed the trunk, Mr. Cotton touched my arm.

"There are a lot of adults in this town who respect you, Dan. I want to ask a favor of you, tonight. If anything happens to me soon, take care of my daughter, okay?"

I could see the worry lines around his eyes. It concerned me that he would ask a seventeen-year-old to take care of his daughter. I couldn't tell him I had already made that commitment to myself, but I could give him a hint. The Glock 19 was for Angel's protection.

"Yes sir. She and Mrs. Cotton can stay here as long as they want. Now, I have a favor to ask." I held out the backpack to him. "Would you keep this for me? Angel and I were shooting this afternoon, and I don't want to get stopped and accused of carrying concealed weapons."

"What's in here?" he asked.

Angel answered for me as she walked up. "Dan's Glock 17. My Glock 19, which Dan is going to let me do farm work to pay off, several boxes of ammo, and a cleaning kit. Good night, Daddy. Let's go, Dan."

She gave her dad a quick kiss, and we soon backed out of the drive.

"What's the rush?" I asked.

"Mom and Dad have had arguments about guns. I wanted to avoid that argument tonight."

Angel reached over and grabbed my leg. "Why did you ask my parents if you could date me?"

I had to shake off the conversation I had with Officer Cotton before I could answer. I actually stuttered a little. "Because you came out wearing a dress and lipstick. You are beautiful, you know. I want their permission to date you. I don't want to run around the farm hiding."

She took her hand off my leg as we turned onto the county road from our drive.

"About this afternoon..."

"Are you breaking up with me already?" I asked mischievously.

"After you had the guts to ask my dad for permission to date me? You are stuck with me, Dan Brock. I never thought I would meet anyone man enough to ask my dad what you did tonight."

"What about this afternoon?"

"Please forgive me for being so forward. I'm new at this dating stuff, and Sarah's attack has me thinking all kinds of crazy stuff."

"I'm just glad we feel the same way about each other. I enjoy being with you, and I miss you when you go home at night. Sometimes, I want to say something to you and realize you have gone home. I don't think our relationship will be all about sex. And I sure don't want your dad or my dad to catch us doing that. Anyway, we have time to plan for that."

She reached for my hand and pulled it to her lips and kissed the back of it. She held it there longer than I felt she should have. When I glanced at her in the darkening evening, I could see her eyes closed tightly as she held back tears. She finally dropped my hand to the console between us.

"I'm scared, Dan. I'm worried about Dad. If these guys raped and beat Sarah, what would they do to me and Mom? If they shot the sheriff, they wouldn't hesitate to shoot Dad. What makes them think they can get away with it?"

"Take a deep breath. I'd give you a big hug right now, but I'm driving." I tried to be lighthearted. There was no way I would tell her what her dad had just asked me. *If something happens to me, take care of my daughter.* I was frightened too.

Five minutes later, we came to the roadblock. They had their blue lights flashing, and you could see them from a distance. They were smart. There was one deputy sheriff parked a half mile up the road from the checkpoint. If anyone turned around to avoid the checkpoint, he would stop them. The checkpoint was at the beginning of a two-lane bridge crossing the Little Red River going into Pangburn. There were three highways leaving town from there, making this an easy bottleneck to catch all traffic before it dispersed in several directions.

There were several cars and trucks ahead of us. Officers were stationed on both sides of the vehicles and they were conducting inspections.

When it was almost our turn, one deputy looked our way and grinned. I looked at Angel. "I've got a funny feeling. Follow my lead."

Angel drawled, "Okay."

The deputies motioned for us to roll our windows down.

"Howdy, you're Dan Brock, aren't you?" The deputy on my side asked.

"Yes sir, do you need my license and registration?" I had already gotten the registration and insurance card out of the console while we were in line.

"Yes, please. Who's your friend?" the deputy asked.

"This is Angie Lewis, a friend of mine and Sarah Young's, from school. We're heading to Little Rock to check on her," I answered, and hoped I lied convincingly.

"Doesn't the new game warden rent a house from y'all?"

"Yes sir. We thought it would be good to have him around in case we had any more cows shot during hunting season."

"Did you see him today, before you left?"

"No sir. I haven't seen him or his family today."

The deputy looked doubtful and disappointed. His partner had shined his flashlight all over the back seat.

"Alright," he finally said and handed my license, registration, and insurance card back. "Y'all drive careful."

"Yes, sir." We rolled our windows up and drove away.

Neither of us spoke for several miles. How did he know so much about me and the Cottons and why he was so curious?

Angel was the first to speak. "Angie Lewis? Who is Angie Lewis?"

Of all the questions I expected her to have, that wasn't the first.

"Angie is also short for Angelina, and Lewis was my birth name before Ben and I were adopted."

"Oh, so it wasn't a random name or some real person I have to watch out for," she grinned. "You just changed my nickname and added your old last name. Are you trying to marry me already?"

"Would you say yes?" I toyed with her.

"Are you asking? Because I don't think you're being very serious. And you can't possibly have a ring."

But I got serious and said, "I'm not serious today, but someday, I will ask you to marry me." Marriage was a topic that Sarah and I never talked about. But it felt natural with Angel.

She turned in the seat toward me and grabbed my hand. "And someday, I will say yes."

We smiled at each other until a glimmer of blue light caught my attention in the mirror. "Blue lights behind us. Call your dad and tell him about the checkpoint. Keep him on the line in case we are getting pulled over."

Angel speed-dialed her dad. She started talking immediately, telling him everything. When she was telling him about the lights behind us, I found a wide driveway to pull into. But then the lights flew past us, heading on toward Searcy. There was an enormous sigh of relief from Angel's phone, and Angel and I sighed as well.

"You should be clear once you reach the freeway. Don't be alarmed if a state trooper follows you there," Mr. Cotton said over the speaker.

"Thanks, Daddy, I love you," Angel replied.

"I love you too, sweetheart," said the deep voice on the other end.

CHAPTER 15

Dan

After a quick stop for a Quarter Pounder for me and fries for Angel, we hit the interstate and headed to Little Rock. A look in the mirror revealed a white King Ranch Ford truck behind us. We held our breath until it passed us and we saw two older ladies in the front. I held my breath so long I had to take a few deep breaths. It wasn't the other Ray brother coming after us. A little further outside of Searcy, another car began to follow us. It was a state trooper. He stayed several car lengths behind us until another trooper took over at the last Cabot exit. That one followed us all the way to the Baptist Hospital parking lot. He pulled up beside us and motioned for us to follow him.

On the southwest side of the large hospital parking lot was a parking deck. We followed him past the front entrance and into the parking deck. We drove around in circles until we reached the top of the deck. There, the trooper leading us pulled up to another trooper's car and an unmarked Camaro. There were two troopers standing between the two vehicles. One was a tall black female; the other was a short white male. The female waved us to a parking space and the trooper who led us here circled around and left the parking deck.

"I suddenly feel like we are in some kind of thriller movie."

"No kidding," Angel said. "I don't think we have taken this seriously enough."

"They have my full attention now," I said.

We opened the car doors, but the officer said, "Hold on, don't exit the car yet. Young man, what's your name?"

"Daniel Brock," I replied.

"And you, young lady?"

"Angelina Cotton," Angel answered.

"Okay, please step out of the car," the female trooper said.

I reached down and pulled the latch to open the trunk, then stepped out of the Honda. I looked at Angel to see her holding her dress down against her legs. The wind was whipping at all of us. I looked back at the female trooper.

She softened her voice a little. "I'm Sergeant Johnson with the Arkansas State Police Special Investigation Division. I may come across as rude and direct. Unfortunately, it is part of my job. Now please open the trunk."

I opened the lid and stepped back.

Sergeant Johnson stepped forward. "Have you opened the trunk since Officer Cotton placed the evidence box in your trunk?"

"No ma'am," I answered.

"Manners and respect. I like that," she said.

"Yes ma'am," I replied.

She moved the gym bag to the side and lifted the duffle. She unclipped the snap and tugged at the bottom of the duffle, gently dumping the evidence box out into the trunk.

Then she stepped back, "Trooper Vega, please take this evidence box back to the lab and dump it in the trash."

"But you can't do that," Angel protested.

"Angelina!" Sergeant Johnson said with such command to her voice that it rocked us both back on our heels. "You were a distraction. A deputy that your father and the Sheriff trusted is delivering the real evidence box as we speak. We didn't think you could bluff your way through that roadblock without getting searched. I wanted them to find it, but it didn't work. I'm sorry we used you. We were trying to find out who is on who's side and it failed."

"What do you mean?" Angel asked, obviously frustrated.

"It doesn't matter. We tried to set someone up, and they either weren't part of the roadblock or they didn't exist. Your father will explain it later."

Sergeant Johnson told us to drive back down to level two and park there. She told us to take the covered walkway which stretched between the parking deck and the hospital and follow the signs to the ICU waiting room. She had a few calls to make and would find us. I thought Angel's dad was intimidating, but Sergeant Johnson scared me.

It was nearly nine p.m. when we found the ICU waiting room. The first person I saw was Dad, talking to a doctor. Dad could get information from doctors when he wasn't supposed to get the information. He would tell the doctors that the family needed a simple explanation of what was going on with their loved one. Dad had been a medic in the army and understood medical terms that most people did not. He would explain his background to the doctors and get the information he needed to share with the families.

Dad was standing at his full height when talking to the doctor, but I could see him physically and mentally deflate when he turned away. Whatever he was told, it was not good news.

We headed through an unusually crowded waiting room searching for anyone we knew and found everyone in one common group. The Youngs, Ben, and Mom, and Mrs. Tatum huddled in one group. Dad was walking toward them. I took Angel's hand and headed to join them.

We were right behind Dad when he kneeled in front of Mrs. Tatum and told her, "The good news is Bull is alive but in critical condition. The bullet entered his abdomen right below the bulletproof vest. It caused a lot of damage to the lower intestines. They believe they have patched all the holes, but will monitor it closely. The bad news is that the bullet severed part of the spinal cord before lodging next to it. They are afraid he may be paralyzed from the waist down. They are moving him to an ICU room to get him stabilized before they decide to do any more surgeries."

She looked at my father. "Thank you, Lloyd, thank you for being here."

She turned to my mom, who was sitting beside her, and pulled her into a tearful hug.

Dad started to stand up, but hesitated. I reached down and offered my arm. "Let me help you, Dad. You've had a long day."

"Thank you, son." He grabbed my arm and helped me as I pulled him up. "We've all had a long day."

I turned to the Youngs and my brother. "Any word on Sarah?" I asked.

I was surprised when Ben spoke instead of one of her parents. But they both sat and looked between me and Ben as he spoke.

"The last we heard was about an hour ago. She is still in surgery. That's all we know."

It was my turn to deflate. I felt the energy leave me as my shoulders slumped. Looking at the Youngs, I said, "I am so sorry. I feel like this is my fault somehow. If I had only talked to her," and I let my words trail off.

"Dan, it's not your fault," Mr. Young said. "We don't blame you. We just want to find who did this."

I wanted to scream. *I know who did it.* But I didn't know, not really. I just had a huge suspicion. Ben was on his feet and had me in a bear hug. Angel eased her hand across my back.

"Excuse me. I apologize for interrupting a moment," a female voice said.

I turned to find Sergeant Johnson watching us closely.

Angel took her hand off my back. "Everyone, this is Sergeant Johnson with the state police. She is here to interview several of us about Sheriff Tatum's shooting."

When Ben let go of me, he had tears in his eyes. I suspected there was something he wasn't telling me, but there was no time to ask.

I turned to Sergeant Johnson. "Who is first, ma'am?"

CHAPTER 16

Dan

Sergeant Johnson had secured an office on the first floor. She didn't take long with Dad. He helped with the search for Sarah, but he wasn't there for any of the exchanges between the sheriff and the Rays. Dad said the best he could do was serve as a character witness.

She took a little longer with Ben, but he didn't hear the exchange between the sheriff and Little John or Donny.

It seemed like she talked to Angel forever, but it was closer to twenty minutes.

When Angel left the office, she looked exhausted. She walked to me, and I stood to meet her. We wrapped each other in a hug. The longer I waited, the more I realized I hadn't taken this situation seriously. I had let my growing feelings for Angel interfere with where my head and heart should be.

"She's ready for you. I'll wait here," she said.

"No. You either stay with me, or I walk you back upstairs to stay with everyone else. I'm not leaving you alone out here." I wasn't leaving Angel alone. Not like we left Sarah.

We walked to the office door where Sergeant Johnson was and stopped. She looked up from her writing and spoke. "Just you, Dan."

"No ma'am. I'm not leaving Angel out here by herself. Either she comes in with me, or I walk back upstairs with her so she can stay with my family."

She looked at her watch and back at me. "Okay, she can come in. Do not look at her for answers and Angel, do not give him any help. Am I clear?"

"Yes ma'am," we both replied.

"Dan, take a seat. Angel, stand behind him. Dan, tell me your version of what happened last night on the launch ramp."

I told her my recollection of what had happened. I didn't stop until I told her about how the deputy ordered us to go straight home because Officer Cotton needed to talk to us.

She made me repeat what everyone said. I had to repeat some statements three times. I had to describe what everyone was wearing down to their shoes. She asked me to describe the inside of the Hummer, item by item.

Finally, she asked, "Tell me about the shoe you saw in the back seat."

When I finished describing the shoe, I said, "Sarah and her mom enjoyed sewing and doing crafts. I think they made those shoes. They're one of a kind."

She reviewed her notes and nodded her head. "Thank you two for helping. I have your contact information if I need anything else. Goodnight."

It was nearing eleven when we walked back into the ICU waiting room. I could tell something was very wrong. The Youngs were not there, and Dad and Ben were leaning forward in prayer. My mother had a very pained look on her face, and Mrs. Tatum was comforting Mom.

"Mom, what's going on?"

She raised her head and focused for just a few seconds on me and Angel holding hands. Then she raised her eyes to my face. "Sarah didn't make it."

A numbness hit me and I felt my knees go weak. It must have hit Angel, too. We both sat down hard in the nearest chairs. The air just left me and I caught myself gasping. Tears formed in the corners of my eyes. "No, no, no."

Angel buried her head against my chest, and I wrapped my arms around her. The guilt I felt was indescribable. I hadn't taken this seriously. Only old people died. We were supposed to live long, happy lives. I never got the chance to apologize. Sarah never got to say what she wanted to say to me. *Tomorrow is not guaranteed,* rang in my head.

I lost the joy of being young and innocent at that very moment. I knew without a doubt, I would kill anyone who threatened the people I loved, which included my parents, Ben, and Angel. And if I could kill the person who killed Sarah, I wouldn't hesitate to do it.

I whispered as quietly as I could, "I'll kill the bastard if I ever see him."

"You'll have to beat me to it," Angel answered. "That could have been me."

* * * * *

It's too late for "I'm sorry" after someone has passed away. That moment of opportunity is gone forever. Those regrets are the genuine ghosts that haunt the living.

Ben handled Sarah's death worse than me or Angel. I think it had to do with him not walking her to her car than the way he found her. He would be upset even if it was someone else, but having known her, had a crush on her, and thinking he could have prevented her death made it much worse. His eyes had a vacant look. Depression had swallowed his soul, and he was waiting for it to come for the rest of him. I had not seen him pray in several days. He was questioning his faith. How could God let this happen to someone as innocent, loving, and caring as Sarah? How could that kind of evil walk this earth as a human being? Ben wasn't finding any answers, and I wasn't leaving him alone until he did.

I could see what Ben was going through, and my heart ached for him. My feelings were on two similar levels. I was dealing with the loss of Sarah also, but just as hard was dealing with my feelings for Angel. She had pushed me away the night we left the hospital. After I dropped her off at her house and Ben and I drove to ours, she texted me; *We didn't get to talk on the way home. You need to deal with your feelings for Sarah before we continue our relationship.*

All I could answer was, *Okay.* I read the message again. She said to *deal with your feelings for Sarah.* Okay, I understood that. Then she said *before we continue our relationship.* That part confused me.

Ben was taking a shower, and I could hear him crying through the door. I grabbed the pillow from my bed and sat on the floor in the corner of my bedroom. I buried my face in it and cried, too. Was I crying for Sarah, Angel, Ben, or myself? It didn't matter. I cried for all of us. I don't know when I fell asleep. We got home after midnight, and it felt like I cried for hours after that.

Ben shook me awake at five a.m. If he was surprised to find me asleep on the floor, he said nothing. "Let's go for our run," he said.

It wasn't the run he wanted, but the distraction of the run. But running often leaves you alone with your thoughts, and thoughts and feelings are two things you can't run away from. Sarah was gone. Murdered. Angel was pushing me away. I wanted to hold her, to make love to her. And Ben, my brother, an anchor of Christian faith, was falling apart.

As I dressed for our run, I grew angry. Angry at the person who caused all this pain. He had to pay for his actions, but how? I threw my jeans at my closet, but there was no release for the anger as they crumpled to the floor.

To my surprise, Angel was waiting at the end of her driveway to join us for the morning run. Had she pushed me away? No, she wasn't pushing me away; she was stepping back and giving me room to grieve and deal with my emotions. I realized she wanted to be close to me, but she wanted me to deal with my pain without substituting her for Sarah. She wanted me to love her, not use her, because I missed someone else. I didn't like it. Her actions confused me, but I respected her enough not to push the subject. I could tell her I loved her more than I ever loved Sarah, and it was truthful. But she would still question whether it was the truth or my pain and misery talking.

CHAPTER 17

Angel

Giving Dan space and time to grieve Sarah's death wasn't what I wanted to do. It was what I had to do before I allowed our relationship to go any further. I knew Dan said he and Sarah were over, but were there lingering feelings? Was our relationship going somewhere? I didn't want to be the senior year girlfriend he dumped when school was out. I was falling for Dan, but I needed to know he didn't break up with Sarah because she was sick. Would he stand by me when times were difficult? I wanted someone like my dad. Strong, loving, and always supportive. I thought Dan might be that man, but he needed space to mourn, space to support Ben.

Dad often said, "When you're too close to a situation, step back and look at the big picture." But I couldn't see it. All I could feel was Dan's arms around me, his fingers exploring my body, and his warm breath in my ear. I wanted to feel that again. But I didn't want him to break my heart, either. Right now, he needed me to be a friend, and I needed him. I'd never lost anyone I knew. I couldn't remember my grandparents. None of my school friends had ever died.

Not only was I questioning Dan and Ben's feelings about Sarah, I was questioning mine. What frightened me the most was that we suspected Dad's enemies.

They had threatened Dad, and me and Mom. I had taken none of this seriously until I learned Sarah had died. Then it all made sense. This was why we had moved my senior year. Dad was trying to protect me and Mom from danger.

And there were Ben's feelings. Did he have more than a crush on Sarah? Or was it the shock and trauma of finding Sarah beaten, naked, and half buried? Crush or not, the second part would cause me trauma. My heart broke for him.

So, when Ben texted me, they were running; I said I'd be ready. And here I was, waiting to join them on a morning run. Ben set a crazy pace, until he broke down crying and screaming, "Why?" incoherently. He sat down on the ground and grabbed handfuls of dirt and gravel and flung them everywhere. I sat down behind him and hugged him. There was nothing I could say, because I didn't know what to say. I just hugged him, cried, and rocked back and forth with him. Dan joined us and hugged us both.

"I love you, Ben. I'm here. I'm here."

I don't know why or how, but I found the answers to my questions in that hug. It was Ben who was grieving the most. He not only lost Sarah, he was on the verge of losing his faith in God. Dan would always be there for his brother. And I knew if we fell in love with each other, he would be there for me as well.

CHAPTER 18

Dan

Funerals are never easy, and Sarah's was no exception. It was held in the high school gymnasium. Ben and I were pallbearers. The Youngs asked me and Ben if we wanted to speak. I respectfully declined, saying my emotions couldn't handle it. It didn't surprise me when Ben said the same thing. Our guilt and our emotions were tearing us to pieces.

Sarah's death shocked the entire community. It appeared the whole high school showed up, plus half of the town. It was the week before school started and depression was the norm. The Youngs owned the insurance agency my biological father started. They were well-known and well-liked. Everyone wanted to show their support for the family. The problem was the state police insisted on keeping the details quiet. Therefore, it left everyone to believe Sarah had lost her battle with leukemia.

Those who knew the truth hurt even more. Sarah had beaten the cancer. She was recovering and getting her strength back. Her mother told me Sarah wanted to thank me for stepping back from our relationship. She had planned the future that she wanted. College and traveling the world were her first steps. Staying at home and living on a farm were not part of that plan. Sarah still cared for me and wanted to be friends. That was a bombshell I didn't expect after our brief confrontation at the lake. I hurt even more for the girl who had been my closest friend outside of Ben and Angel. Worst of all, I felt like God let us all down. How could anyone take the loss of a young, beautiful woman and create something positive from it? I didn't see a way. She had a bright future, one Little John had torn away from her.

There were murmurs and questions about why the coffin had remained closed. There were several poster size pictures and a constantly running slideshow of pictures of Sarah that ran during visitation and before the service.

The preacher, whom Ben and I did not know, tried to be positive and tried to find the silver lining, but he failed miserably. It wasn't his fault. There was nothing positive about it.

Sarah's parents had asked me that morning to reconsider speaking. They knew it would be difficult, but they wanted me to speak at her funeral. I reluctantly agreed.

When the preacher finished his part, he looked at me and nodded. I stood and walked up the steps of the little stage, and I placed my hands on the podium, but I did not look up.

"Until the end of school last year, Sarah and I were boyfriend and girlfriend," I said. "The truth is, we were just close friends. We were an unlikely couple. The farm boy and the beautiful socialite. We talked about our dreams, our plans, and our hopes. She wanted to travel the world, explore new places, and meet new people. She wanted to go to college in Fayetteville, and attend

Razorback football and basketball games. I wanted to stay on the farm and go to college here."

"Sarah had a smile that would brighten your day. A personality that would challenge you to excel and inspire you to be better."

"Last Christmas, the Angel Tree had a lot of kids who needed presents, and people were slow picking them up. We went and selected ten kids' names from the tree. She called several friends, and we went shopping. She raised the money, and we fulfilled the Christmas wishes of ten kids last year."

"Sarah was a saint that cared more about others than herself. This spring, she became aware of a young lady who was invited to prom but couldn't afford a prom dress. She again raised some money and invited the girl to go shopping with her. At a boutique, they found the perfect dress, and the owner made her friend a great deal on her prom dress. It had been pre-arranged by Sarah."

"Sarah, again, took care of someone else's needs. I could tell you more stories where she worked behind the scenes to help people, but you get the picture. She was a fixer. She fixed problems and didn't care if she received recognition or not."

"In memory of Sarah Young, my family and hers will give a two-thousand-dollar scholarship to a graduating senior each year, starting this year."

I had not looked up from the podium while I spoke. There were over a thousand people in the gym. Speaking to so many people would have given me stage fright had I looked up.

We had always blown kisses at school because actual kisses, public displays of affection, were not allowed on campus. I looked at the casket, which was below the podium, and blew a kiss at the closed lid. "Goodbye, Sarah," I quietly said and left the stage. I wanted to pick the podium up and crash it to the stage until it was in a hundred little pieces. I wanted to yell and scream at the unfairness of life. But I did what I was told to do, and I was questioning the societal rules we lived by. I was questioning God and myself.

Seventeen-year-olds should not be asked to speak at a funeral. They should not be asked to lie about the death of the one to be buried. It was a hard afternoon accepting the condolences from friends and high school students who were trying to show support but not knowing how. Many were confused. They had seen her around town recently and were shocked by her sudden death. I wanted to scream that she was murdered, but somehow, I held my tongue.

The graveside service was long over when Ben and I left to find our parents and Angel. Mom and Dad had both tried to engage me and Ben in conversations about Sarah's death since we left the hospital. We had both brushed them off. Now, we were bone tired and they could see it. We all got into Mom's Escalade and headed home.

Angel was sitting between me and Ben and spoke first. "Are we going to do it?"

I looked at Ben, and he was nodding his head.

"Mom, Dad? We want to get away for a few days before school starts. We want to clear our heads."

Mom was driving and looked in the rearview mirror. "I think that's a good idea."

Dad turned in the passenger seat to look back at us. "What about the calves? Do you have a plan?"

"We'll turn them loose in the lot. Would you feed them for me? All you have to do is water and feed them twice a day. They're stressed from the grooming we've done the last three days. This will be good for them, too."

He looked at me hard and then nodded. "I'm proud of all three of you. It's been a stressful week. Where are you going?"

I wasn't used to lying to my dad and what I said wasn't really a lie. "We haven't decided. We are just going to get in the car and drive. I will call you when we get there." I knew exactly where we were going, but Ben and Angel didn't know.

Very little got by Dad. He looked at Ben sternly, almost with disapproval. "Be careful, boys. Angel."

We didn't talk the rest of the way home.

We dropped Angel at her house. Mom and Dad immediately started talking.

Dad asked, "Dan, what's going on between you and Angel?"

Ben answered. "Nothing right now, Dad. They were going to start dating, but Angel backed off and told Dan that he needed to deal with his feelings for Sarah before they could start dating. She's been a big support for us the last three days."

Dad was staring at me from the front seat. I said, "Angel feels horrible about the way she treated Sarah when they met. Ben and I both feel guilty about letting Sarah walk away without protection. We are all dealing with our own guilt, Dad. Each one of us could have done something differently that may have kept Sarah alive. We will never know, and we must live with it. We've become our own support group."

Mom had pulled into the garage. She was visibly crying. Her voice quivered when she said, "You know you can talk to us about anything, right?"

"We know," Ben said. "And thank you."

"No one is blaming you for her death," Dad said.

Neither Ben nor I said anything, and Dad understood that we both felt guilty.

"Okay, you boys need to stop blaming yourselves. Get away and come back home clear-headed. We love you and we are here when you want to talk."

* * * * *

After changing out of our suits, we let the calves loose in the lot. Ben, Angel, and I had worked hard the last few days. We stayed busy from the time we woke until we finally went to bed. We talked little, but I did more talking than Ben and Angel combined. My talking was primarily assigning chores to be done. I had never been ready for show season this early in the year. The calves were all clipped and groomed. Grooming equipment was all cleaned, oiled, and loaded on the trailer. The trailer was cleaned, and the lights were working. The camping section at the front of the trailer was even cleaned and stocked.

We were taught as kids that idle hands are the devil's playground. Our hands weren't idle and our minds weren't either. It was Ben's mind, his mental state, that I worried about. He had broken down twice. The first time, Angel had held him, and cried with him while he cried himself out. The second time was also during our morning run. He brushed us off and just kept running and crying. I knew he couldn't run away from that kind of pain, but he tried.

It was Angel who suggested we get away the morning of the funeral. We had just finished our fifth lap around the farm. No one paid attention to our times, but I believe we broke some personal records. We were bent over with our hands on our knees, trying to catch our breath.

"We need to get away. This isn't working for us," she said.

"I agree," was Ben's surprising response.

"When?" I asked.

"Today. After the funeral," he replied. "Just pick a place, Dan. I don't care. We can take my car and you can drive."

That's how we found ourselves in Memphis, Tennessee at nine p.m. on another hot Monday night in August. We stopped at two motels before using our phones to call a Holiday Inn near the airport with a vacancy. Angel and I dropped Ben off to secure a room while we went searching for pizza. I'd asked Ben to call home and let our parents know where we were.

We picked up three pizzas and found Ben waiting for us in the room. We finished the pizzas and set the empty boxes on the tiny table provided. He sat on one bed while Angel and I shared the other one. We sat cross-legged on the bed, our shoulders and legs touching. I hadn't thought about our actions.

But Ben noticed and asked, "Are you two sleeping together?"

I immediately got angry. "Ben, that's uncalled for."

Ben raised his hand. "I'm sorry. It's the way you two are together. When your bodies touch, you don't apologize or seem to feel like your space has been invaded. It's like you can read each other's thoughts. I see it, but I can't explain it."

Angel put her hand on my arm before I could respond. "No, Ben. We haven't slept together. We barely talked about dating. Dan asked my parents for permission to date me the night Sarah died."

Any sermon Ben was about to give must have melted away. I watched him wither and slump down on his bed.

He took a deep, ragged breath and began talking. "I'm sorry, I wasn't thinking. I was angry because I thought y'all weren't respecting Sarah."

"Is that why you only got one room?" I asked. "You wanted to lecture us on our lack of respect?"

He nodded. "Something like that, and they only had one room. I could tell you had gotten close. I heard Angel say she was going to give you some time and space to deal with any lingering feelings about Sarah. That's why I defended you with Dad today."

Angel squeezed my arm before I could say anything else.

"Ben, I love both of you. You're the brother I never had. Dan has shown me respect from the first day we met. He answered all my questions without putting me down. He never treated me like a dumb girl. And he is the first man I've ever met, besides you, that treated me as an equal. That made an impression on me. Guys have always treated me as a dumb girl to have sex with. Dan is different. You are different. Our relationship is not about sex. It's about love and respect. We enjoy being together."

Ben nodded. "I can see that, and I'm happy for you." I could see the tears forming in his eyes. "Why would God allow something like this? Sarah didn't deserve to die that way. Why couldn't we have talked longer and stopped her from leaving? I can't make sense of this."

My hand covered Angel's as I replied to Ben's questions. "God does not control the evil that walks our earth. You know that. You and Dad have had that debate many times. Dad always says evil is the absence of God. We could beat ourselves up until we die over why we didn't do something differently. Unfortunately, we will have to live with the fact that we didn't."

Angel added, "I know finding her the way you did is ripping you apart. I don't know how you have dealt with it. Maybe God has a plan for you to help women and children who have been victims of this kind of abuse."

Ben lifted his head as if a spark of life had touched him. But then the exhaustion sank in, and he wilted. But it was obvious what Angel said touched a nerve.

I reached across and grabbed his hand. He had not talked this much in several days. It was a good sign. "Pray for us, Ben. Pray for Sarah."

Slowly, he began to pray.

CHAPTER 19

Dan

I awoke to the sounds of freeway traffic early in the morning. My neck and back ached from sleeping in a chair by the window. We were conditioned to getting up at five in the morning, so sleeping in past seven a.m. wasn't something we could easily do.

We talked past midnight. Angel and I shared our dreams with Ben. We were only seventeen, but the last few days made us feel years older.

Ben picked up on Angel's comment about God having a plan for him to help women and children who were victims of abuse. It kept nagging at him and he kept saying it was so insightful.

We had been sitting with our backs against the headboard, talking to Ben when I looked at Angel. She had curled up next to me, laid her head on the pillow, and fallen to sleep. Ben turned the lights off and I covered Angel with a blanket. I fell asleep in the chair. Ben admitted to covering me with a blanket. He said my teeth chattering woke him up in the night. I didn't remember my teeth chattering or him putting a blanket over me. I must have been more exhausted than I realized.

Ben was in a better mood than he had been in several days. He thanked us both for listening to him, even though Angel fell asleep while he was talking. She started apologizing, and Ben forgave her immediately. He said it was her insight that brought him around.

"I'm not likely to forgive myself for Sarah's death. I might never forgive myself. But I can dedicate myself to preventing as much abuse as possible. I don't know how, but I'm going to trust God to help me find a way. Thank you, Angel, for helping me to see that."

Angel replied, "You're welcome. I think it's a worthy goal. You will do well, I'm sure."

"What are our plans today?" Ben asked.

I had one stop in mind, but I would postpone it until the afternoon. "Breakfast first, and then we can go to Mud Island, and after that, the Bass Pro Shops inside the pyramid. This afternoon, there is an electronics store I want to visit."

Ben frowned and asked, "Your laptop is almost brand new. What are you looking for?"

"Not that kind of electronics. This store does remote cameras, security systems, and stuff like that. I don't want to rely on game cameras for security around the farm."

Angel said, "You want a more advanced system than the one you started building yourself."

"Winner, winner, chicken dinner."

Ben asked, "You mean the cameras you made from the old phones?"

"Those are the ones," I said. "I want some kind of system that alerts me when someone besides us or the Cottons are on the farm."

"Sounds like a good idea," Ben said.

I didn't tell Ben or Angel, but I wanted cameras I could set up in our stock trailer at fairs. I wanted to watch our cattle at the fairs with no one knowing. There were other uses I had in mind, but I was afraid I was getting paranoid. I was thinking ahead and coming up with ways and places we could be ambushed.

Ben was right. It wasn't fair that Sarah died that way. It's unfair that Sheriff Tatum might be paralyzed for the rest of his life. I wanted every edge I could find to protect my family and Angel's family.

It was a good day to explore downtown Memphis. It was cloudy and cool for an August day. We visited Mud Island and watched the tug boats push barges past Memphis. The fountain in the Peabody Hotel lobby was famous for its ducks. It was the most elegant place we had seen. It made us country kids feel uncomfortable, so we didn't wait around for the ducks to come down.

We had lunch at a Subway sandwich shop downtown and then spent a couple of hours in Bass Pro Shops looking at guns and archery equipment. After lunch, we decided to head back home that evening. Our last stop was the electronics store.

I spent an hour talking to the owner about what I wanted and he said that was simple stuff. My idea about the trailer and the fairs was a little more complicated, but doable. He didn't like my last idea. But he said he would help me if I purchased the cameras and the software for the farm from him. I agreed to his terms, paid him an advance, and agreed to pay the rest when he shipped it in a week.

We left Memphis at three that afternoon. The usual two-and-a-half-hour drive took a little longer because of my sightseeing tour. We took State Highway 33 north from Interstate 40, passing through soybean and rice fields. We crossed the White River at Des Arc on State Highway 38. That would take us to Searcy, and from there, it was an easy trip home.

The Ray family lived near Des Arc.

CHAPTER 20

Dan

The internet is full of information if you know where to look. You can find property records online. Online listings include incorporation records and the people who file them. It is also easy to find phone numbers and emails. An online subscription to the local paper can provide lots of background information. And the Ray brothers hadn't bothered to hide anything. They couldn't hide anything because their family was so large. They inherited their father's farm, which comprised over two hundred acres of White River bottomland spanning both sides of the river and across Prairie County.

For the three days after Sarah's death, we ran in the mornings, worked around the farm, and groomed calves. When we said our goodnights, we were usually exhausted. My body was, but my mind went a thousand different directions. I couldn't stop thinking while I worked. At night, after I showered and closed the door to my room, I turned the laptop on and the hunting began.

The Ray's great-grandfather had owned over two thousand acres many years ago. Then his estate got divided between twelve children, which comprised five sons and seven daughters, shrinking the farm to almost nothing. I found a blog from one of their cousins which listed the family tree. The great-grandfather had a sizable family, besides twelve children, there were sixty grandchildren, over two hundred great-grandchildren, and a growing number of great-great-grandchildren.

On the second night of the internet hunting expedition, I explored the Ray cousins and their family history online. It was easier to understand why they were so well connected. One cousin was a county sheriff, another worked in the Attorney General's office. Most of them were hard-working, well-respected people. But, going back several years through the local paper explained why the Ray brothers and Little John were the black sheep of the family. There was a long list of suspected criminal activities associated with them. They were only suspected activities because authorities didn't convict them of many of those charges. I almost threw my laptop across the room. I had to control my anger. How could authorities look the other way? Perhaps I was as naive as Dad said.

Finding the Ray home place was easy. The question was, did they stay there? They also owned a hunting club, which I had not located yet. It was well known though, because that was, apparently, the Ray's primary source of legitimate income. They were licensed hunting and fishing guides. I found a sloppy website that had pictures of the twins hosting hunting trips for lawyers, judges, and a few minor celebrities. It was coming together in my mind. They thought they were important and above the law.

The third night, I focused on Little John. It was crude, but I thought of him as the little prick who named his dick. Little John was almost a ghost online. Outside of his police record for petty crimes, the only thing I found was a Yelp ad for Little John's House Painting. I needed more information. I wasn't sure what driving through their community would accomplish, but I was doing every ounce of research I could.

As a hunter, when I decide to hunt a new territory, I scout the area to get the lay of the land. I hadn't decided to do anything, but getting the lay of the land hurt nothing. I would probably end up doing nothing, because I was out of my element. Deer hunting was one thing. Man hunting was totally different.

I couldn't go hunt them down and shoot them. I mean, I could, but it was illegal, immoral, and totally beyond my abilities. Officer Cotton had the skills. This thought made me pause. He definitely had the skills, but he didn't use them, because he was an officer of the law. He was a man with a strict moral code. So were Dad, Ben, and supposedly me. This kind of thinking was leading me down a hole that would make me as bad as Donny Ray and Little John. That thought made my stomach churn. I needed to remind myself that I had a moral code as well.

My phone rang, causing me to lose my train of thought. It was a number I didn't recognize.

"Hello," I answered.

A male voice came from the speaker on my phone, "Hi, I'm calling about the show calves you have listed on the internet."

I had listed several of my calves on a website designed to promote 4-H and FFA members' livestock. I had no contact the first two weeks and was thinking it had been a long shot.

"Yes, sir, how can I help you?"

"Well, my daughter is looking for her first proper show calf. She doesn't like any of the ones we have raised. But she has fallen in love with the pictures of one of your Maine-Anjou heifers. She likes the one with the white spot on its side."

I laughed, "We call her Daisy because that spot looks kind of like a flower."

"That would be the one," he replied.

We talked for thirty minutes about cattle and showing cattle as I drove away from Des Arc. The caller was Charlie Dallier from Colorado and they had their fairs in the summer and early fall; we had ours in the late fall. He wanted a show heifer for his twelve-year-old daughter, who was developing an interest in the farm.

We had just reached the Searcy city limits when I heard Ben sigh from the back seat.

"What's wrong, big brother?"

"Oh, nothing," he replied.

"Spit it out. After what we have been through. You don't need to hold back," I said.

We made eye contact through the rearview mirror.

"Dan, I want to get an apartment in Searcy. I love our home, but this week has filled it with sorrow. I want to make a clean start." His statement stunned me. I knew when classes started, he wouldn't be at home much. But he had never hinted he wanted to move out.

CHAPTER 21

Dan

We surprised Mom and Dad by coming home so soon. They encouraged us to talk about Sarah, until Ben finally replied to Dad, "We are doing good, but if you and Mom feel the need to talk, Dan and I will make the time to listen."

I chimed in with, "We've come to grips with the fact we can't change what happened, but we can be more aware in the future and perhaps protect others. Right, Ben?"

"That's right."

Dad wasn't used to being brushed off when it came to a *deep* conversation with his sons. He certainly wasn't used to us flipping the table on him. He looked at us, smiled, and raised both hands. "Okay, Sarah's death has affected us all. I'm glad you too have leaned on each other."

We were trying to move on. And Ben needed it the most. So, when he mentioned the idea of getting an apartment in Searcy, it started a long conversation about the unnecessary expense. Harding was a twenty-minute drive from home, so why spend the extra money? But Ben prevailed. He needed a change of scenery. He would be home often. And most of all, our trust funds covered it.

I'm the type of person who is slow to get angry. But my anger was building. Every time I thought about Sarah, my anger went up a notch. Every time I looked at my brother and felt his pain, the anger built another notch. The thought of Sheriff Tatum being in a wheelchair made it build a little more. But when I remembered Little John reaching out and touching Angel, I flared red hot.

In my mind, I had decided that it was Little John who had raped and killed Sarah. What kind of man does that? The kind who tells a girl to *Come home with me for a fucking good time.* The kind who thinks it's okay to reach out and caress a girl's face. Or the kind that pulls a pistol because a girl kicked him in the groin. Little John was a psychopathic rapist and killer. His cousin, Donny Ray, was his enabler. But what could I do about it?

It was up to the police to figure out. The police, who weren't on the Ray's side, anyway. How can they have police on their side if they are breaking the law? Dad often told Ben and me that life simply wasn't black and white. There were a lot of gray areas between the black and white.

We caught the calves and put them back in the barn. The heifer I had tentatively sold was in the barn.

The steer I told Mr. Dallier about was in the pasture that needed to be halter broken. We took my four-wheeler out to find him. Angel rode behind me. Her hands found the hair on my stomach and she started tickling me. I never knew I was ticklish there until her hands touched me.

We found the young steer in the pasture close to the barn. He was better than I remembered. I took a few pictures and a short video of him walking around. I would upload and email those before I went to bed. His mother was one of my older show heifers that was too old to show. She would be easy to lure into the barn with a bucket of feed. Once in the barn, we could catch and put a rope halter on him. I explained the process to Angel and said, "We'll do that after we feed in the morning."

We stood in the pasture watching the herd graze. "We have two days before we begin school on Friday. What are we going to do?" Angel asked.

"Well, after our morning run, we will feed and water the show calves. Catch the little steer here. And I think I still owe you a fishing trip."

"Oh, I like the sound of that. I'm ready to go fishing."

Bending down, I kissed her gently on the lips. "I could get used to this. Living with you on the farm."

"Then get used to it. I'm not going anywhere." She pulled my head down and kissed me again.

CHAPTER 22

Angel

The fog was thick on the river when we launched the fourteen-foot Jon boat Wednesday morning. Dan had a few issues starting the motor, but once it started, it was ready. We motored downriver to the Lobo Landing dock. We went inside the little store and bought some wax worms and power bait. Then we motored back up the river to Dan's favorite fishing hole. We anchored in a deep spot where he and Ben usually had a lot of luck. The river was low, which meant the generators in the dam were off. The power company usually ran them in the afternoon this time of year to offset the high electrical power usage during the hot summer. Water from the dam came out between fifty-two and fifty-six degrees. The water temperature allowed the trout to survive in the waters of Arkansas rivers.

Dan told me, "This is my favorite spot for two reasons. The fishing is good and if we are lucky, we'll get to watch the otters play on the bank over there."

I stared at him. He had to be joking. "Otters? Really?"

He winked at me. "Two years ago, it was just a male and female. Last year, there were two babies. I haven't been fishing much this year and haven't seen them. We will get our lines set and be quiet. Maybe they will come out and play."

There are hundreds of books written about trout fishing and I had read one of Dad's. Everyone does it differently. The purists wear chest waders and use fly rods with hand-tied flies. Arkansas country boys and girls use boats or fish from the bank, they use rods and reels with lightweight lines and whatever bait is working. There are catch limits, weight, and length limits, and other rules you must know before fishing. Some areas are designated as catch-and-release areas where barbless hooks are required and all fish caught must be released. Ignorance of the law was no excuse.

We had been fishing for about twenty minutes when we heard a splash behind us and a high-pitched chattering sound. I turned to see what was happening. The otter family had finally shown up and slid down the bank into the river. There were five of them. The family was growing. I looked at Dan and he was watching them play. My mouth was wide open, and I was laughing silently at them. I mouthed to Dan when he looked at me, "Five of them. I thought you were pulling my leg."

He shook his head and grinned at me. It thrilled my heart to watch the otters play. I needed this. Who was I kidding? I think we both needed this. Dan pulled his phone out and took a short video to send to Ben later. They had been fishing together the first time they saw them.

Dan said they kept very few of the fish they caught and often practiced catch and release when they didn't have to. We were using barbless hooks today, so we could release whatever we caught.

The common quote by many hunters and fishermen was, *A bad day of hunting or fishing is better than a good*

131

day at work. Today looked like one of those days. We hadn't had a nibble in the half hour we had been there, but we got to watch the otters play, and that was a treat itself.

As suddenly as the otters came out to play, they disappeared again. Then we immediately heard a boat coming up the river and understood why.

The fog was lifting and we could see the boat coming from downriver. This was a larger boat than ours. The motor sounded like it was jet-propelled. Guides liked jet propulsion over propellers because there was less chance of damaging the motor in low water conditions like today. The river was constantly changing, and rocks and limbs were always being pushed downstream by the force of currents. Propellers were always finding those rocks and limbs.

As the boat drew nearer, I looked at Dan and raised my eyebrows. We drew our Glocks at the same time and hid them discreetly in our laps. The front of the twenty-footer held an older couple, while Donny Ray manned the motor.

Boater courtesy called for the moving boat to slow down to prevent a wave from overturning the anchored boat. Donny slowed before he got to us. I kept my head down, hiding my eyes behind the bill of my ball cap while watching from the sides.

The older man in the front yelled, "Howdy, having any luck?"

Dan replied, "They don't like wax worms today. We're about to try some power bait and see how that works."

"Thanks for the info," he replied. "Good luck."

"Good luck to you also," Dan replied.

Donny glanced up and nodded. Otherwise, he paid us very little attention. I was suspicious, of course.

"Did he not recognize us?" I asked after they were upriver a hundred yards.

"He didn't act like it," Dan answered.

Donny had seemed like the nicer of the three cousins. He had spoken softly and warned Dan to stay out of the fight between Little John and me on the launch ramp. He was also holding a pistol. His brother, who was now dead, had cussed Dan. Dad had a saying, *Beware of the dog that doesn't bark or growl.* I believed that Donny Ray was the most dangerous one of the two living cousins.

I looked at Dan and sighed. "Dan, can we go home?"

"Are you sure? We can go down the river."

"No, let's go home." I kept watching the boat as it went around a bend upriver. He wouldn't come back, would he?

We reeled our lines in and pulled our anchors up. Dan started the motor, and we headed back. The fog finally gave up and let the sunshine glimmer off the water. A great blue heron passed us, flying a few inches above the water as it made its way upriver.

CHAPTER 23

Dan

The beginning of school came like the rushing wind before a storm. Angel and I dropped the top on the Mustang and drove to school on Friday morning. The wind felt good on our faces. We would have a half day with shortened classes. For some reason, the State of Arkansas thought students needed to be eased into school. We went a half day on Friday, took the weekend off, and jumped right into schoolwork on Monday. I asked Mom about it and she laughed. She said it was the teachers who were being eased into school.

Angel and I had three classes together in the mornings. AP English, AP Calculus, and AP Chemistry. The AP or Advanced Placement classes would give us college credit when we passed the AP exams at the end of the year. I wanted to follow in Ben's footsteps. He had graduated high school with a full year of college credit. He was starting at Harding University as a sophomore.

It was my goal to finish high school and be a certified EMT, and take another year to become an LPN. After that, I would study to become an RN. There was the small hospital locally, but I wanted to specialize in emergency room care and the busier location would be in Searcy.

Angel changed her mind about being a game warden and wasn't sure what she wanted to do yet. But college was still in her plans. She would take concurrent classes at ASU-Heber Springs in the afternoon, while I drove north and took classes at UA-Batesville.

Neither of us had thought about getting home in the afternoons. But it became apparent that Friday afternoon we would go in separate directions. Angel didn't have a car of her own and her mom had just gotten a job at school as a teacher's aide. That made the timing all wrong for Angel and her mom.

"Alright," I said. "I'll let you drive the Mustang and I'll drive my truck."

Angel gave me a horrified look. "I can't drive the Mustang, Dan. I don't know how to drive a stick."

"It's okay, I'll teach you."

"Dan, it's a classic. I'm afraid to drive it. I'll ride with you all day long, but I don't want to damage it."

That the Mustang was a classic hadn't occurred to me. It was just a cool older car for me. She was right, it was a classic and she would look beautiful driving it.

"Alright. You drive the Green Machine and I'll drive the Mustang."

She surprised me when she said, "Okay, I'll drive the truck. But you have to buy the gas."

I laughed. "Okay." What else was I going to say? I was in love with this beautiful young lady and I'd give her a piggyback ride to school if that was what she wanted.

After the short school day, we met my cousins, Sissy, and Mike Brock, and Mike's best friend, Bobby Williams, at Sonic for lunch. We sat at a table in the middle of the drive-in. Bobby was an anomaly in our town. He was half black and half Cherokee Indian. He and his grandmother were two of five dark-skinned people I knew who lived in our community.

No one bothered him, though. He and Mike were two of the best athletes in our school. As sophomores, they were probably going to be starters on the varsity football, basketball, and baseball teams. Mrs. Williams, Bobby's grandmother, was an elementary school teacher. Everyone knew her and respected her. She pushed every student in her class to do their best. She and Bobby had moved here from Tulsa, Oklahoma. Mom told me that Bobby's mother was Cherokee and had died of a drug overdose. His father was in prison. She didn't know why. His parents had been track and field athletes and met in college.

Angel had met the members of the cross-country team, but very few of them were honor students. My cousins and Bobby were all honor students. And she met a few more people today in our classes. I wanted her to feel like she belonged. It had to be difficult to finish your senior year in a new school.

There were tons of comments and condolences about Sarah today. Angel and I had told no one we were thinking of dating. I think we still felt a little guilty about our feelings for each other. I couldn't explain why, but we were embarrassed about the timing of everything. But we weren't hiding from everyone.

Sissy asked, "How long have you two been dating?" Then she tossed a tater tot at Bobby and he caught it with his mouth. Sissy was fifteen and a freshman, but she was probably the smartest person in our school.

I wasn't one to lie, especially when she could see right through it. I glanced at Angel, then at Sissy.

"We're kind of biding our time. Sarah's death has affected us all, Ben included. But you are right, we consider ourselves best friends and we will start dating soon."

"I'm sorry, Dan," Sissy apologized. "I didn't think about Sarah. You broke up with her in May. That was three months ago."

"But no one knew we broke up. It was close to the end of school and most people assumed we were still together," I answered.

Angel grabbed my hand. "They'll know we're together Monday when I drive your truck to school."

"Another reason for you to drive the Mustang. No one knows the Mustang is mine," I said, and smiled at her and raising my eyebrows.

Mike and Bobby turned to stare at the Mustang. Bobby blurted, "Dude, if you don't want to drive that sweet ride, then I will."

Mike said, "Dan's been working on that car for four years. It looks awesome, cuz!"

"Thanks, Mike."

Mike asked, "Are y'all coming to the red/white game tonight?"

I looked at Angel. My beautiful Angel. I longed to hold her in my arms and tell her I loved her. Other than a quick hug or kiss, we had kept our hands to ourselves. Angel had been right. I needed time to deal with Sarah's death. The way it happened affected all of us and shook me to the core. I had caught myself looking for her in the hallway at school today, even with Angel there, But Sarah wasn't there. I missed her smile and her bubbly personality. I would never see her again, and I hated the way I treated her the last time I saw her. I was glad I didn't see her the way Ben had.

Angel held my gaze when I asked, "Are you ready to have our first date? Dinner at Arrow's and then the football game?"

She smiled and asked, "Are you ready?"

"I have to move on. And I love you too much to keep you waiting. Do we have a date?"

She blushed when Bobby and Mike started mocking me. "I wuv vu." And other nonsense. Sissy was giving them the evil eye.

I ignored them and kept my eyes on her. Still blushing, she finally looked up and said, "Yes."

I looked at Mike and Bobby. "Y'all laugh all you want. You should have seen Angel kick the guy's butt that we think killed Sarah."

It was out of my mouth before I caught myself. Everyone was looking at me. Angel grabbed my arm. But Sissy asked the question.

"Dan, what are you talking about? Sarah died from leukemia, didn't she?"

I looked at my cousin and shook my head. "Why do you think the casket was closed?"

"Dan, we're supposed to stay quiet," Angel pleaded.

This time, I turned my whole body toward Angel. "Look at Sissy. I can't keep quiet. We need to warn her, so Mike and Bobby can be there to protect her. Besides, how long do we stay silent? It's been two weeks. Do we stay quiet for two months or two years? How long? The girls in our school need to be warned and protected."

Angel's mouth hung open in surprise. She turned to look at my fifteen-year-old cousin and nodded her head.

"You're right," she said, looking back at me. She leaned in and kissed me gently on the lips. "But let me tell the story. Okay?"

I nodded to her and turned to look at my cousins and Bobby. They were staring at me and Angel like we were crazy. We might suffer from PTSD, but we weren't crazy.

"Sarah was murdered." Angel started the story. She told the story as it happened, leaving out very little.

By the time she finished twenty minutes later, I knew they believed her. Sissy had seen Sarah at Walmart and said she looked fine.

Sissy asked, "Why were you asked to stay quiet?"

I answered that question when Angel took a sip from my drink. "The State Police wanted time to process a rape kit and other evidence. They were afraid the guys would run and hide."

I looked at Mike and Bobby and said, "Please do not let Sissy go anywhere alone. Okay?"

They nodded at me and Mike said, "I promise you, Dan, she will always be with one or both of us."

Sissy said, "Dan? Tell Ben I'm sorry about Sarah. And I'm glad you and Angel have found each other."

"Thank you." I looked at Angel. "I think it's time you learned how to drive a stick shift."

CHAPTER 24

Dan

I admit it; I was a horrible teacher. But I laughed so hard I hurt. Teaching Angel to drive a stick shift was a challenge. I hadn't realized how difficult using a clutch could be. She stalled it; she spun the tires, and she screamed at me for laughing. Angel was determined to learn because I told her she needed to know how to drive everything on the farm in case of an emergency. Dad, Ben, and I all volunteered with the local fire department. Knowing how to turn off PTO drives and hydraulics on farm equipment could save someone's life. Knowing how to drive a stick shift could be a life-saving skill. After a half hour of tearing up our gravel driveway, she was getting comfortable shifting from first to second gear, but she wanted to test herself shifting to third gear, so I let her take it out on the county road.

By the time we got back to the farm, she felt comfortable driving it. I planned to let her practice more over the weekend. We had to drive slowly down the drive to our houses because Angel had created a few holes in the road by spinning the rear tires.

Dad met us in the yard after we parked the Mustang in the shop. He watched as we laughed and held hands. "Did y'all have fun tearing up the driveway?"

Dad was smiling when he said it.

"Sorry Dad. Angel was learning how to drive a standard. I'll take the tractor up and level the holes out shortly."

"I know you will. Can I talk to both of you?"

Angel and I dropped our hands. Dad watched us for just a second and a slight smile crossed his face.

He held his hand out toward us and said, "Your Mom and I, and the Cottons approve of your dating. You have been very respectful and acted like adults. You've had the run of the farm and could do anything you wanted. I'm not going to caution you about sex. I think you're both mature enough to deal with that yourself. Am I right?"

"Yes sir," we both answered.

"What I want to say is not going to be easy. I want you to promise me you won't take matters into your own hands."

He looked at both of us and waited for a reply.

I finally said, "Dad, I promise to remain level-headed, but I won't promise anything if Angel is in danger."

"Me either," Angel said.

"That will have to do, I guess," he said and looked at the ground.

"What's going on Dad?"

"This is difficult to say," he replied. "The rape kit on Sarah came back inconclusive. They didn't find a match in the national database. It lets Donny Ray and Little

John off the hook because they refused to submit a DNA test," he said.

Angel sat down on the grass and asked, "Who else could it be?"

I was suddenly angry. "What about the shoe?" I asked.

"Their lawyers argued they found it beside their Hummer and thought it belonged to the girls with them that day. They picked it up and threw it inside. It was easily dismissed."

I kneeled and hugged Angel. I wanted to curse, scream, and beat the living devil out of those guys. But Angel brought me to my senses.

"Dad's still in danger. Probably more than ever now," she whispered.

I looked up at Dad. He had a tear in his eye when he said, "I'm sorry, Angel. But you needed to know."

"Does Mom know?" Angel asked, looking up at Dad.

"She knows," Dad answered.

"I need to go be with Mom."

"Go," I said and kissed the top of her head. "Take the four-wheeler or the Mustang."

Dad and I stood and watched her ride away on the four-wheeler.

"You two have something special going, don't you, son?"

"I think so. My feelings for her are much deeper than anything I ever felt for Sarah. I liked Sarah, but there was no connection like I feel with Angel," I told him.

"I can see that," he said. "Now, would you repair those holes y'all made in the road?"

I knew he was trying to lighten the mood, and gave him a smile when I replied, "Yes, sir."

We both stayed where we were. I finally said, "Dad, can I ask you a question?"

"Of course, Dan."

"How do you tell the difference between genuine love and infatuation?" I asked.

He thought for a moment, as we watched Angel run into her house, and replied, "Infatuation is a one-way street. Genuine love is returned without demands or expectations."

He put his hand on my shoulder. "I think you know what you have, son. Just don't rush into anything. Let it grow." He hesitated another moment before patting my shoulder and repeating, "Let it grow."

"Thanks, Dad."

I called Ben as I walked to the equipment shed to get the tractor. Dad had already called him and told him the news. He was as upset as I was. That shoe was Sarah's. Ben and I were sure one of the Rays, or Little John, killed her.

Ben surprised me when he said, "I'd like to catch them alone on a back road sometime."

I smiled and said, "A preacher shouldn't think like that, Ben."

"I know. Pray for me, Dan."

I told him I would and asked him to do the same for me.

I swapped the hay fork for the front loader bucket on the tractor and headed up the driveway to fix the holes. Once again, I laughed while I dragged the bucket over the holes. Then I rubbed my neck. I might have gotten a little whiplash from Angel's driving lessons.

Fifteen minutes and the drive was in decent shape. I stopped at the Cottons to see how they were doing. Angel walked out, shaking her head. She had changed clothes and came out wearing black leggings and a black spaghetti strap t-shirt. She could look beautiful in anything. I turned the tractor off and Angel jumped up on the running board. She leaned in and gave me a kiss and hugged me tight.

She whispered in my ear, "Mom's acting like it is nothing new. But it bothers me tremendously."

"We must take precautions. But there's nothing we can do about it unless they come after us," I said.

She leaned back out of our embrace and said, "I know."

She lifted her finger to my lips, and I kissed it. Then she pulled it away and placed her hand over her heart. I did the same. Standing on the running board put her breasts about at eye level to me as I sat on the tractor seat. She was teasing me. I leaned my head on her chest.

"Are you ready for our date?"

"I've been ready. Are you?" she asked.

"Absolutely!"

Then she asked, "Can you do chores without me? Mom wants to help me get ready for our date."

"How can I say no? I'll text you right before I take my shower."

She laughed, kissed me, jumped off the running board, and said, "Thank you, Dan. See you soon."

I started the tractor while I watched her jog back to the house. I had to remind myself that I was in love with her, not just her body.

I picked Angel up for our date a little before six o'clock in the Green Machine. She was beautiful. She had her hair in a double French braid that met at the back. As a true country girl should, she wore denim shorts and a red tank top covered by a thin white cover-up that tied in the front. Red, white, and black were the school colors. She was more loyal than I was. I wasn't wearing school colors. She also carried a small red purse over her shoulder.

I wish I could say dinner was a quiet affair. It wasn't. One of Sarah's friends, and our classmate, was our server and she kept giving me the evil eye every time she came to our table. Thankfully, she ignored Angel and focused her anger on me.

I finally asked her, "What's bothering you, Heather?"

She leaned toward me and said, "You really have to ask? You're out on a date with someone else so soon after Sarah's funeral. You asshole."

She never gave me the chance to respond. She just walked away, leaving the customers around us looking at me.

I said for their benefit, "Sarah Young and I broke up in May. She was raped and murdered three weeks ago. The man Sheriff Tatum killed was a suspect."

Heather came back and accused me of lying.

I looked at her and said, "I wish I was lying, Heather. No one deserves to die the way she did. Did you ever wonder why her casket was closed?"

I felt a sinking feeling inside of me. I was upset, but my anger wasn't all directed at Heather. She didn't know the complete story. I turned to Angel and informed her, "I'm sorry, I've lost my appetite."

We were barely halfway through our BBQ sandwiches, but she quietly nodded and asked Heather, "Can we get to-go boxes, please?"

Heather acknowledged her and snapped, "Sure, I'll be right back."

Another server brought us our to-go boxes. She apologized for Heather's behavior and told us she was outside crying.

The server asked, "Why haven't we been told what really happened?"

Angel replied for me, "The State Police needed time to process the evidence and they were afraid the suspects would run. But they refused to submit DNA samples, and their lawyer got the only other physical evidence thrown out. So, the primary suspects are free."

The server asked Angel, "Who are you? How do you know this stuff?"

"I'm Angelina Cotton. My dad's the Game Warden. He's had several run-ins with the suspects."

I took the to-go boxes. "Thank you for the boxes. Tell Heather, I'm sorry I upset her."

We filled our boxes, and I left forty dollars on the table to pay for our bill and a tip. Angel put her hand on my arm as we walked out. The surrounding tables had become silent.

We lived in a community of seven thousand people in Heber Springs, and another fourteen thousand in the surrounding county. It wasn't a small town, but if your name made it into the weekly paper, you were probably known by more people than you knew. Mom and Dad had explained this to me and Ben when we were eleven and twelve years old. They would know if we did anything wrong before we even knew.

I was calling home as soon as I got to the truck. I needed to explain to Dad what had just happened before he started getting the phone calls. As we walked out the door, I told Angel she needed to call her dad and let him know we just informed the community what had really happened to Sarah.

"I'm way ahead of you. Being the game warden's daughter means being known by people I've never seen in my life. Besides, you handled that very well."

"Thank you," I replied. "I'm sorry you were right in the middle of it."

"Dan, I haven't had a dull day since I've known you. I don't expect to start now." She smiled up at me as we walked to my truck.

I opened the driver's side door of the Green Machine, and Angel slid to the center of the bench seat. Our legs were touching as I sat beside her and started the truck.

"I'm still hungry. Let's get a drink and drive to Sandy Beach and watch the sunset."

Angel punched my shoulder lightly and said, "I knew you were still hungry. That's why I asked for to-go boxes."

We finished our BBQ sandwiches sitting on the tailgate and watching the sun go down over Greers Ferry Lake. It was a beautifully peaceful interlude before we headed to the Red/White football game at school. We talked about the lake. I told her the story of J.F.K. coming to Heber Springs and dedicating the dam just a month and a half before being killed in Dallas.

We threw our trash into one of the trash cans in the parking lot, climbed back into the truck, and headed back down Front Street to the school. I parked between the high school and the elementary school, close to the agriculture classroom. I was going to miss taking agriculture my senior year, but I knew most of what would be taught, anyway.

Admission was a few cans of canned goods to be donated to the local food pantry. I had grabbed several cans from our cabinets before I left home, with my mother's permission, of course.

Angel and I held hands as we walked between the old gymnasium and the football field. We were both checking out the cars and trucks parked there. Most belonged to football players, cheerleaders, band members, and coaches. I noticed she was still checking out the parking lot when we got to the gate.

"Is everything okay?" I asked.

"Yeah, I think so. I thought I recognized Little John," she said. Clutching her purse a little closer.

"Are you sure?"

"No," she answered and squeezed my hand. "I don't think it was him. I think I'm imagining things."

The bleachers weren't very full. It was mostly students, and parents of students on the football team, band, or cheer squads. I was looking for my aunt and uncle; Mike and Sissy's parents. Instead, the first people I recognized were the Youngs, Sarah's parents. Angel and I were still holding hands. When she spotted them, Angel tried to let go of my hand, but I held on tight and walked up the bleachers to them. Besides Sarah, they had a son who was a freshman and a younger daughter in the seventh grade. I assumed they had come for the junior varsity Red/White game.

They stood and hugged both me and Angel. Angel was very tense about the situation until we said goodbye. Mrs. Young grabbed Angel's hand, leaned over, and whispered something in her ear. As we moved across the bleachers to my aunt and uncle, Angel grabbed my hand and squeezed hard enough that it hurt.

I looked at her and saw her holding back tears. I stopped and asked her quietly, "What did she say to you?"

She pulled herself together, let out a big breath, and smiled at me. "She said she was glad you found me. That you were an awesome guy and deserved happiness. I was worried she was going to be upset with us for dating."

"She's known about us since we went to the hospital in Little Rock. Apparently, your parents told my parents I asked for permission to date you. They talked about it at the hospital, because I asked the Youngs for permission to date Sarah, also," I said.

"Why didn't you tell me?"

"Because Ben just told me a few days ago, and we've been kind of busy. I'm sorry I didn't tell you. Forgive me?"

Angel looked me directly in the eyes and nodded. I held her eye contact, squeezed her hand. "If we have their permission, no one has the right to say anything. People can say whatever they want. We have done nothing wrong."

I introduced Angel to my aunt and uncle. We talked for a few minutes before the Red/White game started. Angel asked me why I didn't play football and I told her it interfered with farming, livestock show season, and hunting season. She grinned at me then and said she agreed with me about hunting season.

151

Although they were sophomores, Mike and Bobby proved they would be a major part of the football team on both offense and defense. As quarterback and running back, they scored three touchdowns for the white team in the first half. As linebackers, on defense, they held the red team to one touchdown. They showed their leadership on the field by talking and cheering their teammates on continually.

Sissy was a member of the dance team. After their halftime show, they took a third-quarter break, and she joined us, sitting between Uncle Wheldon and me.

The third quarter started differently, because the red team double-teamed Mike and Bobby, every play. The red team scored another touchdown against them. While the first half had been the Mike and Bobby running game, the second half showed off Mike's arm. He threw three touchdown passes and Bobby ran it in for two more short yardage touchdowns. Mike and Bobby were talented players. They just needed more talent to be playing with them.

We waited with Sissy outside the field house for the football heroes to get changed. She invited me and Angel to go get ice cream with them. They laughed and told the rest of the team, "Good game," when they saw us waiting. Bobby slipped away, grabbed Sissy by the arm, and yelled at Mike to come on. We waited on Mike as Sissy and Bobby started walking ahead of us.

Mike finally broke away after a booster told him he played an outstanding game. We headed to the back of the high school, about twenty steps behind Sissy and Bobby. I was congratulating Mike on a great game when Angel pulled both of us out of the way of a white van.

Mike yelled and started trotting after the van, yelling at Sissy and Bobby to watch out for the van.

I watched Bobby fall to the ground. A man stepped out from between two parked trucks and grabbed Sissy. The van stopped, and the man pushed her toward the van. Mike was already ten steps ahead of us, running at full speed now. Angel and I started running as well. Sissy dropped to the ground and Mike made a flying tackle on the assailant. Angel ran toward Sissy. She pulled her Glock 19 out of her purse as the side door of the van opened and an arm reached out to grab Sissy. My beautiful girlfriend ran straight into the van's door, slamming it into the man reaching for Sissy. She then pointed the gun into the van and said, "Freeze or I'll shoot."

The driver had other ideas and hit the gas. Angel took a two-handed aim at the van. I put my hand over the pistol and pushed her hands down. "Put that away. We're on school property and you don't have a permit." I turned to Mike, and he was repeatedly hitting the guy he'd tackled. I grabbed him from behind and got him in a full nelson and pulled him off.

"Mike, Mike. Get yourself together. He's down," I yelled at him as he lifted me off my feet and screamed, "Let go of me!"

Sissy was up by then. And got into Mike's face and yelled, "Mike, Stop!"

As he focused on his sister, Mike relaxed, and I let go of him. She wrapped him in a big hug.

I turned to Angel to find her glaring at me. "Call 911, please," I said to her.

I grabbed Sissy and Mike by the shoulders and instructed them, "Check on Bobby. He hasn't moved."

They turned and ran to him. I looked at the man Mike tackled. I wasn't sure he was breathing. His face was beaten beyond recognition. His mouth and nose were a mess of blood, skin, bones, and broken teeth. The left eye was open and bloody, and the right eye was swollen shut. I knelt and checked his pulse. He was alive, for now.

People began showing up and asking what happened. I couldn't help the guy on the ground. He was unconscious. I figured his head hit the pavement when Mike tackled him. I turned to go check on Bobby when the first police car showed up. Angel was still on the phone with 911.

Sissy was crying when I squatted by Bobby and grabbed his wrist. He had a strong pulse. I asked Sissy, "Did you see what happened? Did he get hit on the head?"

"No, I don't know. It happened too fast," she whimpered.

I carefully started feeling around his head. I found a knot swelling on the back of his head. "He's been knocked out," I told Sissy and Mike. "He probably has a concussion, but that's just a guess."

I stood up in time to see the ambulance pulling in from the cafeteria side of the school. Angel was answering the police officer's questions. I headed toward the ambulance and met the first paramedic by the assailant.

Before he asked what happened, I just told him, "This man tried to kidnap my cousin and her brother tackled him. I'm sure his head hit the pavement when he was tackled, and then he took a beating from my cousin. Our friend was also hit on the head and knocked out as he walked Sissy to her car."

The paramedic nodded at me and said, "Thank you. We'll take it from here."

I took a few deep breaths and tried to clear my head. I asked myself what needed to be done next, but I was interrupted by the police officer. It wasn't my job to take charge. It was his job. I saw the paramedics with Bobby and the assailant. Everything was under control.

The police officer jerked my arm. "Excuse me, are you listening to me? I need to talk to you."

I didn't appreciate being grabbed and wheeled on him and grabbed his wrist. "I'm a volunteer with the Wilburn Fire Department. I'm just making sure everyone is getting treated," I hissed.

Grabbing his wrist was not something I should have done, and he shouldn't have had an attitude, but we both lost it. He tried to put me on the ground, but I was taller and stronger and flung him to the ground to get him off me.

Before I could move, a hand came from behind me, grabbed my shoulder hard and squeezed hard enough to put me on my knees.

"Easy Dan, stay on the ground." The familiar voice of Officer Cotton told me. He let go of me and helped the police officer off the ground.

I looked up at the policeman, who was staring daggers at me. "I'm sorry. You startled me. I'm still on edge after watching my cousin almost get kidnapped."

It was Officer Cotton who spoke first. "Dan, he could arrest you for assaulting a police officer."

The fear rose inside of me, making me nauseous. I had the feeling whatever happened now, it would not be justice.

"I'm sorry," I repeated.

Officer Cotton knelt in front of me and put his huge hand on my shoulder. "Relax and tell us what happened."

I stayed on my knees and told them my version of what happened, minus the part about Angel and her gun. I would keep that a secret. It could get her into a lot of trouble. What I didn't see coming is what happened next.

I didn't get to say goodnight to Angel after our first date, because my cousin Mike and I got a free ride to the county jail in a police car. I was arrested for assaulting a police officer. The officer was still angry at me and made sure he clamped the cold handcuffs tightly around my wrists so they hurt. He tried to force me into the back seat, intending for me to hit my head, but I quickly avoided it. I searched for Angel and found her standing with her dad's arm around her. She appeared angry, and I mouthed *I'm sorry*. She must not have been angry at me, because she blew me a kiss. Mike was arrested for assault and battery on Sissy's attempted kidnapper. While one kidnapper went to the hospital, the others drove away. It wasn't right.

When the officer got into the driver's seat, I started to yell at him. But Mike stopped me. "Dan, we have the right to remain silent. Let's use it."

He was right. It was the building anger and anguish inside of me that put me here. I was ready to explode and beat someone the way Mike had beaten Sissy's assailant. He stared at me until I nodded and let him know I heard him.

CHAPTER 25

Dan

Mike and I were released early Saturday morning. Video footage from the school's security camera showed exactly what we said happened. It showed the guy Mike beat up, pushing Sissy toward the van and another man reaching for her. It didn't show Bobby getting hit, though. The video also showed the police officer grabbing my arm and me turning around. But apparently, it looked like the police officer tripped and fell and I reached for him. I was afraid to ask if it showed Angel aiming her pistol at the van. It was possible that my body hid her actions from the camera, but things happened so fast. The camera was above the door to the Ag shop, but I couldn't remember where we were standing.

I'm just glad Mike's dad, my uncle, was an attorney and knew the judge and prosecuting attorney. He got the high school principal to copy the videotape. He reviewed it and met with the prosecutor at six a.m. on Saturday morning.

As he drove me back to the high school to get my truck, Mike asked for an update on Bobby. They admitted him to the hospital overnight for observation. He had a concussion and had been in and out of consciousness all night. He told us Mrs. Williams and Sissy had been there all night. Mike asked his dad to take him to the hospital after they dropped me off at the high school. I thanked my uncle for getting me out of jail. He thanked me for watching out for Sissy.

I arrived home to find Mom, Dad, Ben, Angel, and Mrs. Cotton sitting at the dining room table waiting for me. The only person missing was Angel's dad. I was sure he was working.

"What's going on?" I asked.

Mom deflected my question with her own question. "Are you hungry, dear?"

"Starving," I answered. She got up and went into the kitchen.

Dad said, "Have a seat, son."

I didn't exactly ignore him, but I walked around the table to Angel instead.

"I'm sorry Angel."

She jumped to her feet and hugged me.

"Some first date," I said.

"I told you I haven't had a boring day since I've known you."

"What's going on?" I said and kissed the top of Angel's head.

Angel released me, stepped back, and asked, "Did they see my pistol on the video? Dad chewed me out for carrying it onto school property. He's never been so angry with me."

I put my hand on her shoulder. "I stopped you from making a bigger mistake."

"When you did that, I was so angry," Angel said. "I wanted to hit you myself, but I put the pistol back into my purse. And then you pulled Mike off that guy and yelled to call 911. Dad heard the dispatch call over the radio and came to the high school because mom told him our plans."

She waited a minute before she asked again, "Did they see the pistol on the video, Dan?"

"Uncle Wheldon said nothing about it. I think my body blocked that view from the camera. If I remember correctly, the camera was above the Agri-shop door. From that angle, I might have blocked you from the camera's view."

Mrs. Cotton spoke then, "She's been worrying all night about going to jail. She worried about you and your cousins. I don't think she slept very much last night. Jonathan lectured her half the night about carrying that pistol onto school property."

Dad said, "Sit and have some breakfast, Dan. Wheldon told me what the video showed, but I want to hear it from you after you've eaten something. Angel has told us her story."

I sat in the chair beside Angel. She had gone to the kitchen and brought me a cup of coffee, followed by Mom with a plate of waffles and bacon. As I ate, Dad told me I received a package after I left last night. Ben said he thought it was the security cameras I bought while we were in Memphis. I had told Mom and Dad about the security cameras. They weren't sure we needed them, but I think last night changed their minds. I would spend the rest of the day installing them.

I had just finished telling them my version of last night's events when we heard a knock on the mudroom door. A knock there meant family or friends, a knock at the front door meant it was someone who didn't know our patterns.

Mom got up and led Uncle Wheldon into the kitchen. Dad stood and greeted his brother and thanked him for taking care of me this morning. He took the last of the eight chairs around our table.

Dad said, "Bring us up to date. What's going on?"

"How's Bobby?" I asked.

Uncle Wheldon looked at me and replied, "Thank goodness he has a hard head. He has a concussion. It's going to take him several weeks to get over it. The police found the steel pipe he was hit with under a truck. He may not play football again this season. The Doctor wants to keep him under observation a few more hours."

He looked at Angel then. "You got lucky. I've watched the video probably twenty times. The video shows your pistol if you are looking for it. It appears just briefly before Dan steps between you and the camera and pushes your hands down."

He hesitated. "There may be enough video there to justify questioning you, but I don't think anyone is going to be looking for it. The first fifteen times I watched it, I saw my daughter on the ground and you hitting the van door into the man reaching for her. The scene also showed Mike tackling the assailant and beating him senseless. So much is happening that it's easy to miss the gun in your hand. I'm just glad you were there last night. Thank you for what you did."

"I'm glad we were too," Angel replied.

"We warned them, at lunch yesterday, to never leave Sissy alone. After Sarah's death, every teenage girl in town needs to be cautious," I told him.

Uncle Wheldon frowned and asked, "What do you mean, Dan?"

I looked at him in shock. "You haven't heard what really happened to Sarah?"

"I heard her leukemia came back," he said, furrowing his forehead.

Everyone at the table kind of deflated. I looked at Dad and Ben. "Can y'all tell him what really happened? I'm calling the Youngs to ask them to go to the paper and tell the truth. People need to know."

I stood up and walked through the house to the deck. Angel followed me, her hand on my arm. I called Mrs. Young, and we talked for twenty minutes. I explained what happened to Sissy last night and asked her to talk to the media about Sarah. She wouldn't promise until she spoke to her husband. But she agreed with me. People needed to know.

Everyone at the table stopped talking when Angel and I walked back into the kitchen.

"What did they say?" Dad asked.

"Mrs. Young agrees that the community needs to know, but she wants to talk to Mr. Young first." I looked at Uncle Wheldon, "Maybe it would help if you called them, and offered to join them. Sissy could have faced the same fate.

"I'll call them," he said, rising from the table. "I'll call on my way back to the hospital."

Angel and I skipped our morning run, but we walked our usual route. We were talking and scouting locations to place the security cameras. Angel was still upset about the pistol. She wasn't upset that she carried it, just upset that she didn't think about the repercussions of exposing the pistol on school property. She never thought about going to jail because she was trying to protect herself. That's what the pistol was for - protection. But society looked at the situation differently. Society looked at a teenager carrying a gun on school grounds differently. Angel's dad told her the number of school shootings across the United States proved that only authorized and trained individuals should be allowed to carry weapons.

"Where is your pistol now?"

"It's at home. In Dad's gun safe," Angel said, wringing her hands.

"He took it away from you?"

"No. I gave it to him. I'm so upset and embarrassed." She looked at me with big puppy dog eyes. "Dan, I can't believe I was so stupid. I didn't take it to shoot up the school."

We stopped, and I pulled her into my arms. "I know Cotton Top. You were only protecting yourself. And last night, you were trying to protect Sissy, and you kept her from getting taken. Thank you."

She let the tears flow, and I hugged her tightly.

"For what it's worth, I ended up in jail," I whispered in her ear, "for assaulting a police officer." I loosened my hug and joked, "I'd share a cell with you if they would let us."

"That's not funny." She let me go and lightly pounded my chest with her fist.

I lifted her chin to look into her eyes. "I'm sorry about last night. Who knew protecting Sissy would get us in so much trouble?"

"Right? I never like it when Dad is angry at me. Mom usually takes up for me, but not last night. She lectured me some more after Dad finished. I wanted to run to the barn and curl up in the feed room and hide, but I wanted to be here when you came home. I still can't believe they arrested you and Mike."

"Mike and I talked about it all night. We got arrested, and no one bothered to chase that van. That wouldn't happen if Sheriff Tatum was here."

"I like him," she said.

"Are you sure? He's the reason I gave you the Glock."

"I can't blame him or you for my stupidity. He would have been the first to tell me to leave it at home."

I released Angel from the one-arm hug I'd been holding her in, grabbed her hand, and continued walking down the logging trail.

"What are we going to do, Dan?"

"We are going to install some cameras," I said.

She yanked on my hand and looked at me with bloodshot eyes.

"No. I mean, about Donny and Little John, neither of them was in that van last night."

"We are going to install the cameras around the farm, in the stock trailer, and on the show display. Those are for security. Then I ordered some other cameras for another purpose."

"What purpose?"

I hesitated, but gave in and told her my thoughts.

"Dan, we can't do that. That's stupider than me carrying a gun onto school property."

"I never said WE were going to do anything. I haven't figured out how to do it yet. And I probably won't. As long as there are so many people protecting them, they won't be caught."

"Promise me you won't do anything stupid." She looked at me with puffy eyes. The tears were about to start again. "At least, not without me."

"I promise. I keep thinking about last night and how it went sideways, so fast. We were lucky your dad showed up to stop me and take you home."

CHAPTER 26

Angel

Ben attended the press conference and recorded it on his phone. When he returned home, he emailed the video to Dan. Dan hooked his laptop up to the television in the living room and we watched it together. We were grounded and weren't allowed to attend.

The Youngs and Dan's aunt and uncle stirred up as much noise as they could. They held a press conference on the High School steps on Saturday afternoon. All the television stations out of Little Rock and several local, state, and even one national newspaper reporter attended. Dan's Aunt Liz was an international marketing consultant, and she knew how to arrange for media coverage. The video showed the large pictures from Sarah's funeral. The school video footage, edited to take out the two seconds showing my gun, showed Sissy's attempted abduction on large screen televisions. There were volunteers handing out USB drives with the video to any media members who requested one.

The video showed the Youngs hugging each other and their two remaining children. They lost a daughter and didn't have closure over her brutal rape and murder, and probably never would. They stood beside Dan's uncle. The Youngs cried while Mr. Brock told the horrible story.

Dan's aunt stood beside his uncle while he angrily expressed his frustration by pounding the podium. "The only people arrested were the brother and cousin who kept Sissy from being abducted. The man Mike tackled and beat up is under guard at the local hospital. But no charges have been filed against him. He obviously committed assault and battery, attempted kidnapping, and probably other atrocities," he shouted.

Ben told us, "Uncle Wheldon called the local Prosecuting Attorney, the one who dropped the charges against you and Mike this morning, and warned him he was going to throw him under the bus this afternoon. He wanted him to be prepared."

The rest of the news conference was about warning people to take precautions. He knew charges would be filed first thing Monday morning and trusted the Prosecuting Attorney to do the right thing.

"There's Sheriff Tatum," I said, grabbing Mike's arm.

Sheriff Tatum was in a wheelchair. He detailed the search and rescue efforts that were organized to find Sarah within minutes after the call. He briefly talked about questioning suspects at the Dam Site Marina the night Sarah went missing and the shootout the next day where one city officer and one suspect were killed and he was wounded in the line of duty.

Ben's video showed most of the high school football team, cheerleaders, and dance team. He said, "The coaches and teachers told them they needed to be there, to stand behind the Youngs and the Brocks and show support, but they didn't explain why." They stood in shocked silence, listening to the news conference. They cried and embraced each other as the truth emerged. It was near the end of the press conference before they finally woke up and came alive. When Mike and Sissy wheeled Bobby, with his bandaged head, through the crowd in a wheelchair, the students went crazy. Before their classmates could swamp them, Sissy and Mike turned the wheelchair to face the TV cameras. Sissy put her arms around Mike and Bobby and said, "My heroes."

That was the end of Ben's video. The press conference was planned with precision. They were careful not to name any suspects, but the reporters went to work doing their jobs, interviewing anyone and everyone who knew anything. When the evening news aired, they knew Danny Ray's name and the name of the assailant in the hospital.

Most of the stations showed Sheriff Tatum cautioning against interviewing the minors who were involved, which included all of us. Ben just disappeared into the crowd and came home. We watched the news until it became a repeated coverage.

It was me who asked the lingering question, "Will it do any good? Will it protect enough girls? Will it put those bastards behind bars?"

My head immediately snapped to look at Dan's mom and dad, and my hand covered my mouth. "I'm sorry. I didn't mean to say that out loud."

Mr. Brock smiled at me. "It's okay. I think you were being kind, stopping at calling them bastards."

CHAPTER 27

Dan

Angel and I started our Monday morning at five-thirty by running five miles around the farm. We fed and watered the show calves and headed to our homes for breakfast and a quick shower before going to school.

We'd finished installing the security cameras the day before and made sure they were working. I moved an old hay wagon from a shed at the Cottons for Angel to park the Mustang. I didn't like leaving the canvas top exposed to weather all the time. We skipped shooting sports practice on Sunday afternoon. We were grounded, anyway.

Mom caught me as I was about to leave for school. "Are you sure you want to let Angel drive the Mustang? That car is special to you."

"I'm sure, Mom. I trust the Green Machine to get me to Batesville and back home. The Mustang will be okay around here, but I don't want to test it on the road yet."

"That's not what I meant."

"Mom, the car, and Angel are both special to me. I love them both." I hadn't meant to proclaim my love for Angel to my mom that way. It just came out. It felt right, though, and I wasn't ashamed of it.

Mom just stared at me. "Yes, Mom. I love Angel."

"You know I want grandkids, but not soon."

I just grinned at her and gave her a kiss on the cheek. "Mom, you won't have grandkids anytime soon. I love you."

I followed Angel off the farm. Man, she looked beautiful driving the Mustang, her blond hair flying behind from the wind blowing in the window. I couldn't decide if she made the car prettier or if the car made her look sexier. Maybe it was both.

I wasn't looking forward to school, though. I had received a lot of texts and phone calls from friends since the press conference asking if it was true. I assured them it was true, and I tried, politely, to tell them I did not want to talk about it.

When we arrived at school, there was a heavier police presence than the one resource officer we normally had. He was rarely seen at the high school in the mornings because he was directing traffic at the elementary school.

The guys stepped up and were walking the young ladies from their cars in the parking lot to the school. It was good to see the press conference had the intended effect. I wondered how diligent they would be a month from now, three months from now, or even a year. The young ladies would never forget. The guys would forget as soon as deer season started.

John Parker met me and Angel as soon as we got out of our vehicles. He gave me a hug, which surprised me, and then he turned and hugged Angel. "I'm sorry about Sarah," he said to me. "The whole leukemia story never added up to me. I saw her at the park when Ben was praying with her and she didn't look sick. Then I watched the news conference yesterday, and it all made sense. Except, why the lie?"

I shook my head and looked at Angel. She read my thoughts and answered for me.

"The state police needed time to process evidence and a rape kit. They knew the guys would flee the state if they knew they were suspects."

"What took so long?" John asked.

"Their DNA isn't in the national database. And their lawyer had the physical evidence thrown out by claiming they just picked it up off the ground and threw it in the truck," Angel responded.

John just shook his head. He looked at the front entrance of the school. I followed his gaze and saw my cousins and Bobby standing there.

"They resemble each other, don't they?"

Not following his comment, I asked, "What do you mean?"

"From a distance, your cousin Sissy and Sarah could have passed for sisters. They both have long, black hair. And the same smile."

"Oh my God," Angel whispered. I looked at her and she was searching in her wallet. "They were after me."

"What?" John and I asked.

She handed me a picture, and said, "This is my sophomore class picture."

It showed Angel with long, light brown hair down to her waist. She handed me her driver's license. Her hand was shaking when I took it. John was looking over my shoulder.

"Triplets," he said. Angel's hair in her driver's license picture was black.

"I put green highlights in my hair for the district track meet. The green wouldn't come out, so I dyed it black." Her voice quavered. "I finally bleached it and cut it shoulder-length in January. I've kept the bleach-blonde look."

Tears formed in the corners of her eyes. "I got Sarah killed."

"No, you didn't," I responded. A little more forcefully than I intended.

"The Rays have police contacts. They got a copy of my driver's license," her voice still quavered. "They confused you and Ben and thought Sarah was me. She was killed because of me."

"No," I said, grabbing her hand. "Even if they thought she was you. They killed Sarah anyway. They're rapists, killers, and human traffickers. There were two more girls on the boat. They took whoever they could find. You don't know they were after you."

"I thought I saw Little John in the parking lot before the game. He could have seen Sissy sitting between you and her parents during the game and thought she was me."

"I think you're reaching. You told me Little John and Donny weren't in the van. The two events may not be related," I said.

She was making sense, but I couldn't let her have a breakdown on the second day of school.

"Angel, you can't take responsibility for their actions. You didn't force them to do anything. It's not your fault. You're jumping to conclusions. Do you hear me? It's not your fault. This all started because your dad arrested Danny."

She nodded at me. "I still feel responsible."

"How? It's your dad they have threatened. And Danny is dead. If they aren't running for their lives, I would think they'd go after Sheriff Tatum now."

"What are you guys talking about?" John asked.

I'd forgotten he was there. "Sorry John, it's a long story. The news conference didn't tell everything. It starts with Angel's father. He's a game warden. He arrested the guy Sheriff Tatum killed. Before the shootout, he and his family threatened Officer Cotton, Angel, and her mom. Because of that threat, Angel thinks they were after her."

"Oh man, I'm sorry Angel," John said.

The first bell rang, indicating we had five minutes to get to our first class.

I was now nervous about attending classes that day. There were too many questions about the entire ordeal. We relived it in every class as the teachers felt the need to counsel students to be vigilant and watchful. During

173

our last class of the morning, our chemistry teacher pushed me too far, and I told the entire story. The class stared at me and then at Angel. I left out the part about them all resembling each other. There was no proof and Angel was blaming herself enough.

I said, "This is the last time I want to talk about it. I've lived through the death of a good friend and I had to lie about the truth. We survived an attack at the lake, the shooting of Sheriff Tatum, who is a friend of our families, and the attack on my cousin Sissy and Bobby. Mike and I even spent a night in jail because of it."

I looked at Angel and she was watching me, the tears rolling down her cheeks. I added, "We have lived with this for weeks. We are tired and just want to move on." I turned back to the Chemistry teacher and said, "I will never forget Sarah. I won't forgive whoever killed her, and I pray for their capture every day. But, please respect the fact that we can't keep reliving it every day. If I have to go through another day like today, I will quit school."

I stood up, started gathering my books, and motioned for Angel. I addressed the teacher again. "With your permission, we'd like to go to the office. I think we need to see that counselor the school is providing."

She couldn't deny us. Every teacher had offered students the opportunity to talk to a grief counselor today. She kindly replied, "I'm sorry, Dan. I didn't mean to upset you and Angelina."

Angel responded for both of us. "It wasn't just you. It's been every class. We've been through police interrogations, hospital visits, guilt trips, and counseling sessions already. We shouldn't have to relive it again, and again."

The principal was in the outer office when we walked in. He took one look at us, frowned, and said, "Go to my office. Mrs. Hazel, hold my calls and any visitors."

After we took our seats, Principal Haden looked at us and said, "You look like you've had a long week, and it's only Monday morning."

I nodded. "I appreciate the school trying to be there for everyone after learning about Sarah's death. Some will need the counselors. But Angel and I have lived through it. And now, in every class, we are reliving it. If we don't tell what really happened, then people make stuff up."

He sighed and said, "I'm sorry. We were thinking of the other students. We never thought it would affect you differently. What can I do to help you?"

"Can we leave a little early today or stay here in the office? I'm going to UA Batesville in the afternoons and Angel is going to ASU Heber."

"Okay Dan, I understand why you are upset, but help me understand why Miss Cotton is involved in all this."

I looked at Angel. "I guess we have to tell the story again." And we did. This time we told the story together, and we even told him about the resemblance of Sarah and Sissy to Angel's driver's license picture.

When we finished, he just looked at us quietly for a full minute. "I'm sorry Dan. Why didn't your uncle tell me about this?"

"Because he didn't know. He didn't know about Sarah until Saturday morning. And he doesn't know everything that we just told you," Angel replied.

I continued, "We have been close to everything that has happened. Even Sheriff Tatum getting shot, it was me that told him Danny Ray was in the grocery store parking lot. We were with Sarah shortly before she was attacked. My brother Ben was the one who found her. We were being interviewed by the state police at the hospital when she passed. And we were walking behind Sissy and Bobby when they were attacked."

Angel shifted in her seat and added, "Dan and I were about to start dating the day Sarah died. Our first date was Friday night, and it ended with him and Mike in jail. My family moving here has been exciting, just not the kind I wanted."

"Do you want to talk to the counselor? If anyone needs it, I would think it would be you two."

I shook my head and leaned forward, putting my elbows on my knees and my hands over my face. "We've had Mom, Dad, and Ben. Although Ben was in awful shape himself when he found Sarah. Angel's dad is the game warden. He's been through a lot and has helped her cope. We just want to stop talking about it and move on. The memories are painful enough."

A knock on the door interrupted Principal Haden. He stood and walked around his desk to the door.

He started talking as he opened the door. "I asked not to be disturbed." Then he stopped, and I heard Mrs. Hazel whisper quietly to Mr. Haden.

"Angel, Dan, you have a visitor," he said as he stepped aside. "Please, come in."

Sergeant Johnson from the Arkansas State Police stepped into the office.

"I just need a few minutes with them, sir. Then I need to see the other students involved in Friday's incident."

"Yes ma'am. I'll call them to the office," Principal Haden said as he stepped out of the office and closed the door behind him.

She looked at us and shook her head. "I came in here to chew your butts out, but it looks like someone beat me to it. Are y'all okay?"

I was still leaning forward, my elbows on my knees. Angel, at some point, had pulled her legs up into her chair and was hugging her knees. Tears rolled down her cheeks, and she stared silently at the state trooper.

I sighed and leaned back in my chair. "When does this end? When do we get to live our lives without looking over our shoulders constantly?"

Sergeant Johnson sighed. She had been standing ramrod straight until I asked those questions. Now she leaned against the principal's desk.

Her response shocked , and I heard Angel gasp when quietly said, "Not anytime soon. They disappeared right after your uncle's press conference, but not before offering an undisclosed amount of money for the deaths of Sheriff Tatum and Officer Cotton."

"We don't think anyone is stupid enough to try anything after that press conference. Sentiment around the state is they have gone too far this time."

I thought about Donny and Danny Ray. How did Donny feel about losing his twin brother? They had a connection, and it was gone now. How would I feel about losing Ben? I would want revenge.

"Donny may let things cool off, but he will get revenge for his brother," I said.

"I agree," replied Sergeant Johnson. "Now tell me what happened Friday night. I've seen the video. Your uncle gave me a copy and let me watch the unedited version. Did you hear me, Miss Cotton?"

Angel, still hugging her knees, whispered, "Yes, ma'am."

"When you turn eighteen in a few weeks, you can get a concealed carry permit. But never carry it onto another school campus in Arkansas again, or I will personally throw you under the prison. Am I clear?"

Angel spoke a little louder this time, "Yes, ma'am."

"You're lucky to have an attorney like Mr. Brock on your side. Now what happened Friday night? Angel, you go first."

Angel told her about the attempted kidnapping. She left nothing out. We even told her about Angel's thoughts about her hair color.

Sergeant Johnson looked at Angel's pictures. "I think you may be onto something. Go back to your natural hair color, though. You're prettier with brown hair."

There was a knock on the door and it opened. Principal Haden stepped into the office. "They're here."

"Thank you, sir. I'm finished with Dan and Angel. If you don't need them, they are free to go."

We stood to go and ended up hugging Sissy, and fist bumping Mike and Bobby as they made their way into the office. Bobby wasn't looking good, but he was determined to get back to normal.

We had barely stepped into the outer office when Angel wrapped me in a hug and started crying. With Principal Haden and Mrs. Hazel giving us disapproving looks, I hugged Angel back. I looked at Principal Haden. "Sergeant Johnson just informed us that there's been a hit put out on her dad and the Sheriff."

That wasn't the only reason Angel was crying, but it shut the adults up. The principal sat down in one of the office chairs used by visitors and sighed. Angel was crying because Sergeant Johnson just said that Sarah and Sissy could have been mistaken for her. Sarah may have been killed because of her. All I could do was hold her. What could I say? At that moment, I knew we were done with school for the day.

Dad often said, "When God wants to send you a gift, He wraps it up in a problem."

I looked at Angel as a gift from God. But the problems she brought with her weren't her fault and they were harder to deal with. Her dad was only doing his job. Then some outlaws took offense to him doing his job and threatened him and his family. Angel and her mom were just innocent bystanders. I had fallen in love with Angel and felt her problems were now my problems. The country boy's way of dealing with a problem was to meet it head-on with the biggest stick you could find.

But I knew that would not work. We had met them on the boat ramp with my cattle prod and Angel's fists and feet. They had guns and weren't afraid of me and Angel. They weren't even afraid of Sheriff Tatum, or Angel's dad. Apparently, they weren't afraid to die, either. I wasn't afraid to die, I just didn't want to die this young. I wanted to grow old with Angel and raise children.

"Dan, I want to go home." Angel brought me back to the here and now. Principal Haden handed me two hall passes that gave us permission to leave campus in case a teacher stopped us.

We left the office and headed to the Mustang. The Green Machine would stay in the parking lot just in case we didn't come back to get it today. I was still protective of the Mustang, and I didn't want to leave the convertible in the school parking lot. I called Mom and Dad and told them we were coming home.

Angel didn't want to talk on the way home. She shook her head no when I asked, and pulled her feet up on the seat, and hugged her knees again. That fetal position worried me. She was going to keep everything inside. She cried, looked out the passenger side window, and whispered, "I'm sorry."

I winced. I had a flashback to a nightmare where Sarah told me *I'm sorry.* It had been weeks since that nightmare, and I had to wonder, after seeing Angel's driver's license picture, was it Sarah or Angel I saw in that nightmare? I couldn't remember the details, and honestly, I didn't want to.

CHAPTER 28

Dan

Mom and Dad met us in the driveway. After explaining our morning and telling them about Angel's pictures and Sergeant Johnson's visit, they understood why Angel was shaken up. Talking to Mom and Dad was better, because they knew the complete story. We just needed to update them on the latest. If we talked to a counselor, we would have to repeat the entire story all over again for them to understand the depth of the pain. That might do more harm than good right now.

Angel let Mom wrap her in a motherly hug that I was rather surprised to see after Mom's conversation about the Mustang with me that morning. Angel was still sniffling and had said nothing during our conversation.

I finally said, "She blames herself for Sarah's death and the attack on Sissy."

"Because you have black hair in your driver's license photo? Don't be ridiculous," Mom replied.

Mom turned and led Angel toward the house. I started to follow, but Dad grabbed my arm.

"Son, I know you want to be here, but let us talk to her. She is going to look at you and remember you dated Sarah. That Sissy is your cousin, and you insisted on warning her. You may not learn anything today, but go to class. We will take care of Angel. I know you are strong enough to handle this. So go to class and be safe."

I hated it when he made points like that. I couldn't think of anyone that I would rather leave Angel with than my mom and dad right now. Together, they had counseled many members of Dad's congregation over the years and helped them through some trying times.

Dad was right. I learned nothing in class that day. We primarily got our syllabus, and the instructor laid out the expectations for completing the EMT One course. I purchased my books from the campus bookstore and headed back home. I put the top down on the Mustang and enjoyed the rumble of the dual exhaust when I pressed the gas pedal. I even floored it on a couple of straight stretches on the back roads and enjoyed the wind swirling around me. It got my heart thumping as I gripped the steering wheel. My eyes squinted, watching the road ahead for any danger, as the odometer reached one hundred. The flicker of a bird flying across the road in front of me caused me to hit the clutch and slow it back down to sixty. I took a deep breath to calm the adrenaline rush. The car could easily have reached one twenty, maybe one fifty, but a pothole or a deer at those speeds could mean death in a convertible. I wasn't ready to die yet. I had already seen a couple of those as a fire department volunteer.

I had not called Mom or Dad, nor had I texted Angel. I trusted everything would be better when I got home. My mind had not been far from Angel all afternoon. We were heading into a busy month with fairs and cross-country meets. Plus, we both turned eighteen before Thanksgiving. I was just a few weeks older than Angel.

When I arrived home, I found my mom, Angel, and Mrs. Cotton in the kitchen preparing dinner. I could see Dad and Officer Cotton through the kitchen window grilling on the deck.

I slipped into the kitchen and gave Mom a hug and a kiss on the cheek. Said hello to Mrs. Cotton and finally touched Angel's shoulder as she stood making salads. I turned her toward me as I leaned forward to see her face. Her eyes were puffy and red from crying, and she gave me a slight smile.

"Hey gorgeous, how're you doing?"

"I'm okay," she answered hoarsely.

I raised my eyebrows at her, and she gave me a quick kiss on the cheek. She said, "I will be."

"Good, I'll be back shortly."

"What's for supper, Mom? Steak?" I asked, walking backward out of the kitchen.

"Ribeye steaks, baked potatoes, yeast rolls, and a salad," she called after me.

"Ben's going to be upset."

"He'll be here shortly," she replied.

I laughed, knowing Mom had invited Ben and he wouldn't miss out on a ribeye steak.

In my bedroom, I changed out of my good jeans and into the worn-out jeans I wore around the farm and put on an old T-shirt. I had taken my shoes off in the mudroom and slipped my house shoes back on after changing jeans. I smelled a hint of perfume. Looking

184

around my room, I spotted a note on my pillow. I picked it up and the scent of Angel's perfume grew stronger. The note read, *Thank you for being there for me. I love you. Angel.*

There it was, in black and white. My heart swelled with happiness. *I love you too, Angel.*

Both families sat around our big dining room table and ate the tastiest ribeye steaks ever cooked. They were farm-grown right on our farm. You couldn't get any better beef. Ben and I could grill when we wanted, but we always conceded to Dad. He was the master at cooking steaks for each person's preference. They always had the perfect amount of pink in the middle. I'd yet to figure out how he did it.

When we finished eating, Angel and I headed to the barn to do the chores. She had been quiet during dinner. We looked at each other while eating, but neither of us said anything. She remained silent on the walk to the barn. As soon as we were in the barn's hallway and out of sight of the house, I grabbed her hand and pulled her to me.

"I found your note." Looking into her eyes, I confessed, "I love you, too."

She responded with a fierce kiss. "I love you, Dan."

Then she pulled me to the feed room, where I unlocked the door. I closed the door behind us with my foot as we headed to the feed pallet. I suspected Ben would be close behind us. We didn't have time for sex, even if we felt up to it.

There was a hurried conversation between us about our feelings in between the kisses. We straightened our clothes and were mixing feed and supplements into five-gallon buckets when there was a knock on the door.

"Y'all okay in there?" It was Ben.

Angel opened the door.

"Yeah, just talking some. It's been a rough day," Angel replied, pouring a cup of Manna Pro into a feed bucket.

"I heard. I'm sorry, Angel."

"How was your day, college boy?" I asked him.

"There's too much free time between classes. I'm thinking of getting a job to have something to do."

Angel looked at him. "You're kidding, right?"

"I'll give it a week or two. If it continues to be this boring and easy, I'll get a job."

"At least you didn't have to relive Sarah's funeral in every class this morning and then tell Principal Haden the entire story and then repeat Sissy's attack for the state police."

He looked at Angel. "I was going to suggest another road trip this weekend, but Dad reminded me you have a meet at Lyon College on Friday, and you need to get ready for the county fair next week." He looked at me and asked, "You want some help grooming calves this weekend?"

"I'll never turn your help down. I definitely want you to help me groom Buster for the state fair. Be sure to take a day off from classes the day before."

Buster was my steer. He was the best steer I'd ever had, except for the one I sold in January to an FFA member in Grant County. It was a toss-up which one was better then. When grooming calves, Ben and I divided the work, and somewhere along the way, he had become better at grooming the steers than I had. He had the touch of making them look better than the competition.

CHAPTER 29

Angel

The first cross-country meet of the season was at Lyon University in Batesville. Dan and I arranged to miss our college classes and ride the bus with the team to Batesville. Normally, there would have been joking about us not taking part in team practices, but the recent events kind of kept everyone quiet.

But the meet went well. John Parker and Dan crossed the finish line in first and second place. Just when I thought Dan had John Parker beaten, he found a burst of energy somewhere and crossed the line just ahead of Dan. I finished first, nearly twenty seconds ahead of second place. Race officials were questioning whether I cheated, but I passed every checkpoint well ahead of the pack after the first lap. I set a meet record in the first race of the season.

It was the boost I needed to get my smile back. I wasn't even breathing hard when I crossed the finish line. By running five miles a day, a three-mile race was simple. Coach Taylor, John, and Dan met me after I checked in with the race officials. I jumped into Dan's arms and screamed, "They said I set a meet record. Was it that fast?"

Coach Taylor and John were both patting me on the back. "Yes, you were," Coach Taylor said and yelled for the next girls' team member to cross the line. Maria was next across the line and came over to me and gave me a high five. "Where did you get those rockets? I never saw you after the starting line." That made us laugh, and Dan pulled me into a hug.

It was good to see Dan smiling again. It was good to be smiling again.

John Parker and Maria showed up at the farm at five a.m. the morning following the Lyon College meet. They said they wanted to see our training program. Maria dropped out after lap four and John was breathing hard after lap five.

Maria asked, "How do you run up that hill five times? That was killing my calves."

"We've built up to it." I said.

"Y'all run five miles a day? Like that?" John asked.

"We sure do."

"Now I know why you are so competitive. Three miles is nothing when you run five every day."

"Hey, there's also the farm workout," Dan said. "You're welcome to stay and help us with chores, bathe eight calves, and haul hay this afternoon."

John stood up. "Let's go home, Maria. I don't think I can keep up with them today."

"I'm with you, John."

"See you tomorrow?" I asked.

"We'll see."

Dan and I walked around the farm after feeding the calves. We had the awkward sex and birth control talk that we had avoided. But I just smiled at Dan and told him I had been on birth control since I was fifteen. I explained most girls took the pill to help control their hormones, which played a big part in acne flare-ups. We agreed we wanted to have sex. But we wanted it to be special.

"Mom has already said something to me about not wanting grandkids yet," Dan said.

"Mine too. But she likes you. I don't think she would be too upset."

"It's not our moms that worry me," Dan said. "I wouldn't want to face either of our dads."

CHAPTER 30

Angel

September flew by with no sign of Donny Ray or Little John. Life was normal. School was normal. Dan and I were competitive in the cross-country meets this year. I won my first four meets. Dan finally beat John Parker at the last meet. I think he let Dan win one. We both recorded times that rivaled state championship times. John and Maria joined us for our morning runs. Coach Taylor was a little upset we weren't at his practices in the afternoons, but he wasn't arguing with the success we were having. I was winning meets. John and Dan were constantly in the top five, and Maria improved from a top twenty-five finisher to the top ten. Dan and I would miss one meet during the state fair, but we had one more meet between the State Fair and the state cross-country championship.

The county and district fairs were successful for Dan. But I got the feeling that he found the lack of competition boring. I even asked him if it was worth all the hard work and effort. He gave me the usual answer, "Of course."

The state fair was the event Dan looked forward to the most. I could only compare it to getting ready for the state track meet. He worked tirelessly, getting everything ready. I worked right beside him, because I wanted to be with him.

We arrived early in the afternoon on the first Monday of the fair. We unloaded the equipment and calves, set up the display and were cleaning up when Ben arrived with food around three o'clock.

He handed me a drink and said, "I know Dan. He'll work you to death before he stops for a drink or food."

"Thank you," and I took a long pull from the straw.

"Here you go, brother."

"Thank you, Ben. Please tell me those are pork chop sandwiches you're holding."

"You know it."

"It's break time Angel," Dan said.

"Thank goodness. I'm already exhausted."

Ben laughed. "We haven't even got started yet. Dan has to check in shortly, then we have to weigh Buster and they have to classify him as an American, British, or exotic breed. We already know he's exotic, but many people try to cheat the system. When we get back, we will touch him up in the grooming chute. Then the fun starts."

"That doesn't sound bad. What do you mean, the fun starts?" I asked.

"Remember the two guys who asked if I would help them clip their steers?" Dan asked.

"Yeah," I answered hesitantly.

"Dan and I have developed a reputation. It will probably be one or two o'clock in the morning before we finish helping people clip calves," Ben answered.

"But they're your competition," I protested.

"Yes and no," Dan said. "You could put the five best steers here in the show ring, and five different judges would place them differently."

"Then why do you do it?"

"Money," Ben answered. "The grand champion steer can bring twenty thousand dollars at the premium sale. But Dan's trying to breed quality show steers and they can sell for a lot of money."

"Wow, now I understand why you are so excited about this."

Ben was right about grooming calves until early in the morning. They finished the last steer about two a.m. I fell asleep in a camp chair next to the show box, listening to the hum of the generator. Dan's jacket helped to ward off the night chill, but I woke up as soon as they turned the generator off.

I don't remember falling asleep. But I must have crawled into the overhead sleeping area of the trailer and fell asleep. Dan woke me when he and Ben left to get breakfast. They locked the door and left me to shower.

They knocked on the trailer door when they returned to make sure I was decent. I unlocked the door for them.

"Is that coffee I smell?"

"Yes, and sausage egg and bacon egg biscuits, too."

I was hanging a towel up after drying my hair. Dan put his hand on my shoulder and I turned to him.

"Good morning, beautiful," he said as he bent and kissed me.

"Hey handsome," I answered after our kiss. "Did we sleep in the same bed and I not realize it?" I laid my head on his chest and hugged him tightly.

"I'm afraid we did. And tonight may not be much better. Let's eat. Ben's waiting to say grace."

CHAPTER 31

Dan

Angel went to the coliseum with Mom and Dad to watch the steer show. We took our time getting Buster ready and were just finishing when they called for the Exotic breed steers to report to the coliseum. I put my long sleeve shirt over my t-shirt and tucked it into my pants. Ben pinned my exhibitor number on my back. I grabbed my show stick and headed to the arena entrance to the coliseum. Ben would clean up and lock up and join Mom, Dad, and Angel to watch the show.

I checked in with one of the show volunteers who organized the classes behind the scenes. It would be several minutes before my class would enter.

My phone rang, and it reminded me to turn the ringer off in the show ring. I looked at the caller ID and saw Charlie Dallier in Colorado. I answered the phone.

"Dan, we thought we would drive down to Little Rock and watch the heifer show tomorrow, but we are here today and thought we would stop by and visit. We are looking at your heifers in the barn. Are you close by?"

"I am waiting to show my steer in the coliseum in about fifteen minutes. Stay there. I'll send my brother to get you and you can watch the steer show with my parents."

"Okay, we'll wait right here."

I hit the end call and then called Ben. He said he and Angel would go get them.

I was excited now. I hadn't seen a steer that would beat Buster. Second, no one drives twelve hours from Colorado to Little Rock, unless they are serious about buying cattle. I was smiling when my exhibitor number was called and I entered the show ring.

There were twenty-five steers in my class, and the judge sorted the class methodically. He started placing the class at the bottom and pulled the bottom fifteen. Buster and I were still in the top ten.

The judge walked around the ring again and pulled the next five, leaving five of us. He placed the last five after scrutinizing the steers from top to bottom. He paid very little attention to Buster, which worried me at first. Then I realized he'd already made his decision earlier. When he pulled the second-place steer and put him in the lineup, he told me to stay put.

First place in our class. To say I was excited would be an understatement. I looked into the stands and found Mom and Dad, who gave me the thumbs-up sign.

The top three places were told to hang around to show for the Grand Champion Exotic steer. There was one more class after ours and Buster's half-brother was in it. I stood outside the coliseum and watched them walk into the ring. There were three excellent steers in that class that I picked to be Buster's competition for Grand Champion. The best one was the one I raised and sold, but I was biased. Scott Langly, a Sheridan FFA member, had bought him and named him Batman because of a white spot on his forehead.

As soon as the last class finished, the show ring assistants lined everyone up to go into the show ring for Grand Champion. I had not seen Scott and Batman exit when they had the first steer enter the show ring. He won his class. He was waiting for me to enter, with Buster to line up behind me. I couldn't help it. I gave Scott a high five when I entered the ring. We were both grinning from ear to ear.

Batman beat Buster. He took Grand Champion Exotic Steer. The steer from the class before me took Reserve Champion and Buster took third. The judge told me he couldn't place Buster any higher because he wasn't as finished and ready for market as the two he placed ahead of me. I told him I was still thrilled because I raised and sold the Grand Champion.

The last part of the steer show was to bring all the breed champions back to show for Overall Grand Champion and select which steers went to the Sale of Champions. Buster didn't make the cut, but I was proud of Scott and Batman.

I headed to the barn and found Ben, Angel, and a young girl who must be Hannah Dallier. I forced myself to smile when I saw her, but my heart fell to my stomach. She was tall for twelve, very pretty, with waist-length black hair. She could have passed for Sarah Young's sister and I could see Ben wasn't dealing with it very well. He was trying, though.

"Congratulations, little brother."

Angel gave me a quick hug and kiss. "You did good."

I looked at Hannah and stuck out my hand. "You must be Hannah. What did you think of the steer show?"

She smiled shyly, but recovered and said, "It was interesting. I thought you should have won, though."

"I did win," I said and smiled. "The Grand Champion steer was Buster's half-brother, and he was the Overall Reserve Champion. Even though I didn't show him myself, I feel like I won because I raised him."

She nodded at me and looked at Buster. "Can I pet him?"

"Sure, start at his shoulder and neck, then move up to the top of his head. He likes to be scratched behind the ears."

I looked at Ben and Angel. They were both a little pale. I was tired, but I could see I needed to take the lead here.

"Ben? Angel? Would you take Buster back and clean him up? I'd like for Hannah to introduce me to her parents."

I watched them both sigh in relief. Turning back to Hannah, I saw she was grinning because Buster had lowered his head for her to scratch. I handed the lead to Ben and my show stick to Angel.

"Hannah, let's go meet your parents."

"Okay." And she backed away from Buster.

"Have you shown cattle before?" I asked as I watched Ben and Angel lead Buster away.

"No. But Dad showed cattle when he was in FFA."

She watched with me and then said, "I don't think they like me."

"They don't have anything against you, Hannah. It's just that..." I hesitated. Then I pulled my phone out and unlocked the screen.

"We lost a friend recently. My old girlfriend, before I met Angel. You resemble her a lot. Here. Let me show you."

I scrolled through my phone and found a picture of Sarah and showed it to her. She stared at the picture and then at me. She could see the resemblance.

"What happened to her?"

I took a deep breath and blinked away the tears that were forming. "I'm sorry for getting emotional. It's a long story. Let's just say she was murdered and Ben was the one who found her."

She looked sad. I reached out and touched her shoulder. "Hey, it's not your fault that you remind us of her. It's just a shock. We will adjust. You just be you. Don't do anything different, okay? Just understand, we are going to be very protective of you."

"Why?"

"Because the day Sarah died. She and I had an argument. Ben and Angel were there. We all feel guilty because if we had done something different, my friend might still be alive. Come on, let's go so you can introduce me to your parents."

They were still taking pictures of the Champions in the arena when we walked down to where my parents and the Dalliers were sitting. Hannah ran down the steps to her parents.

They stood, and we introduced ourselves.

Charlie Dallier was a tall, skinny man. He was clean shaven and handsome, but had the sunken eyes of someone who was sick recently. *That's why he asked if I would deliver the calves. He wasn't physically up to driving a truck and trailer for nearly twenty-four hours.* His wife was an older version of Hannah. *No wonder Ben and Angel were so shaken.*

"Dan, you have some impressive cattle. The pictures and videos don't do them justice," he said.

"Thank you," I replied. "I've been working for five years to build the herd. It's finally paying off."

"We've talked to most of the breeders here. Hannah pointed out that three of the five we talked to were exhibiting in Little Rock and asked if we could come down and watch the show."

"Good idea, Hannah," I said. "Kind of one stop shopping, eh?"

Hannah gave me a big smile and said, "Yep, but Daisy is still my favorite."

"She's getting to be a favorite of mine, too. She has a chance to win the whole show tomorrow."

"Really?" Hannah asked.

"She might. You want to go see her again?"

She looked at her dad, and batted her big eyes, "Can we, Dad?"

Mr. Dallier looked at me. "You're a good salesman, Dan." Looking back at his daughter, he said, "All right, let's go."

CHAPTER 32

Dan

I didn't see Ben or Angel when we passed the grooming chutes, which meant they were probably rinsing Buster off before bringing him back to tie him up for the night.

I told the Dalliers I felt Daisy was the best heifer of the seven I had, followed by the oldest heifer, which was bred and was due to calve in another month. Most judges would place the oldest heifer first because she was bred and doing her job.

I enlisted Hannah's help to feed the calves, and she jumped right in to help. Her mom and dad were talking to my parents and watching me instruct Hannah on what to do. I had made some friends, even if they didn't buy cattle from me. I knew getting Hannah involved and feeding my calves would help her decide if showing cattle was something she wanted to do.

Angel was leading Buster back from the wash stall. I looked past her for Ben.

Angel didn't look happy. I met her a few steps away from everyone and she wrapped me in a hug, still hanging onto Buster's lead rope.

"Ben couldn't take it. He left."

"Oh, Lord," I said and pushed her away enough to look into her eyes. "It's going to be okay. He's going to be okay. We are okay. I told Hannah about Sarah and she understands. So, please take a little tough love from me. Suck it up, I need you. Okay?"

She inhaled a sobbing breath, and then slowly let it out with puckered lips. She nodded her head and said, "Okay." Looking at me closely, she asked, "How is this not affecting you?"

I remembered my EMT training. *It's not your emergency. It's their emergency and your job is to remain cool, calm, and collected and focus on following procedures that will ultimately save their life.* Under any circumstance, it was good advice. Especially when emotions ran high.

"Just like my cousin Sissy is not Sarah, Hannah is not Sarah. I focus on what needs to be done now, not what I couldn't do in the past. She's just Hannah. Can you help her finish feeding while I talk to Dad?"

"Sure." But she didn't look sure as she took another long, shuddering breath.

"Hey," I said, so she would look up at me. "I love you."

At that, she smiled at me, and laid her hand on my chest, "I love you more than you will ever know, Daniel Brock."

I told Dad what was going on with Ben and he immediately pulled his phone out of his pocket and called him. I explained to the Dalliers and showed them a picture of Sarah. Mrs. Dallier gasped when she saw the picture and said that could have been her senior picture.

"She was your ex-girlfriend?" Mrs. Dallier asked.

"Yes ma'am," I answered. "But Ben was the one who found her and it really shook him up. That's why it bothers him more than me."

Even Mr. Charlie looked shaken at that news.

"In the meantime, would it be okay if I asked Hannah to stay with me and Angel in our camper tonight? Mom and Dad do not want Angel and I to be unchaperoned. And we have to be back by four a.m. to get ready for the eight a.m. show."

The Dalliers watched Hannah help Angel pitchfork manure into the wheelbarrow. Her mother frowned. I'm sure it was because her little girl was getting dirty. But Hannah was enjoying it, which was obvious from her ear-to-ear grin. Even Angel was laughing at Hannah now.

Mr. Charlie looked at his wife and asked, "Well?"

Mrs. Dallier melted, "Okay, but you will keep a close eye on her right?"

"I promise Angel or I will be with her at all times," I answered.

I stepped toward Hannah and got her attention. "Hannah, would you like to stay with me and Angel in the camper tonight? You can get up early and help us get the calves ready to show."

I didn't think her smile could get any bigger, but it did. "Can I Mom?"

Her mom said, "Yes, but you stay close to Dan or Angel at all times, okay?"

"Dan, are you sure about this?" my mother asked.

"Mom, it would be midnight before we got home and we would have to leave again at three. We would get very little sleep. And I don't know if Ben is coming back. It's not worth it to get two hours of sleep, and I know you wouldn't approve of Angel and I staying by ourselves."

She held up her hands and said, "Okay, okay. You're right."

Dad returned and told us, "I can't get Ben to answer his phone."

"He will be okay, Dad. He just needs a little time. Hannah has agreed to spend the night with me and Angel, just in case Ben doesn't return."

"Are you sure about that?"

"I'm already tired Dad, I don't want to drive home just to turn around and drive back."

Dad sighed. I could see him remembering the early years when he was here working with us to get calves ready to show.

"You're right. You need to rest tonight, because you show early tomorrow morning, then load everything up and drive home and unload it all again."

"Thank you, Dad."

We said goodbye to Mom and Dad, since they weren't sure they would be back to watch tomorrow's show. Dad had to make a hospital visit to one of the oldest members of our church and I assured him it would be okay if he didn't make it.

Mr. Dallier retrieved Hannah's suitcase and left it in our sitting area while we were cleaning up around the grooming chutes and loading the generator back into the truck to use with the camper.

Hannah watched everything we did and asked intelligent questions about why we did things a certain way. When we were finished and ready to go to the camper, Hannah looked at Angel and asked, "I need to go to the restroom. Will you go with me?"

"Okay, the one here is not always the cleanest. Can you handle that?"

Hannah frowned but said, "I'm a country girl. I can handle it."

Angel looked at me and smiled. "We'll be right back."

It always amazed me how scattered my grooming equipment became on show days. The only thing missing was a rope halter. They were cheap, and I bought them by the dozen, so I wasn't worried about losing one. I walked through the calves and made sure their lead ropes were tied well.

Barn three and four were joined with a covered walkway between them. One side held a wash pen for the cattle, the other side held the men's and women's restrooms. I saw Hannah stop in front of the door and look toward the bright lights of the carnival rides.

She was standing where I could see her. She had apparently finished before Angel and stepped outside to get fresh air. I walked toward her. A young boy ran up to her and grabbed her arm, and tried to pull her out of the doorway. Hannah resisted and sat down, fighting the boy. I started running to her and thought I heard Angel scream her name. Angel and I were almost to her when Ben stepped out of the darkness and clamped his hands on the boy's arm and his neck.

"Let go of her," Ben commanded.

"I have an extra arm-band. I just wanted her to go ride some rides with me," the boy said.

"Just let go of her," Ben commanded one more time. He squeezed his arm and neck until I knew the boy was hurting. He released Hannah, and she jumped up and wrapped herself around Angel.

The boy squirmed and yelled at Ben, "Let go of me! You are hurting me." He swung a fist at Ben. But Scott Langly caught the swing before it made contact. Several more guys and an older man in a police uniform followed Scott.

The uniformed man looked like an off-duty police officer. He was wearing his uniform but no duty belt. He stepped forward and asked Ben, "What's going on here?"

Ben said, "He grabbed the young lady, and it looked like he was trying to kidnap her."

"No, I wasn't. I have an extra arm band and just wanted her to ride with me. You got to believe me." It was armband night at the carnival. Buy an armband and ride all the carnival rides you want all night.

I stepped toward him and asked, "Did Donny Ray put you up to this? Or Little John?"

"Who? I don't know who you're talking about. I was just trying to have some fun."

The uniformed man looked at the boy. "In the barns, we're all family. These kids compete like hell in the show ring, but in the barns, they're all one big hick family who will kick your ass if you hurt one of their own. Am I clear?"

The boy was nodding and whimpered, "Yes, sir."

"Let him go."

Ben and Scott relaxed their grips, and the boy jerked free, slipped through the crowd, and ran. Scott and his friends laughed at the boy as he ran away.

Ben turned to Hannah and asked, "Are you okay?"

She nodded yes, let go of Angel, and hugged Ben. "Thank you for coming back."

Ben was a little shocked, but gave her a gentle hug back and said, "You're welcome."

I looked at Scott and his friends. "Thank you."

"Anytime. We're all one big hick family, right?" Scott said, grinning.

I had to laugh. "You know it."

As he started to turn and follow his friends, he stopped and said, "I saw the news conference about your cousin and the other girl. I'm sorry."

"Thank you," I answered as he turned away. He did not know how close I had been to the "other girl" and he didn't need to know.

I turned to Hannah, who was staring at me. She had let go of Ben and was standing by Angel, holding her hand. "Are you okay, Hannah?"

She nodded and then asked me, "Are you okay? You looked angry."

I laughed. "I'm fine now that you are okay. Do you still want to stay with us? We can call your mom and dad."

"No. I'm good here. I think I understand now what you told me earlier about you being protective. Thank you."

I looked at Ben and he said, "I'm alright. Just needed some time. I'm sorry I left you and Angel to clean up everything."

"I helped clean up," Hannah volunteered.

"Yes, you did," I said. "And thank you very much. Are you hungry? Because it's time to get some dinner and get ready for bed."

Ben looked at me and cocked his eyebrow at me.

"Let's go get some chicken sandwiches and head to the trailer."

As Angel and Hannah headed back into the barn, I stepped close to Ben and told him, "Hannah agreed to chaperone tonight, in case you didn't come back. Have you talked to dad yet?"

He nodded at me. "Dad chewed me out pretty good."

"I'm sorry, he doesn't understand," I said, but Ben cut me off and started following Angel and Hannah.

"He understands. He told me it would take time to get over it, but I had to deal with it now. People needed me more than I needed to run and hide. He said I was dealing with a version of PTSD and I should consider counseling. I don't want a counselor. I just want to forget." He took a deep, shuddering breath and stifled a cry. "I just want to forget."

I didn't know how to respond, but I reached over and put my hand on his shoulder. "Ben, I may not know the right thing to say, but I can always listen if you need to talk. I can always pray with you if you need to pray."

"Thanks, Dan."

CHAPTER 33

Dan

At four a.m., Ben and I were up and walking to the barns. We had showered the night before while Angel and Hannah watched the Midway from folding chairs perched atop the trailer. I awakened Angel and told her we would be back at five. We would feed and water the calves and return to get her and Hannah. I did not want them walking across the fairgrounds without me and Ben.

The Maine-Anjou show started at eight a.m. and I owned seven of the twenty-one entries. I had competition in four classes, which meant I was going to need help to show heifers in the Grand Champion drive. I found Scott Langly in barn four and asked if he and a couple of friends would help if needed. He agreed, and I told him we would show in the Equestrian Arena at eight.

Ben, Angel, and I each led two heifers to the Equestrian Arena. I asked Hannah to lead Daisy, and she eagerly agreed.

As a junior exhibitor, it was my job to show each entry individually in their class. During the championship round, the class winners would show against each other. That's when I needed help to show my calves. I showed Daisy first, and

211

after I brought her out of the show ring, Ben grabbed her and started teaching Hannah how to show her. Angel helped me get the next entries ready to show.

As I expected, I needed all the help I could get to show my calves. All seven won their class. I was a little embarrassed that it became the Dan Brock Maine Anjou show. The oldest bred heifer won grand champion and Daisy won reserve champion. Hannah showed Daisy and had difficulty containing her excitement when she received the big pink reserve champion ribbon.

For me, it was a bittersweet dream come true, marking the end of my junior livestock showing career. I could still show livestock in the open division and sell calves to junior exhibitors. I took a deep breath as I led the grand champion from the show ring.

Ben caught me wiping a tear from my eye and gave me a nudge. "Your last state fair as a junior, but not your last state fair. You did well, Dan. Very well."

"Thanks, Ben. I appreciate your help. You've been beside me the whole way."

The Dalliers were waiting when we left the show ring, and Hannah, with a show stick in one hand and Daisy's lead rope in the other, hugged her mom and dad. Ben headed to the barn with two heifers. Angel and I waited and watched the family reunion. The big smile on Hannah's face said everything. She was carrying the large pink reserve champion ribbon in the same hand as the show stick.

Angel nudged me. "I think you just sold some cattle."

The Dalliers walked over to where we stood. Mr. Dallier held out his hand, "Dan, we would like to talk business. Hannah wants to buy Daisy, and the steer you told us about. If he's as good as the ones you have here, he's a dandy. Plus." He looked at Hannah and smiled. "We would like to buy your Grand Champion heifer. Her calf would be of age to show next year. And she'll need a younger heifer."

Mr. Dallier shook my hand the whole time. He finally let go when he stopped speaking.

"Yes, sir, we can make a deal." I looked at Hannah and asked, "Did you have fun showing Daisy?"

She nodded, "I sure did. Daisy showed herself. I just led her around the ring."

"That's because I train them early and work with them every day. Would you like some pictures with her? There's a State Fair backdrop on the north side of the coliseum."

She turned to her parents, who were grinning and holding hands. "Can I? These will be pictures I can look at until we get them home."

Her dad said, "I think we have time. But we have a long drive home, so let's be quick. Okay?"

"Yes," was Hannah's reply while giving Daisy a hug around the neck.

We led the calves back to the barn and took the two champion heifers for pictures. We walked through the barns until we could cross the street to take pictures. The backdrop wasn't being used, and we had it all to ourselves. We took several pictures together, and then Hannah took several solo pictures. As we finished up, I turned and saw a man on the street leaning against a neon green Dodge Charger watching us. His long, blond, stringy hair was tucked behind his ears. Sunglasses covered his eyes. It was Donny Ray. My phone buzzed in my back pocket. I quickly answered it, worried about Angel.

Ben said, "Little John just walked through the barn with another man."

"Is Angel, okay?" I inquired.

"Yeah, your buddy Scott was here with his friends. There were too many of us for them to try anything."

Donny Ray lowered his sunglasses, and we made eye contact and he sneered like he knew something I didn't. When Little John and the other guy walked up to Donny, the sneer disappeared. He stared at me with a look of hatred as they got into the car to drive away.

"Thanks Ben," I said to my brother. "I'll be back shortly." I put my phone back in my pocket.

The Dalliers were watching me. For the first time, I noticed Mr. Dallier had the left side of his blazer pulled back, exposing a badge and a shoulder holster.

"Who were those guys, Dan?" Mr. Charlie asked.

I gave him the quick story about Angel's dad and the sheriff shooting Danny Ray. He nodded. "If there is anything I can do to help, just let me know."

"Thank you, I will," I replied. "What kind of job do you have?"

"I'm the deputy sheriff in Cheyenne County. There is a lot of land and very few people. I've been recovering from a knife wound I got while breaking up a domestic disturbance."

"I'm getting stronger, but this trip has taken its toll on me. It does my heart good though, to see Hannah this happy. You have gone above and beyond to make this a memorable experience for Hannah. Thank you again for that."

We said goodbye, and I headed back to the barn. I still had to bathe and blow dry my champion heifers. Or rather Hannah's heifers. Suddenly, that job felt like a bigger responsibility. I was taking care of someone else's cattle now.

CHAPTER 34

Angel

I wanted to be brave and pretend that Little John walking through the barn was no big deal. But it was a big deal. They knew us, now. They knew me, Dan, and Ben.

When Dan led the heifers back into the barn, he made eye contact with me. I know he could see the fear in my eyes. He was almost back at the stall when the alarm sounded on his phone. It was the security camera alarm that let him know someone was tampering with the trailer.

I moved to Dan's side. The security app on his phone showed Little John with his hand on the camper door. Barely in the picture behind him was Charlie Dallier. I was in shock. Were the Dalliers part of their group? No. We watched Little John raise his hands and slowly back away. Then he turned and walked away. Mr. Charlie was holding his revolver. We watched as he holstered it and took out his cell phone.

I jumped, and Dan nearly dropped his phone in surprise when it rang. It was Mr. Charlie calling. He wanted to let Dan know what happened. Hannah was so impressed with the trailer she wanted her dad to see it. Dan told him we had watched it on video and thanked him for protecting the trailer. He told us to be careful and to watch our backs before saying goodbye.

I said, "They know exactly who we are, don't they?"

"They do now," Dan answered.

This was getting crazy. I feared for my life. We were constantly dropping things and bumping into each other as we watched every person who walked past. I didn't talk and instead I let the fear fill my mind with thoughts of Sarah. Had this been an attempt to abduct me? Possibilities flowed through my mind until I believed they were there to kidnap me and force Dan to save me. They wanted us both. I already felt responsible for Sarah's death. I would not let Dan die because of me.

We spent the next few hours bathing the calves, cleaning the stalls, and packing up everything we wouldn't need again. Whenever I looked at Dan, I could see the worry lines around his eyes. I came close to tears a few times, but I would stand up straight, hold my head back, and take deep breaths until I got myself under control.

It was after two o'clock when Ben helped us load the last of the equipment into the trailer. All we had to do now was untie the calves and load them and two folding chairs into the trailer after the eight o'clock release time and head home.

"Anyone hungry? I need a pork chop sandwich," Ben said, more cheerfully than any of us felt. When I said I wasn't hungry, I think Dan knew we needed to talk. Dan asked Ben to get all of us a sandwich and bring them back to the trailer.

We sat on the tailgate of the truck and Dan asked me, "What's going on in that pretty head of yours?"

He reached for my hand, and I snatched it away. What came out of my mouth was the most incomprehensible flow of apologies, curses, tears, and doomsday gibberish I had ever spoken. Dan was shaking his head. I know I wasn't making any sense until I said, "I love you too much for you to get hurt. We have to breakup."

"And I love you too much to let you fight this battle alone. Even if you breakup with me, I will still be around to protect you. I'm not going anywhere. Do you hear me?"

I nodded. I knew he wouldn't walk away, but I had to try. Somewhere during the conversation, we both stood up and were facing each other. He reached for my shoulder to caress it and I hugged him. This was not what I intended to happen. I wanted to breakup to protect him, and instead I'm holding onto him like a crying baby.

"Oh no, oh no, I am so sorry," he said. "I didn't see it until now."

"What do you mean?" I sobbed.

"They came after both of us. But Scotty and his friends stopped them from getting you, and Mr. Charlie, with his badge and gun, stopped them from getting me."

"Why would they want you?" I thought I knew why, but I wanted to hear his thoughts. I hoped they made more sense than the gibberish in my head.

"They parked where I would see them put you into the car. Donny Ray wouldn't want to leave a witness. They were counting on me to stop them. I think they were planning to kill me in front of you, or take us both."

We both hugged a little tighter until we heard an "hmm, hmm," behind us. We turned to find our dads standing behind us. I let go of Dan and rushed to my dad, who hugged me tightly. Dan hugged his dad, too.

I asked Dad, "How long have y'all been standing there?"

"Long enough to know Charlie Dallier was right. You need us, and we are here."

Dan nodded and said, "I hate to admit it, but yes, we do."

I asked Dad, "I'm sorry, did you have to take off work?"

"No sweetheart, I'm off today and tomorrow. Is there a place we can talk privately?"

"The trailer," Mr. Brock replied.

Ben showed up as we were entering the camper portion of the trailer. He made excuses for not getting enough sandwiches.

Ben said grace and attacked his sandwich. Dan and I just kind of stared at ours. I think Dan lost his appetite as soon as he realized what Donny Ray's plan could have been.

Dad looked at us carefully. "If you're not going to eat, then tell me what happened. Don't leave out any details." When he set the recorder on the table, my stomach dropped again. We had accidentally escaped a serious situation.

We told our stories and answered questions for forty-five minutes. He watched the video showing Little John and Mr. Charlie five times before asking for a copy.

Then Dan remembered the cameras on the show display around our cattle. They had been constantly recording since we set up. It took Dan a few minutes to find the videos of Little John. The last part of the video showed Little John staring at me and giving me the double middle fingers.

Dad encouraged me and Dan to eat our sandwiches. Ben grabbed a couple of bottled waters out of the fridge for us as we each took tentative bites. While we ate, Dad made a phone call. The call wasn't on speaker, but I could hear the voice on the other end and recognized Sergeant Johnson of the State Police. Her last words to Dad were loud and heard by everyone in the trailer.

"John, you have no cause to take action. I believe you and the kids, but without a crime, all you have is speculation. Send me a copy of that tape, please."

"Yes, ma'am," he replied. "What about harassment? Could we get them for harassment?"

"Maybe. But I want them on bigger charges. You're spinning your wheels, John."

I asked Dad, "There's nothing you can do?"

He didn't speak, he just shook his head no.

"How long is this going to continue?"

Again, he just shook his head.

"Dad, you've never lied to me. Don't start now. How long is this going to last?"

His response made me wish I hadn't eaten my sandwich.

"Until someone else dies," he said and pulled me into a hug.

CHAPTER 35

Dan

I awoke at five a.m. and sent Angel a text - *Ready for our morning run?*

Her response was quick - *Meet you at the end of the driveway.*

I wasn't sure how she would respond after our dads interrupted yesterday's conversation. She avoided talking or making eye contact with me yesterday, and she hadn't responded to my text messages last night. I didn't know if we were still dating or broken up. Her answering me this morning made me feel slightly better.

Angel had left early and rode home with her dad. My dad stayed and helped me load the calves and he rode home with me. We pulled the truck and trailer into the lot and unloaded the calves. We took their halters off and let them loose. The show season was over. We would slowly decrease the grain we fed them and get them ready to go back to the pasture. Except for the ones we would deliver to Colorado.

I stretched when I left the house and trotted down the road to meet Angel. I would normally slow down and let her fall in beside me. But this morning she stood in the middle of the road waiting for me.

I slowed my jog to a walk and stopped right in front of her.

She reached for my hand and looked into my eyes.

"Daniel Brock, I love you with all my heart, but I will never forgive myself if you get hurt because of something Dad did on the job. I want to spend the rest of my life with you, but I need to know how you feel about me."

I felt a wave of relief wash over me. Since she used my full name, which she had never done, I used her full name. "Angelina Cotton, I love you more than life itself. I would be empty without you. You aren't getting rid of me without a fight. I want to spend the rest of my life with you. To raise our children here, on this farm. I want to grow old with you and watch our grandchildren grow up. I don't know how I can express my love any clearer than this. If you need me, I will be beside you. Now stop trying to breakup with me, because I'm not going anywhere."

She dropped my hand and hugged me tightly. I returned the hug. My little speech came out of nowhere, but I meant every word.

Mr. Cotton's voice came out of the darkness. I didn't hear the gravel crunch under his feet until he spoke. To say he frightened us both was an understatement.

"She needed to hear you say that, Dan. I needed to hear it, too. Thank you. Now y'all start your run. I'll be watching for you on each lap. If you don't show up on time, I'll come searching. This afternoon, after school, I'll start training you both to fight and defend yourself."

We took off jogging. We didn't say a word until we were up the hill.

"What did he mean by training us to fight and defend ourselves?" I asked.

"Exactly that," Angel answered. "He's going to teach us military combat tactics just in case we are attacked. That way, we stand a better chance of defending ourselves."

"I thought you knew a lot about self-defense already."

"I thought I did too. But Dad said he hasn't taught me how to fight dirty."

"Oh," was my response. "I thought kicking Little John in the balls was fighting dirty."

"Apparently not to Dad."

We didn't speak for the rest of our run. We didn't need to. The feeling of undying and devoted love was there between us. That would carry us for the rest of our lives.

We missed three days of school and had lots of work to make-up. Both from our high school classes and college classes. The day flew by and we quickly found ourselves in Officer Cotton's physical combat training.

Day one consisted of me learning the basics of how to stand and maintain my balance in a fighting stance. How to make a proper fist and block punches. I was proud of myself for holding off Angel's punches and kicks until she grabbed my arm and swung her legs around my neck and flipped me to the ground. Mr. Cotton called time and chastised Angel for using advanced tactics against me on our first day.

She just smiled at me and said, "I'm sorry. I just wanted to remind you who was the top dog."

Rubbing my neck, I said. "I already knew that, Cotton Top."

Looking at Mr. Cotton, I asked, "Can we call it a day? I still need to unhook the truck from the trailer and catch up on homework."

With Angel's help, I parked the trailer in the barn. One look inside the camper part and I said, "This is going to wait until the weekend. I don't remember leaving it like this."

"Well, we did," Angel said. "I'll help you clean up."

"Thank you. Let's unload the truck, then we can feed and go study."

"I'm hungry. What's your mom making for supper?" Angel asked.

"She said something about venison steak."

"I know where I'm eating," Angel said. "I'll go get my books and let Mom know."

"And I'll let my mom know we're having a guest."

I kissed her long and hard before she started jogging back to her house.

CHAPTER 36

Angel

Friday afternoon brought our last cross-country meet before the state championship next week. This one was on the War Memorial Golf Course in Little Rock. We were running against teams we hadn't seen all season. That could mean better competition, or not. I wasn't worried about the race; I was worried about Donny Ray and Little John. Could they know I would be here? Would they show up here?

Dan was watching me closely. I was quiet most of the morning. He finally said what I was thinking. "You're worried about Donny Ray and Little John."

I nodded and said, "Yeah."

"We stay with the team. We are safer in a large group. If you go to the restroom, go as a team. Okay?"

I blew out a big breath and said, "Okay."

I noticed John and Maria had turned around and were listening to us.

John asked, "Did something else happen at the State Fair?"

Dan nodded. "We were lucky. It really shook us both up."

"We've got your back. Right, Maria?" John said.

"You know it," Maria added.

The meet occurred with no issues. John and Dan placed fourth and fifth. They started their kick too late, and they knew it. There were three guys from one school running side by side and blocking the running lanes.

The girls' meet was a little different. Maria hadn't placed above fifth at a meet yet. I told her to stay with me and I would be her pace runner and help place in a top five. What I didn't tell her was I wanted to stay in the pack today. I didn't want to separate myself from the other runners the way I normally did.

There was only one problem. There was one girl, about my height and build, who started smack talking and challenging everyone.

She yelled, "This is my race! My time to shine. My time to win."

She was intimidating some of the runners. I was smiling though and whispered to Maria, making her laugh. The girl walked up to me and Maria.

"Did I say something funny?"

It was Maria who spoke. "My teammate here has already set three meet records. In fact, she has won every race she ran this year. You want to win? Then stick with us."

There wasn't time for more taunting because a race official yelled, "Runners to the line."

The starting pistol sounded. We sprinted the first two hundred yards to get in front of the pack.

We would make three laps. Maria and I led the first lap with the taunting girl about five yards behind us and another pack of about ten girls ten yards behind her.

The second lap shook things up. We were still leading by fifteen yards. The taunting girl had fallen back into the pack that was now down to six girls. As we passed coach Tucker, he yelled for us to maintain the pace. We were ten seconds ahead of Maria's best time.

Half-way around the last lap, I would normally start my kick. I had encouraged Maria to start her kick earlier also, and I made this race about Maria. If she maintained the pace, she could win.

The last lap seemed to take forever. As we rounded the last corner, still in the lead, followed closely by the pack of six.

As soon as I could see the finish line, I yelled, "Now!"

Maria took off sprinting. I let her get ahead before I started my sprint. The rest of the pack tried to sprint, but it was obvious they had nothing left. The taunting girl was nowhere to be seen.

I could have beaten Maria across the finish line. Instead, I maintained her pace right behind her and encouraged her the whole way. Maria won her first cross-country meet. I'm not sure who was happier, Maria, me, or Coach Tucker.

Maria and I sat together on the bus ride home, forcing John to sit with Dan. I still had some planning to do. Tomorrow was Dan's eighteenth birthday, and I wanted it to be special.

CHAPTER 37

Dan

I wanted to spend the day with Angel, but Mom and Dad had a different plan. They wanted to take me car shopping for a new or slightly used car or truck. All I wanted was to be with Angel.

"I have all the vehicles I need. I have the Green Machine, the Mustang, and the dually."

It was Dad who explained their thoughts. "Son, it's true, you own all those vehicles, but you're letting me drive the dually. Angel drives the Mustang, and that leaves you with the Green Machine. You need a backup. We need a backup. Your Mom and I want you to have a vehicle that will get you to college reliably. And we will all have a backup if one breaks down."

It made sense. I couldn't argue with his reasoning. I'd already had concerns about the drive train on the Green Machine, because it was starting to grind and make noises. All the bearings and joints had been greased, but it was still wearing out.

"Okay," I sighed. "What's the plan?"

"We go car shopping tomorrow," Mom said a little too cheerfully.

I got the idea something was up. So, I decided not to play along and see what happened.

"Can we postpone until another weekend? I haven't thought about another car or truck, and I don't know what I want."

"All the more reason to go shopping," Mom replied.

"I still need to finish cleaning the trailer out from the State Fair. Clean the gear up for next year and get the truck and trailer ready to take the Dallier's calves to Colorado. I'm still behind on school work and I really don't have the desire or the time to go shopping for a new car."

It was Dad's turn to speak up. "Dan, we will leave here at ten o'clock in the morning. Get as much work done as you can in the morning and be ready to go at ten. Okay?"

I knew something was up then. Dad never gave me an ultimatum. I tried one last trick.

"Can Angel go with us?"

"I think Mrs. Cotton said something about Angel having a hair appointment tomorrow morning," Mom answered.

I wanted to say something like: *Thank you for planning a surprise birthday party for me, but don't you think I'm a little old for that?*

But what if I was wrong? What if they weren't planning a surprise party? I would look like an idiot, and worse - I risked making them feel bad because they didn't plan a surprise party. I decided to keep my mouth shut and play along. Even though I was irritated, I knew whatever they were planning; it was out of love for me.

Angel and I were jogging our first lap at five o'clock, Saturday morning. The first lap was a warmup lap before we picked up our pace for the last four laps. We often talked during the first lap and not talk at all the last four laps. Today we jogged all five laps and talked the whole time. Angel was going to help me clean the trailer up and get it ready for the Colorado trip. She wasn't sure her parents would let her go, especially after the incident at the State Fair. I hadn't thought about that. I wasn't sure my parents would let me go to Colorado either, even if Ben went along.

Angel's dad sat on the front porch drinking coffee and watching us make each lap. He was never far away, and he knew our lap times better than we did. Angel had informed him that morning we wouldn't be pushing ourselves very hard after the race the day before and not to expect our normal faster final four laps.

We stopped at the end of her drive on our last lap. Her dad spoke from the porch.

"You guys are consistent. Your last lap was the slowest, and it was only fifteen seconds behind the others. Your middle three laps were less than five seconds apart. I'm impressed with your timing."

"Thanks Dad," Angel replied. She looked at me and said, "I'll change clothes, eat something, and come help you clean the trailer. See you soon." She winked at me and walked towards her house.

I jogged back home and instead of doing the same thing Angel was doing; I headed to the barn and started feeding the calves and horses.

The trailer needed to be unloaded before wasting the rest of my day looking for a new vehicle that I didn't want. As a family, we might need an extra one, but I didn't feel like I needed a new car. It was something that Mom and Dad could buy without me. I was getting angry, and I knew I shouldn't. I took a deep breath and focused on what needed to be done.

Angel walked up as I was trying to decide what to tackle first. She was wearing her camo ball cap with her hair in a ponytail stuck through the size adjustment loop in the back. It made her look natural and down to earth. I loved that look, especially when she smiled.

"Staring at it will not get it done," she said and smiled at me. "And happy birthday."

"Thank you," I said. "My parents want me to go shopping for a car today. I don't want a new car. I was hoping to spend the day with you and have a date tonight."

She gave me a hug. "That sounds like a wonderful idea. But Mom was insistent on me getting a haircut today. Maybe we can plan something later."

"I don't know," I answered. "This whole thing smells like a surprise birthday party to me."

Angel said nothing and just hugged me a little tighter. That told me that something was up.

I loosened my hug and said, "I'll put the bucket on the tractor and we can get the show box and other things off the top of the trailer. Then I can organize, clean it, and put it up later."

"I?" Angel asked. "Where am I going to be?"

233

"I'm sorry," I said and caressed her face. "We can do all that later."

It was nine twenty when we emptied the last of the show supplies from the trailer. We still had the camper portion to clean, but I would do that tomorrow. We gave each other a long kiss goodbye. I wanted more, but it would have to wait for another time.

CHAPTER 38

Dan

My parents definitely had something planned. Instead of shopping at the dealers in our own home town, or even Searcy, they headed to North Little Rock. We finally stopped at a Chevy dealership.

We got out of Mom's Escalade, which screamed "they have money" to the salespeople. Dad started talking to the salesperson, who was asking tons of questions and giving suggestions. Dad finally said, "It's going to be his. Maybe you should ask him."

"Well, all right then. Is this your first vehicle? What color do you want?" He questioned without taking a breath or letting me speak. I looked at Mom and Dad and shook my head.

"What's the cheapest thing you have on the lot?" I asked the salesman.

"I'm sorry. What?"

"You heard me. What's the cheapest car you have here?"

"Daniel!" Mom said.

I ignored the salesman for a moment and spoke to Mom and Dad. "I'm sorry. Let me buy a clunker and I'll take it home and rebuild it like I did my truck and the Mustang. I don't have any desire to buy a new car or truck."

Dad was about to say something, but the salesman beat him to it. "So, you got a Mustang, huh? Is it a new one?"

"It's a sixty-five. Rebuilt from the ground up. I did everything but the upholstery, and the paint job, myself."

This time, the salesman picked up on my sarcasm. "Let me give you folks a few minutes to talk. I sense some tension here. Just wave at me when you're ready."

"Daniel, what's your rush to buy a car today?" Mom asked.

"Gee Mom, I don't know. What is the rush for us to go car shopping today? This wasn't my idea, remember?"

It was Dad's turn now. "Daniel, apologize to your mom. That was uncalled for."

I sighed heavily, but I said, "I'm sorry, Mom. But you both know me better than to pull this stunt. How many weeks did I research trucks before we ordered the dually? It's not my style to buy something on a whim. You know this. This shopping spree screams, 'We have to get Dan away from the farm today.'"

"So, your answer is to disrespect us, and waste our time?" Dad asked.

"No, Dad. Let's do this. Let's go get some lunch. We can discuss what kind of car you and Mom are thinking about, then we can test drive a couple. But I'm not driving anything home today without taking my time and doing my research."

Mom and Dad looked at each other. "All right son," Dad said. "Where would you like to eat? It's your birthday."

We stopped at a popular buffet restaurant. I asked them several times what they had in mind for a backup vehicle. They weren't too concerned about an extra vehicle, they just wanted me to have a dependable car or truck to drive to college. I kept using the word car. They kept mentioning the word truck. Their faces kind of went blank when I said I would prefer a small economical car, because I already had two trucks, and I had the Mustang as a sports car.

We spent several hours test driving cars that afternoon. Everything I owned was a Ford, but I wasn't stuck on a single brand. I wanted to do some research before I made a commitment.

Our trip home was quiet. Mom and Dad had mentioned test driving trucks several times that afternoon. I finally asked them if there was something wrong with my rationale. No, no, there was nothing wrong with my rationale.

When we finally got home and turned the curve to drive past the Cotton's, it was obvious I had guessed correctly. There were cars parked everywhere and Mom and Dad were grinning from ear to ear until they saw my face. And then there was the brand-new silver Ford F-250, 4X4, with an extended cab and a big blue bow on top. Angel was sitting in the driver's seat and several of my friends were sitting in the back of the truck.

When Mom stopped the Escalade in the garage, neither of my parents said a thing. I said, "I'll play along. But all I wanted was a quiet day at home and a date with Angel. And we will talk about the truck later."

My Dad said, "Daniel, we did it because we love you."

"I know, Dad. That's why I'm not angrier than I am. I love you too, but this is not what I wanted."

I got out of the Escalade and put on a fake smile and walked to the truck to the cheers of "Surprise" and out of sync strains of Happy Birthday.

Angel flashed me a huge smile, but all I could see was beautiful layered brown hair. That was her hair appointment. She dyed her hair back to brown, and she was beautiful. She opened the truck door for me, but I just stood there.

Ben yelled from somewhere, "Burgers are ready!" And that took most of the crowd away.

"Climb in. Let me give you a tour of the truck," she said.

"Later. Let's go eat."

"You don't want to even look at the truck," she said. She saw right through me.

"It's just a truck. I can't take my eyes off you."

She stepped down out of the truck and I pulled her close for a kiss, but she raised her hand between our mouths and said, "You don't like it, do you?"

"I don't know, I haven't looked at it. I don't want it, if that's what you mean."

"You're being ungrateful. Your parents, me and Ben, and your friends went to a lot of work to plan this."

"I just wanted to spend the day with you. Me and you. How is that being ungrateful?" I asked.

"You are being selfish, Dan. Your parents and Ben love you and they are proud of you. I love you and I'm proud of you. You're always encouraging the surrounding people. You've encouraged and pushed me in ways I can't explain, and I love you so much for it. But, please don't be selfish, Dan. This party was partly my idea, and I want you to be happy and have fun."

That hurt more than a slap in the face. She was right. I was being selfish.

"You're right. I'm sorry. I'm tired and stressed, Cotton Top. I've treated Mom and Dad rudely, today, because I didn't want to go car shopping."

"Then come on. You're going to apologize right now." She took me by the hand and led me into the house, and I apologized again. Then she led me onto the deck to find Ben and told me to thank him for everything he did to help organize my birthday party.

I learned something about Angel that evening. She could be a force to be reckoned with. I learned from everyone there that Angel didn't help plan my birthday party; she planned it all. Angel invited every guest and made me thank them for coming. She enticed Mom and Dad into taking me car shopping, which meant I owed them another apology.

The biggest surprise of the night was when I realized I was having fun. I stopped and squeezed Angel's hand to get her attention. I put my palm against her face and she leaned into it. Looking her in the eyes, I said, "Thank you. I love you." And I bent down and kissed her long and hard.

Angel looked up at me and said, "You need to take your birthday present for a test drive. Let's go to Sonic for some ice cream."

"Wait. There's no cake and ice cream here?" I asked.

"Nope. We decided the best way to get you to drive the truck was to make you go get your own ice cream." She pulled an envelope from her pocket and produced a stack of gift cards.

Now I was really embarrassed. They knew exactly how I would react to this party and the truck, and they played me very well. My cousins were here, members of the cross-country team and the 4-H shooting sports team. There were fifteen people there, not counting me and Angel. She gave gift cards to everyone and told them it was for ice cream or whatever they wanted at Sonic.

We created a seven or eight car parade into town and pulled into Sonic with lights flashing and horns honking. I had to admit; the truck was nice. Everything worked like it was supposed to. The Green Machine had its flaws and the biggest flaw was its age.

Sonic is a drive-in restaurant where you park and place your order at a drive-up kiosk. Because this Sonic was close to the lake, they added extra parking, walk-up kiosks, outdoor tables, and a kids' playground.

We parked and claimed the two empty tables in the walkup area. Everyone had ordered, and we were hanging out and enjoying ourselves for thirty minutes when three guys in their early twenties showed up and told us to move. They claimed we had taken their tables.

I turned to the one talking and told him, "We will be glad to share. There are two tables."

He stepped towards me and I could smell the alcohol on his breath. "These are our tables. We left to run an errand, and you took our tables.

241

Y'all need to leave." He raised his fist like he wanted to fight.

"Like I said, we will share," I responded, and moved my feet into a fighting stance. I handed my shake to Angel.

"You're not listening to me," he said and threw a slow punch at me, which I blocked much easier than Angel's quick punches. "I'm going to kick your ass."

I blocked two more punches and when he tried a sidekick; then I grabbed his leg, stepped in, and kneed him in the groin. He hit the ground, groaning, and holding his crotch.

I looked up at his friends and found Mike, Bobby, and more friends surrounding them.

"Your friend is drunk. Take him home and let him sober up. We don't want any trouble," I said.

I watched them carry him away. Angel moved to my side and said, "Did you learn to fight like that in one day?"

I laughed a little. "He was drunk. I knew what he was going to do before he did. That wasn't a fight."

We broke up the party a little later, and everyone headed home. Angel and I took the truck for a drive. We found a lonesome logging road, parked the truck, and turned off all the lights. We cuddled, talked for a while, and watched for shooting stars. Then things got heated. We made some memories and Angel gave me a reason to keep the truck. It was a wonderful birthday, after all.

CHAPTER 39

Dan

John and Maria joined us for our Sunday morning run. We jogged the first lap and discussed our last race. John and I lamented getting caught behind the teammates who blocked us. Angel saw them and that was why she and Maria sprinted the first two hundred yards to get into the lead. John and I agreed it was a good idea and a tactic we would use as well.

We pushed ourselves as hard as we could on the middle three laps. Angel and Maria were behind us, but not too far behind. We slowed down to let them catch us. They were less than a minute behind us, which were outstanding times.

We finally finished cleaning the trailer early Sunday afternoon, before heading to shooting sports practice. All the show equipment was unloaded and stored. The camper was cleaned and sheets pulled off the beds and put into the laundry. I had already hooked a hose up to the gray water tank and drained it. I would flush the clean water tank later and refill it right before the trip.

We shot muzzleloaders that afternoon. Angel didn't own one and used one of the club's muzzleloaders. She had a difficult time getting used to it, but her target groups got smaller the more she shot. She was so competitive she was upset that she was the low scorer on the last round with a score of eighty-five out of one hundred.

It gave me the idea of getting Angel a new muzzleloader for her birthday next month. I know it's not a romantic gift, but it is one that a girl like Angel would love. Okay, I would get her something else, a little more special. We weren't ready for an engagement ring yet, and I didn't think our parents would approve. But a true promise ring, that would be perfect.

The state cross-country championships were held on the infield of Oakland Horse Race Track in Hot Springs. The track was one-mile around and that made the course for the cross-country race shorter than a mile. To get 5 kilometers inside the track, the starting line and the finish line were in different places, which could be confusing if you weren't aware of where they were. Our school was in the class 4A division and would have about two hundred participants in the boys' division, and one hundred and sixty in the girls' division. Coach Tucker said we would start in staggered heats, meaning the faster runners could lap the slower runners from previous heats, creating confusion.

John and I got lucky and started in the first heat. We sprinted the first two hundred meters and found there were ten other runners with us.

We slowed our pace to about three-fourths of our sprint speed. Two runners passed us, but the rest stayed in a tight pack with us.

When we made the first pass, Coach Tucker was yelling five forty-five. John and I looked at each other, wondering if he meant five minutes and forty-five seconds. That was a record time for us, if we could maintain the pace. We soon caught and passed the two speedsters who passed us at the start. I knew there were several runners still with us, but I wasn't looking back at this point to count how many. John Parker and I were breathing hard. We had pushed ourselves this week and knew we were okay at this pace.

Two runners moved up beside us, but we held our pace. As we finished the second lap and started the last lap, Coach Tucker yelled, "Twelve forty! Twelve forty. Keep it up." I vaguely heard Angel and Maria yell for us. We were running sub seven-minute miles, which was a great time for us.

At what John thought was the halfway point of the third lap, he hit my arm, a signal, and we sped up to nearly a sprint. We started lapping the slower runners. Race officials were trying to get the slower runners to move to the right and get out of our way, but it was of little use. We lapped more runners, John passing them on the inside, and I was passing them on the outside. I could hear another runner breathing right behind me. I could see two runners right behind John. We were a pack of five or more runners.

As soon as I could see the ribbon being pulled across the finish line, I yelled, "Sprint!" John and I gained a two-step lead, but it wasn't enough. Three of us crossed the finish line in an almost dead heat. Race officials determined another runner crossed the line first. John was second, and I was third. I felt elated. I'd never finished above thirtieth in the state meet before.

Angel and Maria jogged a little on the infield to warm up, while the remaining male runners straggled across the finish line.

When the girls' race started, Angel and Maria sprinted the first two hundred meters to get out front. They weren't the only ones, though. Other runners ran with them and created a pack of fifteen to twenty runners.

After the first lap, Angel was running easily, but Maria and the rest of the pack were struggling. After the second lap, Angel led by twenty meters. Maria and the pack were still behind her, but the pack was down to about ten runners.

Angel must have surprised all the runners with her sprint at the end. She won the race by nearly thirty meters. The pack split up and spread out as they crossed the finish line. Maria finished in seventh place. She was grinning from ear to ear when she hugged Angel.

John and I found them and celebrated with them. Maria told Angel, "The girls in the pack kept saying you would get tired and drop back soon. When we hit the halfway point of the last lap and you started your kick, I told them, 'She's gone. You won't catch her now.'"

We laughed at Maria's comment. I gave Angel a hug and a quick kiss. We were at a school function and we were supposed to behave accordingly. I didn't care, though.

Coach Tucker found us and congratulated Angel on what should be a State Championship. We would know for sure when all runners had finished. He told me and John, our finishes were official, we had placed second and third. He looked at Maria and said, "And you are the most improved runner. You barely made the top fifty finishers last year, and this year you finished seventh at state. That's outstanding!"

We made the two and a half-hour trip back home on the school bus. We laughed and sang as a group. Angel and I whispered to each other. Cross-country season was over. Now we would focus on shooting sports, hunting season, and school. A particular topic was how were we going to convince our parents to let us go to Colorado together.

When we reached the school, the parking lot was empty, except for a few cars. I parked my truck at the end of the lot, close to the basketball gym. It was a brand-new truck, and Angel and I didn't want it scratched or dented up. John Parker turned and asked, "Hey, can I drive your truck around the school?"

"Sure, but no horsing around."

Maria popped up beside him and asked, "Can I ride with him?"

"Why not?" I said, grinning. "Angel and I will unload the cooler."

Angel and I grabbed the handles of the cooler and we were right behind John and Maria getting off the bus. I dug into my pocket and handed John the keys.

"It's got a remote start. Does it work?" he asked.

"I don't know. I haven't tried it."

We were barely off the bus when John touched the remote start button. That's when we heard a whoosh and saw my birthday present go up in flames.

Angel and I dropped the cooler. I turned back to the bus to grab a fire extinguisher which was stored just above the steps under the dash. Angel must have had 911 on speed dial. By the time I turned around with the fire extinguisher, I could hear sirens. I stopped as soon as I saw my truck. The fire fully engulfed it. The little fire extinguisher in my hand would not make a dent.

John looked at me with pleading eyes. "I'm sorry Dan. I didn't know that was going to happen."

Disbelief and shock took over my thinking.

Coach Tucker brought us all back to reality. "If you hadn't tested that remote start, you could have been sitting in that truck when it went up in flames."

I suddenly wanted a remote start on all my vehicles, including my tractors.

"It wasn't your fault," I said. "I'm just glad you weren't in it."

I stepped toward John and pulled him into a bear hug. Angel and Maria joined us for a group hug.

We ended our hug when we heard the sirens get louder. Five minutes was a good response time for a volunteer fire department, but the truck was already a total loss. They had the fire doused in just a few minutes.

I was so shocked by the fire that I forgot to call Mom and Dad. That was not a call I wanted to make. Coach Tucker made it easy when he said, "I've already called your parents. They're on their way."

"Thank you," I said. I sat down in the middle of the parking lot and just watched the firefighters as they put out any remaining flames.

Angel sat down beside me. "Do you think this was Donny Ray and Little John?"

"I don't think so. I've had this truck for less than a week. How could they know it was mine?"

"It just seemed well timed," she answered.

"Yeah. Thanks to you, I was beginning to really like that truck."

We watched the firefighters weave in and out of the black smoke. Angel laid her head against my shoulder and rubbed my back, trying to console me, just as the firefighters extinguished the last flames.

Mom and Dad arrived at the school. Angel and I had not moved. We just sat watching them clean up as they watched and waited to see if there would be any more flames.

Mom came directly to me and Angel. As we stood up, she pulled us both into a hug and asked, "Are you okay? Was anyone hurt?"

Dad had given us a quick inspection and walked to the firefighters instead.

"Yes Mom. We're okay. I'm upset and disappointed about losing my truck. That's all."

"The main thing is that you are both okay. What happened?"

I briefly told her the story about John trying the remote starter, and then the truck went up in flames.

I looked at the truck again. The firefighters had opened the hood of the truck, and they were inspecting the motor. Officer Cotton must have been right behind Mom and Dad. He had his flashlight out and was surveying the engine. I watched as he pointed at the battery and said something to Dad and one firefighter. He glanced at us, then took out his phone and made a call. He stepped away from the truck and started yelling into his phone. I could only hear two words: "attempted murder." Those words cut my legs right out from under me.

"Oh God," I whispered. I hit my knees and began shaking. It was Donny Ray and Little John. I closed my eyes and a vision of Angel and me burning inside the truck popped into my head. I could feel the heat and flames and hear our screams. Then the scene changed to John and Maria. I watched as they screamed and pounded the windows. Their faces turned to charred blobs and exploded into ashes, forcing me to open my eyes and breathe. The smell of burned rubber was making me sick.

We had just survived a murder attempt. I turned and searched for John and Maria to be sure they were alive.

My phone vibrated in my back pocket. I had all notifications turned off except for phone calls, text messages, and my security cameras. I didn't care about any of those things, but instinct or programmed reflex made me take it out.

It was a text message. *Did you and the little bitch survive?*

I was already shaking from fear. But this turned it to anger. I squeezed the phone hard enough to almost crack the screen before I relaxed and Angel yanked it away from me.

She ran toward Officer Cotton. "Dad, you need to see this."

Mom knelt beside me. "Be still Daniel. What did it say?" I realized I'd been rocking back and forth.

"They wanted to know if Angel and I were still alive."

"What?"

I had to take a few breaths before I answered. "It was intentional. They tried to kill us, Mom."

"Why? Why, you? Why, Angel?"

"I'm not sure. They want to hurt Officer Cotton for arresting Danny Ray. I guess they think they can hurt him most by hurting or killing Angel." I had to shake those visions.

Until this moment, I had looked at Donny Ray and Little John as being stupid country boys who wanted revenge against Officer Cotton. Now they had targeted me and Angel and they had the audacity to ask if we survived?

I must have been rocking back and forth again because Mom asked me if I was okay.

"No Mom. I think we just survived a murder attempt." Those visions. Where did they come from?

I watched as Officer Cotton handed my phone back to Angel and pointed toward me. He said something to Dad and Dad nodded. Dad put his arm around Angel and they started walking back.

Mom and I stood up before they reached us. Angel was crying and let go of Dad and hugged me hard.

Mom asked, "Was it intentional?"

I opened my eyes and saw Dad nod yes.

"Daniel. Angel. We are going home now," Dad said.

Angel let go and grabbed her gym bag and purse. I turned to see Coach Tucker, John, and Maria, and other team members watching. I waved goodbye, and John made a "call me" symbol with his thumb and little finger to his ear and mouth. We got into the Escalade and Mom started driving home.

Angel handed my phone back once we were on the road. She motioned for me to unlock my phone. I did, and she took it back and went straight to my messages.

Did you and the little bitch survive?

Someone had responded with *Yes.*

You should have died, was the response.

"Who sent that?" I asked.

"Dad thinks it was Little John. He said Donny wouldn't gloat about it."

"Did we really just escape an attempted murder?" I asked her.

"Yeah! I think we did."

CHAPTER 40

Angel

Dan reached over and grabbed my hand. I know he did it to comfort me, but I was too shocked to be comforted. One look at his face made me realize he was seeking comfort instead of comforting me. A dizzy feeling washed over me. I couldn't process everything that was happening.

I was worried about Dad. He had been so angry and upset. He had called his boss, and then Sergeant Johnson, with the state police, and yelled at them both. I could hear them yelling back, but I couldn't tell what they were saying.

Other than Mr. Brock, Dad was the most morally righteous man I knew. The law was the law, and it was not to be broken. But the anger he expressed today showed him in a new light. He was at a breaking point, and I was worried about what he would do to protect me and Mom.

I looked at Dan. A tear rolled down his cheek. I wanted to reach over and wipe it off, but his straight-forward stare told me he was angry. Maybe I needed to wipe the tears from my eyes. I could feel them burning from the smoke. And the horrible burnt rubber smell. I was worried about Dan now. What had I gotten him into?

I had already tried to breakup with him twice, to protect him. But he wouldn't let me, and I was glad. I loved him more for it. It was too late now. They had burned his truck up attempting to kill us, and used his phone to taunt him. Dan was slow to get angry. Dad said that was a good thing, and he liked that about Dan. He said Dan would keep his cool under pressure. Dad had also said it could be dangerous. Because when he struck out, he could hurt a lot of people.

I squeezed Dan's hand to get his attention.

He looked at me. "Does your mom know what happened?"

"I don't know," I replied.

"We'll drop you off. I'll take care of the chores, and then I will call you."

"Dan? Are you okay?"

"They don't care about the law. They do whatever they want, and that scares me."

"Me too," I answered.

"What's your dad doing?"

"I don't know. And that scares me even more."

Mom met me on the front porch. She was crying and wrapped me in a hug that only a mother can give. It wasn't long before I was crying too. She didn't speak. She didn't have to. I knew Dad had already called her and told her what had happened.

"Did Dad say where he was going?"

"No. But you know where he's going. He's so angry, he'll kill them if he finds them," Mom said.

She was right. I knew where Dad was going. He was man hunting, and he could walk right into a trap.

Mom had dinner ready, but neither of us ate much. There was an old swing on the back porch of our house and that's where we went after cleaning up dinner. It was Mom's favorite place to sit because of the view. It was only a few yards from the river, and when the water was up, you could watch and hear it rush by the farm on its way south.

The squirrels and birds came to the feeders she had put out, and the occasional deer would show up and graze at the edge of the woods. I had strict instructions not to deer hunt off the back porch - from Mom, not Dad or Dan. She enjoyed watching the wildlife, and didn't want them disturbed.

There was a chill breeze coming off the river, and it cooled the porch. We settled into the swing next to each other and pulled a blanket over us. We were silent for a while, and then Mom started talking.

"I met Jonathan the summer after graduation. I was living at home and working at a diner in Clarendon. Roger was the guy I had been dating. I thought we were getting serious, and I even slept with him a few times before he broke up with me. He'd been seeing someone else and got her pregnant. They got married, had a boy, and they stayed together until this summer when she died from cancer."

I asked, "Is he the one who called you? The one Dad was upset about?"

"He's the one. Anyway, Jonathan showed up with all his big muscles and his big smile, and started flirting with me. I thought he was wonderful and would be a pleasant distraction, so we started dating. He was three years older and was about to become a sergeant in the Marine Corps. Before I knew it, we were making out and having sex in the back seat of his car."

"Mom, that's more than I want to know."

"I'm sorry. He was home on a two-week furlough, and I found out two weeks after he went back to active duty that I was pregnant with you. He called me every night after he left and told me how much he missed me, and wished I was there with him."

"I was afraid to tell him I was pregnant, but I finally told him. He surprised me by being excited, and asked me to marry him."

Neither of my parents had told me this story, and I had asked them several times how they met. I wasn't sure why she was telling me now, so I asked her.

"Your dad and I have had our difficulties. He has always been protective of me and you. When we were stationed in Quantico, awaiting his next assignment, another off-duty marine made a rude remark about me, and Jonathan nearly beat him to death before they pulled him off the guy."

She sighed as she continued the story.

"I never understood exactly what happened next. We thought he would receive a dishonorable discharge. But somehow, he received an honorable discharge, and we moved back to Jonesboro, where we attended college."

"I always wondered why he left the Marine Corps. He seems to brighten up when he talks about it," I said.

"He was a good Marine. But I think every Marine has an anger issue. For the most part, they learn to control it until they get pushed too far. Once they are pushed too far, they become a well-trained fighting machine that doesn't stop until they destroy their enemy or they die trying to destroy them."

I shivered at her comment. "Why are you telling me this, Mom?"

"I'm afraid your dad is out for revenge. It's one thing to make threats. Those are just words. It's another to attempt to murder his daughter. You and I are the most precious things in the world to him. He won't stop until they are in jail or dead."

We rocked in the swing silently for a few more minutes. Mom stopped the swing and stood up.

"I know it's early, but I'm going to take a shower and go to bed. If you're going to stay up, call Dan to sit with you."

I stood up and hugged her. "Thank you for talking, Mom."

She smiled and kissed my cheek. "You're not my little girl anymore. You're a grown woman who needs to know the truth. Goodnight, sweetheart."

That seemed a strange comment. I was a grown woman who needed to know the truth. Was there a hidden message in there? If there was, I couldn't figure it out.

CHAPTER 41

Dan

As soon as we were home, Dad pulled me into a hug. "We could have lost you today."

"I know, Dad. I know."

"How are you feeling?" he asked as he released me.

"The shock is wearing off and I'm getting mad. They destroyed my truck, and they taunted me. They tried to kill me and Angel. How am I supposed to feel, Dad?" I reached out and gently grabbed his arm, knowing I had raised my voice a little louder than I should have.

He blew out a breath. "That's a good question, son. I don't know."

He tried to get me to talk more, but I just said, "Dad, I have chores to do. Let me take care of the animals and if I feel like talking, we'll talk then, okay?"

He nodded his reluctant agreement and let me go to the barn. I had one of those spells where I did all my chores by routine memory. They were so routine I didn't have to think about doing them. My mind was off blowing up cars and beating up Donny Ray and Little John. I didn't want to kill them. I wanted to inflict so much injury and pain that they begged to die.

Eventually, I came to my senses. I might beat one of them in a fair fight. But that was the problem. They wouldn't fight fair. They had more people, more cars, more time, and more experience doing crazy psycho stuff to get into your head. Fear is what they wanted us to feel. They wanted Officer Cotton to come after them so they could kill him. If they did that, would they stop? I couldn't answer that. I could only hope that Officer Cotton survived, and if that was the case, they wouldn't quit until he was dead, or they were in prison.

They were getting closer and closer to killing someone, which meant they were tired of playing mind games. They were getting serious now. I needed to talk to Angel. Her dad was walking right into a trap. They would kill him tonight, if they could.

I stopped in the middle of the feed room with another bucket of grain. What was I going to feed? I was so engrossed in my thoughts I had finished feeding everything and was about to start all over. Was it muscle memory? I had physically done my chores without mentally being there. That scared me. I always needed to be alert to my surroundings. If there had been another trap set, I would have missed it.

My phone rang. Caller ID showed it was Angel.

"Hello."

"Dad's in trouble. He left his truck parked to do some recon. When he came back, a window was busted, and he had a flat. He wanted to know if we could come pick him up."

"Sure," I replied. I had a spooky feeling about this. "I'll bring Mom's Escalade. Get his location and I'll pick you up out front."

I called Dad and told him what I was going to do. He was in the Escalade before I left the barn.

Why did he call Angel? Shouldn't he have called another law enforcement agency? This thought worried me. Maybe the burning of my truck had me looking for traps everywhere. Dad backed the Escalade out of the garage.

I went to the Escalade and found Dad in the passenger seat. "I'm coming with you, son, and I brought this along." He handed me my Glock.

I raised my eyebrows at him.

"Don't worry. I've got mine. This could be a trap," he replied.

"I've thought of that. Why didn't he call another law enforcement agency?"

Dad smiled. "Exactly."

We picked Angel up at the end of their drive.

I asked her, "Why didn't your dad call the local law enforcement?"

"He is out of his jurisdiction, and the local sheriff is Donny Ray's cousin."

"Did he call or text?" Dad asked.

"He called. He wanted me to know it wasn't a trap, but it's a trap," Angel said.

I took my foot off the gas pedal. "What do you mean?"

"Keep going," she urged. "He carries two phones. A work phone and a personal phone. He never uses his work phone to call me or Mom. That's what he called me on, so I know something is up."

"Ok," Dad said. "Where is he, and what's going on?"

"His GPS locator in his personal phone says he is on a launch ramp near Georgetown, on the White River."

"Set us up for directions," I said.

We drove in silence for the next forty-five minutes. It should have taken an hour, but I did a little speeding on the back roads.

It was nearly ten when we reached the dirt parking lot of the boat ramp. The GPS tracker said we were within a hundred yards of the phone we were searching for. I drove a circle around the dirt parking area, before we spotted the Game and Fish truck parked at a secluded corner.

I put my headlights on high and drove toward the truck. Officer Cotton was sitting in the driver's seat watching us, but he wasn't moving. He didn't wave, nod, or move like he recognized us.

One side of his truck tilted downward, showing he had a flat on the front driver's side. His lips started moving, like he was talking to someone. Angel's phone rang.

"It's Dad," she said.

"Hello?"

I could hear Officer Cotton's voice, but I couldn't understand what he said.

"Ok," Angel answered. "We'll be careful."

Dad spoke first. "Angel? What's going on?"

"He was ambushed, and knocked out. Then they handcuffed him to the steering wheel. He smelled gas when he woke up and thought of Dan's truck. He used Alexa on his work phone to call me without using his hands," she said.

"They may have set up another fire bomb like they did in Dan's truck. If we open the door, it could release a trigger and ignite it," Dad answered.

"Yes, sir. I guess so."

Dad turned to Angel. "Did you bring your Glock, Angel?"

"No, sir."

Dad handed her his pistol, a Glock 17, like mine. "I don't think you will need this, but you and Dan keep watch while I talk to Jonathan."

"Yes, sir."

I stopped twenty feet from the truck and left the Escalade running. We kept our pistols unloaded when holstered. Angel was familiar with our holsters and the process we followed. I removed my Glock from the holster and then the loaded magazine from its separate pocket, then slid the action back to chamber a cartridge.

It was dark. I scanned the trees and darkness toward the river. Someone could watch from the other side of the river, and I wouldn't be able to see them. I moved to the back of the Escalade, away from the headlights. Angel had done the same. Dad found us as we were scanning the area. I was wondering what we were looking for. I had seen nothing, and the frogs and bugs were performing a symphony, which usually meant no one was close.

"Angel. Your Dad says you keep a special key on your keyring. Do you know the one?"

She gasped. "They threw his keys away?"

"No. Just the handcuff keys."

She reached into her pants pocket and pulled out her keys. She selected the handcuff key and handed it to Dad, but he refused it.

"Come with me," Dad said. "Dan, keep your eyes on the surroundings."

Appropriately chastised, I immediately resumed my watch. I looked toward the river and saw something move in the moonlight. I glanced away and back at the river again. "Dad? Movement on the river," I said. Hopefully, just loud enough for him to hear. I moved around the Escalade and turned off the lights and ignition.

That's when the gunshot sounded from the river. I fired off three shots and heard, "Shit! Get out of here. Go, go, go!" Then I heard a boat motor revving up and heading away.

"Dad? Angel? Are you okay?" I asked. I was breathing harder than I realized.

"We're okay, son," he said calmly. "Can you turn the lights back on?"

When the headlights were back on, I discovered I was shaking. I'd never been shot at, or shot at anyone before. Moving to the back of the Escalade again, I was shaking even more.

The crickets and frogs were quiet now. I was searching the darkness for movement when Dad said, "Dan, we're coming to you."

I heard Dad, Angel, and Mr. Cotton approach me.

"Where were you standing when you shot Dan?" Officer Cotton inquired.

"About where I am now."

He turned his flashlight on and shown it on the ground and scooped up the three shells my pistol ejected.

He handed me the shells. "Put them in your pocket. You were never here tonight."

He turned to my dad. "Thank you for coming. I need to call this in. I'll be okay now."

"We can stay if you need us," Dad said.

"No. Y'all need to be gone before someone comes to check out those gunshots. There is a house close by and they report everything they think is illegal activity here."

He turned to Angel and pulled her into a hug. "Thank you. I love you. Now go home and make sure your mom is okay."

We could hear a siren in the distance.

"Time for y'all to go. I'll be okay."

"Be careful, Dad. I want you to come home," Angel said. She gave him another quick hug before getting into the Escalade.

I moved to the driver's side of the Escalade. Dad held the door for Angel to get in and closed it for her. I was moving as soon as Dad closed his door.

CHAPTER 42

Angel

Dan started driving before I had fastened my seatbelt. "Which direction were the sirens coming from?" he asked.

"South," his dad replied.

"Then we are going north."

"Slow down, son. Stay calm. Stay under the speed limit," Mr. Brock advised him.

"What happened?" Dan asked.

"They knocked him out," I answered. "Then they put him in the truck and handcuffed him to the steering wheel so he couldn't get out. They set up a fire bomb on the floor of his truck. If someone opened the truck door, the light switch in the door would spark and set the gas on fire." I fought the urge to scream before I said, "It would have burned him alive." I let loose a growl of frustration then.

"How did he get out without opening the door?"

Mr. Brock answered that question. "Angel climbed through the window and unlocked the cuffs. They both climbed out the window. He left everything in place, so it could be investigated."

"Why did he want us to leave so soon?" Dan asked.

Mr. Brock said, "He's afraid you might have shot at innocent people in the boat."

"Oh," Dan said. He stopped asking questions and went silent.

I was still angry, but I was getting myself under control. Dan's single word response to his dad's answer told me he had not considered his shots to be anything but self-defense.

There was a single shot, and it didn't seem to come anywhere near us. Was it coincidental? What if Dan had shot someone? Dad would handle it. He would protect us and Dan. What did he tell Dan? *You were never here tonight.* My Dad, who never questioned or broke the law, was doing both tonight, because he loved me and Mom. Even before today, Dad had said it would take someone being killed to end this.

Mr. Brock's voice brought me out of my thoughts.

"Dan, you did the right thing tonight. You thought we were being shot at, and you shot back. That's why I posted you there."

"But what if I shot an innocent person?"

"There were no innocent people there tonight. They didn't have running lights on their boat because they didn't want to be seen. When we get to Searcy, I need you to stop at Walmart. Your mother will kill me if she sees blood all over her Escalade."

Dan and I responded at the same time.

"Dad, are you hurt?"

"Mr. Brock?"

He responded, "I think it caught my shoulder. It's just a scratch, but it's bleeding more than I thought it would."

"Dad, let me stop and look at it."

"No, son. We'll get some towels and bandages at Walmart. Just drive a little faster, but be careful."

This brought me out of my self-pity mode. I expect it did Dan as well, because the speedometer was hitting seventy on the straight stretches. He slowed to the speed limit as we neared the city limits and slower speed signs appeared.

"Dan, do you have any cash?"

"Yes, Dad. About forty bucks," Dan answered.

"Good. Give that and your ball cap to Angel. Angel, I need two dark-colored towels, large feminine hygiene pads and athletic ankle tape. That's all. Go through self-checkout and be casual. Okay?"

"Okay. Tampons? What about disinfectant?" I asked.

"They absorb blood extremely well, and the tape will hold it on. The towels, for obvious reasons. We have disinfectant at home. The priority is to stop the bleeding,"

Dan handed me his wallet and ball cap. He dropped me off at the door closest to the pharmacy. It only took a few minutes, but it seemed like a lifetime. I had to admit; the purchases were brilliant. I was still wearing my sweats, and no one would think twice about me buying feminine hygiene pads or ankle tape. And the cash and ball cap were to help conceal my identity. I understood where Dan got his reasoning skills from.

I was out of the store in less than ten minutes. Mr. Brock had moved to the back seat as well.

"All right, Angel. Time for your first lesson in field-dressing a wound. Can you handle it?"

"Yes, sir."

"Dan, take us home."

I helped him get his jacket and shirt off, only to wonder how bad it really was. He had bled a lot. His shirt and jacket were soaked.

"Now, take one towel and wipe off my shoulder and arm. Can you see where the bleeding is coming from?"

"Yes, but how can a spot that small bleed so much?" I asked as I pressed the towel against it.

"Medication. I'm on blood thinners."

"Hold the towel, please. It looks more like a rope burn," I said.

He held the towel with his other hand, while I opened the tape and the feminine pads.

"Dan, I need a little light," I said.

"Pull into that car wash. Don't turn on the interior lights." Mr. Brock added.

Dan pulled into one of the empty bays and from the light it provided, I put the pad onto the wound and wrapped it with tape.

"Help me get this shirt and jacket back on," he instructed me. "Dan, let's go."

I used the second towel to wrap around his arm in case it was leaking blood. We rode the rest of the way home in silence.

Dan drove to his house and helped his dad inside. Mrs. Brock met us in the kitchen. One look at her husband and she immediately took over.

"Lloyd, what have you done?"

"Nothing I won't survive," he replied. "Dan, clean the car and burn the trash. Clean your gun and put it away. Then go stay with Angel until Jonathan comes home."

"But," Dan protested.

"No buts, go now. Your mother will help me from here."

"Yes, sir."

We found a little blood in the Escalade and cleaned it. We bagged the towels and the stuff I bought from Walmart and combined it with the kitchen trash and carried it to a burn barrel near the barn. It was where Dan burned hay strings to keep livestock and wildlife from getting tangled up in the leftover strings.

Then we unloaded, cleaned, and oiled the pistols before putting them back into the safe.

When we started the walk to my house. I asked Dan, "Are you okay?"

He put his arm around my waist as we walked, a reminder of how chilly the breeze off the river was.

"No, are you?"

"I'm not sure I'll ever be okay."

We fell asleep on the couch waiting for Dad to come home. The stress of the day, chill of the night air, and the comfort of being in each other's arms under a warm blanket must have woven its magical sleep on us about midnight. Dad finally came home about five thirty in the morning. He woke us up and reminded us we had school and chores to get done.

Normally, he would have yelled at us for doing such a thing as falling asleep together. Instead, he thanked Dan for staying with me. He told us everything was okay. Except, his boss suspended him for a week. His normal erect posture was gone, replaced by sagging shoulders and bags under his eyes.

When he asked how we were, I was the one who blurted, "Mr. Brock was shot. It was just a burn wound. He bled a lot, but he's going to be okay."

Dad sagged even more. He looked from me to Dan. Dan looked up at him and asked meekly, "Did I hit anyone?"

"Not that I know about. No one showed up at any hospitals last night for gunshot wounds, anyway."

"Good," Dan said.

"Dan, tell your dad I'm sorry, and I'll apologize in person later. I need to get some sleep right after a shower."

He stood to leave. "You be extra careful today. I can't let them beat me."

Us! Beat us! I corrected him in my thoughts.

CHAPTER 43

Dan

I jogged home in the chill air. It was late October and the morning temperature must have been near forty. I did my chores first, feeding and watering the calves, before heading to the house for a shower and breakfast.

Mom was waiting when I came in. "I know your father said to stay with Angel until her father came home, but that didn't mean all night, Daniel."

"Yes ma'am. I fell asleep on the couch." She didn't need to know Angel and I fell asleep on the couch together, in each other's arms.

"How's Dad?" I asked. Quickly, changing the subject.

She sighed before she said, "Sleeping. I cleaned him up and re-bandaged his arm. He will be okay after he gets some rest."

She sighed again. I could tell she had something she wanted to say, but she was reluctant to say it.

"Your Dad told me what happened. Are you okay?"

"Not really, Mom. They burned my truck trying to kill me and Angel. They attacked Officer Cotton and set a booby trap under his feet, and they shot Dad. I'm scared, Mom. Someone I love is going to die."

I didn't expect that to come out. I hadn't been thinking about it, but it was the truth.

Finally, Mom relaxed and hugged me. She held me tight for a while.

She smelled my clothes. "You stink. Go take a shower and I'll fix you some breakfast."

"Thanks, Mom." I raised my arm and sniffed as I went to the shower. Stale sweat and smoke from my burned truck brought back the great memories of the state meet and the horrendous memories of my burning truck.

Mom sat with me while I ate. I told her what Officer Cotton had said. That he was sorry for everything that happened and he would apologize to Dad later today.

"Daniel, I know you love Angel, but someone is going to get killed and I couldn't stand for it to be you."

"Mom, I don't want anyone to be killed. And as much as they may deserve it, I don't want Donny Ray or Little John to die. I just want them to leave Angel and me alone."

There was a rustling sound behind me, and I turned to find Dad standing in the kitchen doorway.

I stood and hugged him. "Dad, how are you doing?"

"I'm a survivor, son. But I need some of that coffee and breakfast I smell."

I pulled out a chair for Dad and went to the coffeepot. Mom started his breakfast, and I fixed his coffee. Black with one teaspoon of sugar. He often said he needed the sugar to prevent him from being a grouchy old man all day long. Something to sweeten him up, he would say.

"You need to head to school or you are going to be late," Mom said.

"I don't feel like school today." But I headed to my room to get my books when I remembered they were in my truck and were now ashes. The books were replaceable, but my notes were not. I would have to borrow and copy from others to recover that loss.

I turned around without going to my room. Mom asked me when I returned to the kitchen, "Where are your books?"

"Burned up in the truck," I answered. "I can replace the books, but I can't replace my notes."

Mom was a retired high school English teacher. Losing books and notes hit her hard. She gave me another hug before I left.

"I love you, Daniel Brock. Be careful."

"Love you, Mom. Love you, Dad," I said as I grabbed the keys for the Green Machine off the rack in the mudroom.

I texted Angel as I walked to the truck I'd driven for the last two years. The Green Machine was my first truck. It was a love of labor that Dad and I had rebuilt from junk. I was now determined it would be my primary vehicle for a long time.

The Green Machine was an antique. A forty-year-old truck that was built in simpler times. There was no computer in it. There was no button to change from two-wheel drive to four-wheel drive. You had to get out and manually turn the knobs on the front hubs to lock the four-wheel drive in. It was simple, and I liked it. Most times, I don't like technology.

With farm equipment, simpler was better. Dust, dirt, rain, and sun could always destroy the electronics on farm equipment. There was some technology that I liked. The internet was great for research, and my security cameras, for example, had already proven their value at the State Fair.

It was late afternoon when my phone let me know one of my cameras was recording. Fortunately, I was on a break between classes. I quickly pulled up the video and watched Little John and Donny Ray getting out of a boat on our launch ramp.

"Shit!"

I called Officer Cotton's number, and he barely answered before I told him what I'd seen. His response was an even quicker, "Thanks," before he hung up.

My next call was to Dad. But Dad barely answered before I could hear gunshots in the background.

Dad's response was, "I've got to go, Dan."

"Shit!" I grabbed my brand-new notebook and told the professor I had an emergency and needed to go.

I ran to the Green Machine. There were no shortcuts to get home. It would take nearly an hour to get there. I called Angel. She would be in class too. I left her a voice message. It was all I could do.

I called Angel five more times on the way home. She didn't answer, and that worried me even more. Had they kidnapped her? Why wouldn't she respond to me?

I tried calling Mom, Dad, and Officer Cotton and no one answered. Were they all dead? No. It couldn't be.

School buses were a curse on anyone in a hurry, and they were making me angry today. It seemed they were everywhere and stopping every two minutes.

I thought about using my red emergency responder light. But I wasn't responding to a call, and I would break the law to use it under false circumstances. Once I crossed over the county line and into my home county, I might chance it. I would almost be home by then, though.

Why wasn't anyone answering? Ben. Did Ben know what was happening? I called him and got no answer.

The school bus finally turned onto a side road, and I floored it. I eased back on the gas when I hit sixty-five. The Green Machine didn't do well at high speeds, but I was getting upset, not knowing what was happening.

I was tempted to call Sheriff Tatum. But I wasn't sure that was a good idea. If Officer Cotton was trying to keep things quiet, I didn't want to blow it. If the Sheriff was already there, I didn't want to interrupt him.

I tried calling Angel again. Still no answer. This was driving me crazy.

Finally, my phone rang. Sheriff Tatum was calling me. My heart sank, and I almost wrecked the truck.

"Hello?" I answered frantically.

"Dan, how soon can you be home?" Sheriff Tatum asked.

"I'm almost there. Ten to twelve minutes. Is everyone okay?"

"Hurry home Dan. Need to get a copy of the video from your security camera. See you soon."

He hung up on me. He sounded casual, like everything was normal. What's going on? I banged my hand against the steering wheel and screamed in frustration.

I finally hit the county road to our farm. When I got to our drive, there was a deputy patrol car blocking the road. I drove right past our drive, to the logging road, and turned onto it. No one was keeping me from getting home today. I would drive through my fences if needed. The sheriff's new van was parked at our house, but I couldn't see any more cars or anyone else on the farm.

The Green Machine had barely stopped rolling before I was out of the truck and running to the house. Breathing hard and nearly in tears, I barged in to find Mom, Dad, Sheriff Tatum in his wheelchair, and Officer Cotton sitting at the dining table drinking coffee.

I lost my temper and yelled, "Why couldn't any of you answer your phones? I've been calling for the last hour and no one would answer. What's going on? I thought you were all dead."

Mom stood to give me a hug. Dad calmly said, "The power has been out. Our phones only work when your Wi-Fi is working. You know that, son."

"And Angel, she hasn't responded to my calls. Is she okay?"

"She's fine Dan," Officer Cotton answered. "She forgot to charge her phone last night, and it's dead. There's a deputy at the college monitoring things."

I let go of Mom and sat down at the table. "What's going on? I heard shots in the background when I called Dad."

"Jonathan fired several warning shots into the ground after you called. They must have run after that. There was no one at the boat ramp when we inspected it," Dad said.

Sheriff Tatum asked, "Can I get a copy of that video, Dan?"

"Without power, I'll have to go pull the memory chip out of the camera and copy it to my laptop."

"Then get busy, Dan," Dad said.

Officer Cotton went with me. We retrieved a ladder from the shop and put it into the back of my truck. It was too far to the boat ramp to carry a sixteen-foot extension ladder. Using the truck was easier.

The camera was up in a tree and well hidden. Officer Cotton held the ladder while I climbed up to it. It was battery operated, and this reminded me it was about time to change the batteries on this camera. It was one of my most active cameras because of the activity on the river.

I removed the SD card and climbed down the ladder. I was still very upset. But I had no one to blame for that. I asked Officer Cotton, "How do we stop them?"

"You let me work that out, okay? I need you to take care of Angel if something happens to me. That incident last night made me realize I'm not invincible."

"Why are you carrying Angel's Glock?"

Officer Cotton sighed. "I couldn't use my service pistol, because I have to record and report all shots I take with it. I have an off-duty pistol, but I grabbed Angel's first because it was on top." He said nothing else, leaving me to assume that firing his service pistol would involve a lot of explanation he'd rather not do.

"It's a very accurate pistol," I said.

It only took a few minutes for me to copy the video from the SD card to a thumb drive using my laptop at the kitchen table. Everyone was watching the video on my laptop as I copied the file.

Sheriff Tatum let out a heavy sigh as he watched the video. I think he hoped I was lying about them being on the farm.

The video showed Donny Ray, Little John, and another man getting out of the boat. Mom watched until Little John started unzipping his pants to relieve himself. The third man did the same. Donny Ray walked up the ramp and looked at the farm. He suddenly ducked and ran back to the boat. It must have been when Officer Cotton fired his shots.

"Fired those shots into the ground, right Jonathan?" Sheriff Tatum asked.

"I didn't say where they went into the ground, Sheriff."

I was watching Little John trying to tuck his manhood back into his pants. The problem was he hadn't stopped peeing yet and ended up peeing his pants. I started laughing out loud. I would have to tell Angel about this.

"Dan, why are you laughing?" Dad asked.

"I'll show you in a minute when I finish recording."

I replayed the video and told them to watch Little John. The Sheriff reacted first with a loud outburst of laughter. "He pissed his pants!" We were all laughing, and it relieved some of the tension.

Until I noticed the third man. He hadn't ducked. He finished peeing, looked around and up in the trees and spotted the camera. Then he pulled his cap down and walked back to the boat.

"Who is that guy?" I asked.

"I don't know," Officer Cotton answered. "But I want access to your cameras now. You calling me could have saved our lives today. I want the best picture you can capture of the third man. I'll ask the Game and Fish, and the State Police to run a check on him."

"Send it to me too, Dan," the Sheriff said.

"Ok, I'll have it done shortly."

It took me a few minutes to get a decent picture of the third man. Then I tried to sharpen the image, but I had little luck. I sent both pictures to Officer Cotton and the Sheriff.

Mrs. Cotton knocked on the mudroom door. She had come home and discovered the electricity off and the phones not working without the Wi-Fi.

I was installing the security video app on Officer Cotton's phone as he told his wife what happened. I had to admire his honesty with her. But her response broke my heart.

"Jonathon, let's move. Let's go somewhere far away. Somewhere they can't find us. We can start over. We have Angel to protect."

I didn't want to lose Angel. I couldn't lose her.

Officer Cotton's response frightened me even more, though.

"What about Dan and his parents? I can't leave them unprotected. They would come after Dan to find Angel. To find me and you."

He moved to her and cupped her face in his huge hand. "We have friends here. We are safer here than we are running away."

"He's right," Sheriff Tatum said. "Federal and state agencies are already investigating them for numerous charges. It's only a matter of time before they are in prison."

"Can you arrest them for what they did today?" Mrs. Cotton asked.

"Not really," the Sheriff replied. "Yes, they were trespassing, but they could argue they only stopped to relieve themselves without the intention of doing harm. Jonathan's warning shots could get him in more trouble than they would get into. Other than the picture Dan gave us, no one else needs to see this video."

Dad had watched the video when I replayed it and had watched the third man, as well. "That third guy is former military. He didn't duck from the gunfire. He looked around and spotted Dan's camera. Dan, you need to move that camera to a new location."

"I will, Dad." I agreed. The man spotted the camera. But my second choice for a camera location didn't provide nearly as good of an angle.

Angel rushed through the mudroom door without knocking. That surprised me, because she always knocked. But she went straight to her mom and dad and they enveloped her in a three-way hug.

"What's going on?" she asked. "What's happening?"

Officer Cotton explained what happened and tried to make it sound like it was nothing. But we all knew this was a turning point. This was a private war now.

CHAPTER 44

Angel

I forgot to charge my phone last night. It's no wonder with everything that happened. I meant to cuddle with Dan on the couch for just a little while, and then get up and do all the things I normally do before going to bed, but I fell asleep and didn't do any of those things.

I'm surprised I could sleep at all. Yesterday was one of the most eventful days of my life. It was crazy. I became the girl's 4A cross-country state champion. Dan placed third in the boy's 4A cross-country meet. Then Dan's truck burnt up because Donny Ray and Little John tried to murder us. And last night went down the mountain faster than a speeding snowball.

They tried to get fancy and murder Dad, and shot Mr. Brock. So far, today was a quiet day. That was until I got into the Mustang and put my phone on the charger and turned it on and found five messages and more missed calls from Dan.

I didn't listen to them; instead, I called him back, and the call went straight to his voicemail. I listened to my first voicemail, and it said, "The security cameras caught Donny Ray and Little John on the farm. I'm heading home. Be very careful."

The call time from the message told me he should already be home. Was he okay? Were Mom and Dad okay? Dad was at home. Did he call Dad?

I called Dad. No answer. I was just putting the Mustang into reverse when a deputy sheriff knocked on my window, scaring me half to death. I rolled my window down less than two inches like Dad had taught me, and the deputy smiled.

"Sheriff Tatum wanted me to tell you everything is okay at home. The power is out on the farm and they can't get a phone signal without the Wi-Fi. Be careful going home," he said as he turned away.

I put the car back into park. I sat there for several minutes and took deep breaths to keep from screaming before I could drive. Then I did my best to drive home like it was a regular day. The ASU-Heber Springs campus was less than three miles from home, and it only took about seven minutes to get there. Mom's van was at the Brock's house, so I drove straight there.

When I stopped the car, my heart was pounding fast with all the possibilities. The feeling of desperation was rising inside me. I ran inside the Brock's home without bothering to knock.

Mom and Dad were both there, and I ran to them. Relief washed over me like the water from the river running just outside our houses.

Dan was there, but I needed to know Mom and Dad were okay. Dad really. He was the one these creeps were after. He was the one they wanted to hurt.

Dad gave me some lame story about what happened. I'd get the full story from Dan later. My hand felt the first-place medal from the cross-country meet in my jacket pocket.

I pulled it out of my pocket. "We should have been celebrating last night," I mumbled. "Instead, we were fighting idiots."

"What's that?" Mom asked.

"I won the state meet yesterday, but everything else just went up in smoke. Literally."

Dad apologized, "I'm sorry, Angel."

"Dad, it's not your fault."

"No, I'm sorry. I forgot to ask, sweetheart. Congratulations. I'm so proud of you," he said, and hugged me again.

I heard Mr. Brock ask Dan how he did. Dan held up three fingers.

"Really? Great job son. I think these two deserve a little celebration after their accomplishments and everything we've all been through. The evil deeds of men shall not wreck our lives."

"Amen," Sheriff Tatum replied. "And with that, it's time for me to go back to the office. Dan, can you help me out, please?"

"I'd be glad to, Sheriff."

This is what I loved about Dan's parents. They didn't need big things or events to have a celebration. Mr. Brock would celebrate breathing fresh air. But, I guess, winning a state championship is a big thing. This is what we should have done last night. In a perfect world, Dan's truck would still be running. My Dad would not be humiliated. And Mr. Brock would not have been shot.

Mom reached over and rested her hand on my shoulder. "I'm sorry, Angel. I didn't even think about asking how the meet went. There was so much happening yesterday."

"It's okay, Mom. I only remembered because the medal was in my pocket."

Mr. Brock pulled a pan of steaks out of the fridge, and Mrs. Brock began moving around the kitchen.

"We had planned to grill these last night as a celebration for your accomplishments, but life got in the way," Mr. Brock said. "Angel, why don't you see if Dan needs some help?"

"Okay," I replied, but I found his suggestion a little suspicious.

I stepped out of the garage to find Dan closing the sliding van door and tapping the side to let the sheriff know it was closed.

"Hey you," I said.

"Hey yourself," he said and stepped forward to pull me into a hug and kissed me.

"I love you," I told him.

"I love you more."

Playfully, I hit him on the shoulder, "Let's don't start that."

"What's going on inside?" Dan asked.

"I'm not sure. Your Dad pulled steaks out of the fridge and told me to come out and check on you."

"Yeah, sounds like they're scheming up something for our best interest," Dan replied.

"Speaking of that, I'm not sure it's a good idea for you and me to go to Colorado alone."

"Agreed. I thought about asking Ben, but he just got a new job. I think I'll ask Mom and Dad. Would your dad feed and water the horses for me if I can't get Ben to do it?"

I nodded my head, but I had another thought. "Why don't we ask my dad to go? If he is still suspended, then he would be free to go with us."

"I like that idea even better," Dan said. "Dad's not healthy and the wound doesn't help any. He knows my routine here."

"So, what really happened today?" I asked him, breaking our hug.

"As corny as it sounds, exactly what your dad told you. Except Little John peed all over himself, trying to get back into the boat when your dad fired shots at them."

"I'd like to see that."

"It's a little obscene, but I might show you the video," Dan answered.

"How are they going to cook without electricity?"

"Dad will grill the steaks. And our stove is gas. We have power outages often during the winter. If the power is out for very long, we will hook up the generator for the fridge and other minor things."

"Oh, what about lights?" I asked.

"Kerosene lamps," Dan said. "Come on, let's go see what they are talking about."

Mom was helping Mrs. Brock in the kitchen with the light provided by a kerosene lamp, like Dan had said. Dad was talking with Mr. Brock as he grilled steaks on the deck.

Dinner was rather quiet. We were all lost in our own thoughts. There was an occasional question about the state meet, but neither Dan nor I were very excited about answering.

Finally, Dan broke the silence and asked, "Mom, Dad, Mr. and Mrs. Cotton, I need to deliver calves to the Dalliers in Colorado this weekend, but I don't want to make the trip by myself."

Mr. Brock said, "We discussed this earlier and think it best if you go by yourself if Ben can't go."

"That's nearly twenty-eight hours of driving, Dad. I was hoping to ask Angel and Mr. Cotton to go with me."

My Dad and Mr. Brock looked at each other. It was obviously an option they hadn't considered.

"If I'm still suspended, I would be off work," Dad said casually.

Mom smiled and chimed in, "You have vacation days built up that you could use if they take you off suspension before then. It would do you good to relax a little."

"That was an option we hadn't considered," Mr. Brock said. "Jonathan, what do you think?"

"I think I need to prepare for a trip," Dad said.

Dan and I smiled at each other. We had spent a lot of time with each other, but it never seemed like it was enough. Even though we lived about a hundred and fifty yards from each other, it seemed like a million miles at night. And after sleeping in his arms last night, I didn't want him to be far away in Colorado and leave me alone.

We were cleaning up after dinner when the lights came back on. That's when we heard the big power company truck coming down the road.

Dan and I went out with our dads to see what was going on. The driver stepped down out of the truck. I think Dan's dad knew everyone locally.

"Charlie, how are you?" Mr. Brock asked.

"Good. But I'm curious, Lloyd. Why would someone cut a tree down across the power line on your property?"

Mr. Brock looked at my dad. "Jonathan, you want to tell the story?"

Dad said, "I'm a game warden and I live next door. I've made some guys upset, and they've threatened me and my family. They tried to come onto the farm today. They must have cut the tree to keep us from calling the Sheriff."

Dan had been holding my hand and let go. "Something is wrong here. They had to cut that tree after I called you. I called you and Dad, and neither of you would have received the call without the power on."

Dad stared at Dan. His brow furrowed in thought. "The power was out when I came here to talk to Lloyd. There must have been more of them, and they were waiting for a signal that the power was out. They didn't know about the cameras then, but they do now."

CHAPTER 45

Dan

We left the farm at midnight, on Friday night. Angel laid down in the back seat of the truck and took a nap. Officer Cotton rode shotgun while I drove the truck.

Cheyenne Wells, Colorado, was a twelve and half hour drive from the farm. Add an hour and a half for fuel stops and restroom breaks and that would make the trip fourteen hours. I couldn't believe Mom and Dad wanted me to drive twenty-eight hours in two days by myself. They were thinking about other factors, but did they not realize how far that was?

I hadn't thought about it when I agreed to make a nearly sixteen-hundred-mile round trip to deliver show calves.

Angel and I had talked about getting away and having an adventure by ourselves. There was more than one fantasy floating around in my head about sleeping together in the camper without hiding from our parents or my brother. I ached for the freedom of adulthood where we could get married and do what we wanted without sneaking around. I had already ordered the promise ring and a matching engagement ring for later. There was a jeweler in Batesville on my way home and I stopped after class one day. I would give her the promise ring next week on her birthday. I planned to give her the engagement ring on Christmas Eve. If we survived that long.

Instead of being teenagers longing for adulthood, and the freedom to sneak around and occasionally have our alone time, we were looking everywhere for Donny Ray and Little John. We were being pushed into being frightened people who were afraid of every sound, every bump in the dark. I didn't like being afraid to open my truck door or answer my phone. There was no joy in looking over my shoulder or waking up from a nightmare in a burning truck.

I mentioned my fear to Officer Cotton. I couldn't think of him as Mr. Cotton. He was a game warden, and I thought of him as an officer of the law, not Angel's dad, or possibly my future father-in-law. It was a title of respect and a little fear. But it was mostly respect.

Officer Cotton said, "It's psychological warfare, and it can be more effective than war itself. The entire Cold War between Russia and the U.S. was about psychological warfare. Each side was saying, look how many nuclear bombs we have. We can remove your entire country from the face of the earth. That creates fear in humans and they act respectfully toward one another, even though they would rather kill each other."

He hesitated before he continued. "Donny Ray and Little John aren't as afraid now as they used to be. I know they have some law enforcement on their side, but it's like they have someone more powerful on their side now. They aren't afraid anymore, and that scares even me. What they did to me at the launch ramp the other night, that wasn't Little John or Donny Ray." He looked in the back seat to make sure Angel wasn't listening before he continued. "They never would have gotten that close to me. And they would have just killed me. That was someone else. I think it was the third guy on your video the other day."

"I see. Who is this powerful person? Who could that be?" I asked.

"They have a cousin who is married to a lawyer who works for the state's prosecuting attorney. That's a powerful contact, but it's not enough to make them feel invincible. I can't figure it out."

"From what you and Sheriff Tatum have said, I assume they are dealing drugs and kidnapping girls. Isn't that human trafficking?" I asked.

"Yes. They are being investigated by the DEA, FBI, the Arkansas State Police, and who knows who else. But no one seems to get anywhere," he answered. "I got chewed out for arresting Danny Ray and his clients. But I didn't know they were under investigation by other agencies. I was just doing my job. The arrest of Danny Ray's clients for duck hunting violations resulted in them breaking federal laws and losing their guns, trucks, and licenses for several years. They were also fined several thousand dollars. Danny Ray lost his truck, boat, and boat trailer, his guns, and his guide license, and was fined several thousand dollars. The total loss was nearly a half million dollars in equipment and fines. The clients blamed Danny Ray. And he blamed me and wanted revenge."

That was the first time I'd heard what started the feud, and I was shocked. It was their fault. They broke the law and blamed the person who caught them. That was a loser's mentality in my mind.

"Losers," I muttered.

"Exactly," Officer Cotton replied.

He looked into the back seat to check on Angel. He said, "Dan, I have a favor to ask."

"Okay," I said.

"Angel has always wanted a Jeep and her mom and I have found a used Jeep that we would like to give Angel for her birthday. I know you are letting her drive the Mustang, and we appreciate that very much. But would you be upset if we gave her a jeep?"

I grinned. "No sir, I wouldn't. She deserves a little payback for my birthday party. You can even use the shop if you need to work on it."

He grinned back at me. "She worked hard planning your birthday party. But you enjoyed it, right?"

A flood of memories came back to me about that day, but I shook them off and replied, "Yes sir, I did."

"What are you guys talking about?" Angel asked sleepily from the back seat.

"My surprise birthday party," I answered.

I looked at her in the rearview mirror as she ran her fingers through her hair. She smiled. Probably remembering my surprise, our trip to Sonic, or us making out in the truck. "Yeah, that was fun, wasn't it? But don't get any ideas about doing the same thing for me. I just want our families to celebrate my birthday."

Officer Cotton said, "Don't worry sweetheart, we'll honor your wishes."

"Dan, are we stopping soon? I'm feeling a little carsick."

We were nearing Kansas City, and we made our first stop for fuel, bathroom breaks, breakfast, and coffee. We were close to the halfway point. If I could hold up for the time driving, we would be there by noon mountain time or one o'clock central time. We were ahead of schedule.

Angel and her dad swapped places, and she sat up front with me and Officer Cotton tried to get comfortable in the back seat. That wasn't easy for a man of his size. I ate a breakfast biscuit and sipped on a large coffee after we got back on the freeway.

I settled into line with three or four semi-trailers around Lawrence and followed them across Kansas. Angel and I chatted about school, hunting, and other minor topics while avoiding the obvious elephant, Donny Ray, and Little John, that was in our lives.

I scrutinized every vehicle that passed for Little John or Donny Ray. It was unrealistic that they would follow us this far, but I couldn't dismiss the thought. I was also worried about Mom, Dad, and Mrs. Cotton being left alone on the farm.

We exited the interstate at a little town called Oakley. We fueled up at the truck stop before continuing. You couldn't fuel this truck just anywhere. The truck and trailer were a lot like driving a semi because they were nearly as long.

We arrived at the Dallier farm a little after one thirty central time. Hannah met us where their long drive turned onto the county road. She was riding a four-wheeler. She had a huge grin on her face and waved for us to follow her. The driveway ran straight to what looked like a small house on a rise. But it wasn't a small house. The drive was a mile long and the house and barns grew larger as we got closer.

We passed a pasture with an oil well in the middle of it. Several more fields with overhead irrigation systems. If this was all the Dallier's farmland, then they had a vast farm.

Hannah turned off the drive and led us down a side road toward some barns. There was an equipment shed as large as a football field that held several tractors, combines, and semi-trucks and grain trailers.

Hannah led us toward a smaller building where several trucks and an SUV parked. There was a sign on the building that read Dallier Farms. Hannah rode through two wide open gates and waved for me to follow. This was a fenced-in lot that I assumed cattle were unloaded from trailers after closing the gates. The fence and gates were six feet tall and made of rods welded to metal posts. I could see a water trough. And there was a horse barn attached to the office building we just passed. That was probably where Hannah's new show calves would be stalled.

Hannah whipped her four-wheeler around, throwing dust and dirt behind her, and closed the gates behind us. I smiled at Hannah's riding skills.

"She rides a four-wheeler like you do, Angel," I said.

"Just what do you mean by that?" Angel asked.

"With confidence," I replied.

I stopped the truck in front of another set of double gates, and we got out. Hannah rode up and hopped off the four-wheeler and gave me and Angel a quick hug. She held her hand out to Officer Cotton.

"Hi. I'm Hannah Dallier. You must be Angel's dad."

Mr. Charlie and several other people emerged from the building. He yelled, "Hello! Y'all get those calves out of the trailer. After that ride, they will be worn out."

I waved and replied, "Yes, sir." We moved to the back of the trailer and opened the gate. On a normal quick trip, I would have tied their halter lead ropes to the side of the trailer and forced them to stand up. On this trip, I took their halters off and let them move around the trailer and lay down if they wanted.

"Dad was worried about hauling them so far," Hannah said. "Did you have any trouble?"

I yawned. "Just staying awake," I said and smiled.

I opened the gate and swung it open wide. The older heifer was the first one out, followed by Daisy and the young steer. I heard a whistle from the fence.

One guy commented, "You picked some good ones, Charlie."

"Naw. Hannah did that. She picked the little heifer. I picked the big one, and Dan recommended the steer."

The steer picked that moment to run and buck. Daisy chased after him. The big heifer searched out the water trough and went for a drink. We walked over to the fence where Mr. and Mrs. Dallier and two men were standing.

"When's the heifer due to calve?" one of the two men asked.

"Around Thanksgiving," I answered.

He nodded and spit tobacco on the ground.

Mr. Dallier said, "Hello Dan. Angel. And you are?" he asked Officer Cotton.

"Jonathan Cotton. Angel's dad."

"It's good to meet you. I'm Charlie Dallier. This is my wife, Marie, my cousin Devon Dallier, and my foreman, Chester Donovan." We shook hands and said hello.

"Hannah, let Dan pull that truck around and we'll go inside and eat some lunch. Are you guys hungry?"

"Starving," answered Angel.

The foreman, Mr. Donovan, looked at Officer Cotton and asked, "Were you ever in the Marine Corps?"

"I was, but I'm a game warden now, for the Arkansas Game and Fish Commission." Officer Cotton answered hesitantly. "Do I know you?"

"You may not remember me. I was only under your command a few weeks before you left the corps, and I was forty pounds lighter back then. I'm glad you landed on your feet after Quantico, Sarge. Let's go eat," Mr. Donovan replied.

The door to the office building opened into a common room with four desks in each corner. There was another door straight back which led to the kitchen, a restroom, and, to my surprise, a bunk room. Beyond that was the feed and tack room for horses. I hadn't seen horses, but it made sense that a farm like this would have a few horses.

Lunch was sandwiches and chips. Like most farm families, lunch was usually a light meal.

Officer Cotton and Mr. Donovan talked quietly during lunch. It was apparent they had served at the same locations and knew many of the same people. It's strange that you could drive for sixteen hours and run into someone you knew.

Mr. Charlie took us on a tour of the farm after lunch. He didn't show us everything. He said there was no need to look at every wheat field because they all looked the same. The farm was over five thousand acres and planted to wheat and soybeans each year. They ran cattle on nearly a thousand acres of what he called the breaks along the Smoky Hill River.

I was exhausted after driving for thirteen hours straight and from the lack of sleep. Angel and Hannah kept jabbing at me to keep me awake.

I stayed awake, though, when he started talking about cattle and their grazing patterns. That was my type of farming.

CHAPTER 46

Angel

I felt bad for Dan. He was exhausted. I had seen him tired before, but he was barely staying awake. His head was nodding and even his speech was slurring a little.

Mr. Charlie saw it too and headed back to the farm headquarters. He suggested to Dan that he should get a couple of hours' sleep before we had dinner. Dan apologized for being so exhausted, but Mr. Charlie brushed it off. Dan didn't argue. He said goodbye, gave me a quick kiss on the cheek, and headed to the trailer.

"I'll bet he doesn't even take his boots off," Hannah said.

"He'll take them off," I said.

I wanted to go nap with him, but Hannah had other ideas. She wanted to show me the barn and her newly purchased show supplies.

After the tour, we went back inside and listened to the adult conversation, as Hannah referred to it. It was mostly Dad and Mr. Donavan swapping Marine Corps stories.

The conversation changed when Mr. Donovan asked Dad about being a Game Warden. Dad said he had enjoyed every minute except for the last year. He told the story of the Ray brothers and Little John. I heard parts of the story I'd never heard before. By the time he finished telling the story about Sarah being killed, and the Sheriff's gun fight with Danny Ray, everyone was caught on every word.

But he looked at me and stopped. "I'll tell the rest after dinner tonight. Part of the story is Angel's and Dan's. In fact, I'll let them tell you their side of the story." He looked around the room. "Where is Dan?"

"Sleeping," I said. "He could barely stay awake for the farm tour."

Dad surprised me when he said, "Dan's a good young man. I couldn't have picked a better boyfriend for Angel than him. He is much more mature than I was at his age."

I don't know why his comment surprised me. I just didn't expect him to be so approving of Dan. Wasn't it the job of parents to disapprove of their daughters' boyfriends? I had never had a boyfriend before I met Dan.

Hannah went with me to wake him up.

"I still say he went to sleep with his boots on," she said.

"We'll see," I said.

I pounded on the door and yelled that Hannah and I were coming in, just in case he had done more than take his boots off. We entered the camper section and found Dan sitting on the couch, head leaned back against the wall, with one boot on and one boot off. Asleep. I didn't know a person could sleep like that.

All the noise we made entering the trailer hadn't awakened him. My heart ached for him. This was the reason he had spent the last few years breeding and raising cattle. To sell show calves and develop a reputation. Now he was too tired to enjoy it.

I leaned down close to his face and cupped his stubbly chin in my hand.

"Hey, it's time to wake up, sleepyhead."

He moaned and moved his head, then slowly opened his eyes and smiled at me.

"My Angel," he whispered and closed his eyes.

I wasn't as gentle this time. I slapped his shoulder. "Hey, wake up and come join the rest of us for dinner. You've been sleeping for two hours."

"Ten more minutes," he mumbled.

"No. Wake up. I know you're tired, but you can sleep later."

"Okay, okay."

He lifted his head up and rubbed his neck.

"How did you fall asleep like that?" Hannah asked

He stared at Hannah for a few seconds, like he was realizing she was there for the first time.

"I don't know. One minute, I'm taking my boots off. The next minute, Angel is waking me up."

"You didn't get your boots all the way off," Hannah pointed out.

"I didn't sleep much either."

Hannah giggled at his comment, and I couldn't help but laugh.

"Come on Dan. Let's get your other boot on, so we can go eat dinner," I said encouragingly.

Dinner was BBQ brisket and all the fixings. Dan and I needed to start running again, or I was going to gain a lot of weight. Mr. Donovan brought his wife, but Mr. Charlie's cousin didn't come. They, of course, asked Dad to finish his story.

We moved from the dining room to their living room. Dad looked at me and Dan and said, "I've told enough. It's time for y'all to tell your side of the story."

Dan was confused, but I assured him he would catch on quickly. I started my story at the lake, where we met Little John and the Ray brothers for the first time. I told them about all our encounters up to Dan's truck burning up.

Dad finished telling them about being ambushed, and Dan's cameras letting us know they were on the farm. He quietly left out Dan's firing at the boat, and Mr. Brock being wounded at the river. He told us before that no one needed to know that information. We needed to pretend it didn't happen.

It was Dan who commented that we didn't know who the third guy was. We had his picture, but no one could identify him yet.

"Do you have his picture with you? I'd like to see it," Mr. Charlie asked.

Dan looked through his phone for the pictures of Donny Ray, Little John, and the Mystery man. Mr. Charlie inspected the pictures, shook his head, and passed the phone to his foreman. It was Mr. Donovan who identified the mystery man.

"I'll be damned. Are you sure you don't recognize this man, Jonathan?" he asked.

Dad shook his head. "No."

"Think back to the Corps. Think about the guys who were in the bar that night you got into that fight."

I watched as Dad raised his eyebrows. He pulled his phone out and scrolled to the pictures Dan had sent to him. He studied the picture and finally shook his head. "I have no idea," he said.

"He looks like the man encouraging Ronaldo to fight someone. He was the one who looked around the bar and picked you out for Ronaldo to fight. Are you sure you don't remember him?" Mr. Donovan asked.

"No. I was newly married and was trying to settle down with Angel's mom. We weren't aware of anyone else that night except the people at my table. I wasn't aware of what was going on until - what was his name? Ronaldo? Until he started cussing me. Even that didn't bother me. He could say what he wanted about me and that wouldn't bother me. But when he started talking about my wife, that was different. She didn't deserve to be called..." Dad looked at me before he continued. "What he called her that night. I put him on the floor with one swing. But he wouldn't stay down. I had to beat him unconscious before anyone pulled me off."

Dad sighed heavily. "I regret beating him like that. We should have fought together, not against each other."

"It may not be him. May I send this picture to some of my old contacts and see if anyone remembers him?" Mr. Donovan asked before he continued without an answer. "You weren't given much of a choice. If it had just been a fight where you both walked away, you would have both received reprimands and gone on about your careers. But you put him in the hospital. How did you get out of that situation?"

"One of my guys in my platoon did me a solid. His dad was a U.S. Senator, and he stepped in and made it all go away, provided I leave the Corps. I agreed, because I didn't want to leave Angel and her mom. That's when we went back to Arkansas and I used the GI bill to go to college."

I listened to Dad's story, but I was curious about something. I asked Mr. Donovan, "What happened to the guy that Dad fought? And how would this other man get involved with Donny Ray and Little John?"

"The guy your dad fought became a decorated Navy Seal, but he died in Iran or Iraq. I don't know how the others met. I'll let you know if I find out who he is."

We left the Dallier Farm around five thirty Mountain Time, which would put us back home around seven on Sunday evening. Dad insisted we take a different route home. Dan drove south until we hit I-40 in Amarillo. From there, it was my job to keep him awake and talking until we were home.

CHAPTER 47

Dan

The trip to Colorado was exhausting. But the sale of cattle, new friends, and the possible information about the third man with Donny Ray and Little John had lifted our moods.

That was until Officer Cotton was told he would remain suspended for another week until they could schedule a formal hearing about his case. I could tell he was worried when he asked me if there was anything he could do around the farm to help pay the rent that month. I told him not to worry about it. But I wasn't a person who would accept charity, and I knew he wasn't either. So, I asked him to brush hog parts of the farm that I hadn't gotten to yet.

When I told Dad what I had done, he chastised me. I explained my reasoning, and he apologized and said I did the right thing and he was proud of me.

Angel's birthday was on Friday and I could tell she was worried more about her dad than her birthday. Her parents bought her a 1997 Jeep Wrangler TJ. It was a used vehicle and needed basic repairs, like brakes, ball joints, and tires.

I hadn't used the farm shop much since I finished the Mustang, so I eagerly encouraged Officer Cotton to use it so he could make repairs and hide it from Angel. Since he was also brush-hogging, he could come and go from the shop without Angel being suspicious.

The night before her birthday, we took a walk around the farm. We walked the roads that we normally ran in the mornings. When the moon was just above the eastern treetops, I stopped and grabbed both of her hands in mine. I had a present to give her and didn't want it to compete with the Jeep her parents were giving her. I had a lump in my throat and butterflies in my stomach. It was one thing to joke about getting engaged and married at our age, but making that commitment was frightening and exciting at the same time.

"Angel, our parents wouldn't approve of us getting engaged yet, but I want to give you the next best thing."

I let go of her hands and reached into my pocket, and pulled out the promise ring I ordered a few weeks earlier and picked up this afternoon. It was part of a set that included the promise ring, an engagement ring, and a wedding band. Maybe I was getting ahead of myself. But tonight, I was only giving her the promise ring. I wouldn't tell her about the set until I gave her the engagement ring.

"Will you accept this promise ring as my promise to love you and always be yours?"

There was more I had planned to say, but she immediately said yes. She let me put the ring on her finger and hugged me fiercely.

"Are you crying?" I asked her.

She stepped away from me and wiped the tears from her eyes. She looked at me again, stepped forward, and kissed me gently and slowly this time.

"I love you Dan. This is the best birthday present ever," she said. She held the ring up in the darkness, trying to get a good look at it.

"I don't know about the best birthday present ever. Wait until your actual birthday tomorrow."

"You didn't get me another present, did you?"

"Yes, but nothing like this. Besides, I'm not the only one giving you a present," I said teasingly.

"What? What am I getting?"

"I can't tell."

She begged, and I teased her all the way back to our houses. When we got back to her house, she ran to the porch where there was light, so she could see the ring.

"Dan, is this a real pearl?"

"Yes, with two small diamonds on either side."

She gave me a frightened look. "I'm afraid to wear this. What if I damage it or lose it?"

"I understand. Take it off when we are running or working. I don't want you to lose it either. That's why I also got this." I handed her a small box with a gold necklace. "You can put it around your neck, so you won't lose it."

We both had schoolwork to do, but we hugged and kissed each other on the porch for a long time. I left her on the porch and began my walk home. Neither of us did much schoolwork that night. I was too happy to concentrate on studying.

Officer Cotton was waiting for my text when I arrived home from college. We had quietly planned a little surprise party for Angel. I drove past the main road leading to our houses and drove the Green Machine down the old logging road to our house. I walked to the shop and opened the door. The Jeep looked great. The top was down, and the roll bar sported a new coat of black paint. It was thoroughly washed and waxed. Then there was the enormous bow attached to the roll bar. I was sure she was going to love it.

She might be a little jealous that I got to drive it first. But she would forgive me. I texted Officer Cotton that I was leaving the shop. I started it up and drove it to the Cotton's.

The Cotton's led Angel out of the house. Despite being blindfolded, she still wore that beautiful smile.

I pulled the Jeep up close to the porch and turned the motor off. Mrs. Cotton pulled Angel's blindfold off and started singing Happy Birthday.

After several rounds of hugs, Angel asked, "Can we go for a ride?"

"Of course," Officer Cotton said.

* * * * *

There are givers and takers in this world. The givers will let you have whatever you need, including the shirt off their back, as the saying goes. The takers will take everything you own and then try to make you feel guilty when you have nothing left to give. I had nothing left. Donny Ray and Little John were my takers, and I was no longer giving.

I was nursing a two-day-old headache from the wreck. My left arm was broken, and I had bruises and cuts all over me from being thrown from the Jeep. First responders and paramedics found Angel and Officer Cotton still buckled in the Jeep. Officer Cotton was dead, and Angel was unconscious. No one knew I was there until the tow truck driver spotted my unconscious body in the brush and called the ambulance back to the scene.

I remember Angel driving the Jeep down the highway with the top off. She and her dad were in the front and I was riding in the jump seat in the back. Then there was a loud bang, and the Jeep started rolling sideways. I remember nothing after that. Sheriff Tatum told me that someone had shot out the windshield and another shot had killed Officer Cotton. Officer Cotton must have jerked the steering wheel because he was shot, or he was trying to protect Angel from getting shot. He suspected it was Donny Ray and Little John, but he had no evidence. He needed me or Angel to remember what we saw. Officer Cotton's action caused the Jeep to flip and start rolling off the highway and down an embankment.

I was told by several people who had seen the mangled jeep that Angel and I were lucky to be alive. I didn't feel lucky. And my beautiful Angel didn't look lucky. Her face, right arm and back were bandaged from hours of surgery and the removal of hundreds of pieces of safety glass from her skin, face, and scalp.

Sitting by Angel's hospital bed, I held her icy hand. My thoughts bounced all over the place. One minute I was praying, the next I was plotting how to exact revenge against Donny Ray and Little John. They took Officer Cotton's life. They took the joy of Angel's eighteenth birthday and turned it into a day of mourning. Angel would never have another happy birthday without remembering it was the day her father died. You can't possibly celebrate life and mourn it at the same time.

My parents, Ben, and Mrs. Cotton, were in and out of my room and Angel's room. The nursing staff kept running me out of her room and ushering me back to mine. I would wait a few minutes and go back to Angel's room. When no one was around, which wasn't often, I would move close to her bed and talk to her. She wasn't in a coma, but on meds to make her sleep. The doctor said she needed to remain as still as possible to let all the little scars heal. I didn't know if she could hear me or even understand me. But I needed her to know I was by her side.

"Hey. I just want to tell you how much I love you. I've got this plan in my head. It started with the promise ring for your birthday. Next will be the engagement ring for Christmas. Then we can slip away during spring break. Just you and me. We can plan our wedding, our future, and how many kids we want to have. I'm not leaving you. I'm here."

Angel lost her father. I thought I knew how Angel would feel when she woke up. She would want revenge. Let me rephrase that. We would get revenge - together.

Dad pulled me aside and said, "Son, I know you want revenge for what happened to Angel. But don't fall from grace. Remember Exodus 14:14 *The Lord shall fight for you, and you shall hold your peace.*" I kept my thoughts to myself and let him pull me into a hug. I couldn't tell him it was too late. My fall from grace had already begun. Where was the Lord when Officer Cotton needed him? Where was he when Angel needed him?

The doctor turned off the drip of medicine that made Angel sleep. He told us to call him when she awakened. Mrs. Cotton and I were with her when she woke up. She looked at her mom.

"Hey sweetie," her mom said.

"Mom." She turned to look at me. "Dan," she whispered.

She looked back at her mom. "Where's Dad?"

Her mom cried and shook her head.

"DAD!" she screamed. "NO!"

She beat the hospital bed with her fists and kicked her feet. She screamed for her dad. Mrs. Cotton pressed the call button for the doctor. The sound of running feet in the hallway made me think it was unnecessary. Angel's screams had already called him.

Her flailing arm tore the IV out of her arm, slinging saline solution and blood over the three of us. I grabbed her arm and held it down. Mrs. Cotton grabbed her other arm and held it.

"Angel. Angel, your mom's here. I'm here. I'm by your side. Angel, I won't leave you, Angel. I will never leave you."

She looked at me, but didn't speak, while a nurse put the IV back into her arm and restarted the drip to let her sleep. Just before the drip kicked in, she stared at the foot of her bed, as if someone was standing there. She closed her eyes and whispered, "I love you, Daddy."

The End of Book One

The Burden
of Our Sins
Avenging Angel - Book Two

Coming Soon

Tony C. Franklin

ABOUT THE AUTHOR

Tony C. Franklin

Tony C. Franklin is a true Southerner, born and raised in Southeast Arkansas on the Arkansas, Louisiana border. He currently lives in Batesville, Arkansas, and is working on his next novel. You can feel the Southern grit and philosophy just behind the words of his poetry, short stories, and novels. To follow Tony, sign up for his newsletter at www.tonycfranklin.com.

BOOKS BY THIS AUTHOR

Programmed To Steal

A hacker can't always hide behind their computer screen. Especially, when the person hacked is a hacker also. Jess is determined to get revenge for her high school classmate. But she is not prepared for the quick and violent actions taken against her and her friends. Can they survive and take down the villain? Run, fight, or die. What do you do?

The End of the Road

Poetry and Selected Stories

The End of the Road is where the trail begins. We can choose to go alone or travel with friends. We can mourn the past, or anticipate the future. The poetry and short stories in this book do both. Hopefully, you can find joy in both the future and the past.